PRAISE FOR LOIS LANE: FALLOUT

"Readers are in for a treat. A spectacular prose start for DC Comics' spectacular lady." —*Kirkus Reviews*, STARRED REVIEW

"Bond cleverly reimagines star reporter Lois Lane as a teenager today. . . . delightful." —*Booklist*

"Step aside, Katniss: it's time for a teenage journalist to take over." —*The Hollywood Reporter*

"So it's basically Lois Lane in a Veronica Mars-esque plot, which sounds like all kinds of awesome." —*Entertainment Weekly*

"This project should appeal not only to YA readers, but fans of the heroine who may have felt neglected with 20 page comics lately." —*The Examiner*

"This is a story with a strong female protagonist. Lois is smart and gutsy . . . an enjoyable ride." —*VOYA*

"Gwenda Bond concocts an intelligent novel that moves faster than a speeding bullet . . . May this be the first of many more." —*Shelf Awareness*

"A perfect read for anyone who loves a good mystery, with some romance, and a tenacious lead character." —*SupermanSuperSite*

"*Lois Lane: Fallout* is an innovative and overdue revitalization of Lois Lane, and stands on its own as a stellar YA debut for the character." —*The Comics Journal*

PRAISE FOR LOIS LANE: DOUBLE DOWN

"In a sea of series that keep the characters status quo and rehash the same mysteries with different names and doodads, this is a godsend. A must read for comics fans and mystery enthusiasts alike." —*Kirkus Reviews*, STARRED REVIEW

"Superhero fans wishing for a fuller backstory on Superman's love interest will find it hard to wait for the sequel, which seems like a sure thing." —*Booklist*

"Fans yearning for Lois Lane action, both young and old, can find her once more in Bond's book." —*The Examiner*

"Gwenda Bond takes everything that fans loved about that book and throws even more entertainment into its sequel . . ." —*Fantasy Literature*

"Who knew a journalist could wield so much power . . . and win so many hearts." —Charlie Holmberg, author of The Paper Magician series

Lois Lane: Triple Threat is published by Switch Press
A Capstone Imprint
1710 Roe Crest Drive
North Mankato, Minnesota 56003
www.switchpress.com

Library of Congress Cataloging-in-Publication Data is available
on the Library of Congress website.

ISBN: 978-1-63079-084-4 (paperback)

Cover design by Lori Bye
Book design by Bob Lentz

Printed and bound in China.
010738S18

LOIS LANE

TRIPLE THREAT

GWENDA BOND

SWITCH
PRESS
a capstone imprint

CHAPTER 1

"You're smiling like your world domination is nigh," Maddy said.

"Always," I said as I fell into step beside her on the bustling sidewalk.

This time my world-domination smile was because I'd spotted our *Scoop* colleagues James and Devin waiting in front of the fancy old movie theater up ahead, as prompt as I'd known James would be.

It was a beautiful spring evening in Metropolis and a group of us were converging uptown for the first showing of *Madwoman*, a biopic about my hero Nellie Bly and her early days of groundbreaking journalistic exposés. I was determined to do my part for its opening weekend success. Support the things you love with your dollars . . . and make your friends support them too. Especially when journalism is involved. This was my motto. Or one of them, anyway.

Maddy led a hearty crew that also included her perfectly coiffed twin sister Melody, Maddy's paint-spattered boyfriend Dante, and our gaming-happy friend Anavi. James had volunteered to get to the theater early to procure tickets. I'd needed to stop by the *Scoop* offices en route. I had a feature to file about how boys could know when they were being creepy and, um, well, *stop* being creepy. It had been inspired by a topic on the upstart online gossip hub Loose Lips and a long thread by guys who were wondering whether they were part of the problem. Our boss Perry White hated Loose Lips' crowdsourced news style, but we'd found ideas for several stories there—and just not revealed the source of our inspiration to him.

"You got the tickets, right?" I asked James by way of greeting as we met in front of the old-school marquee. He was tall, glossy-haired and -toothed, and born with a silver spoon but also a sense of fairness and a good heart.

Devin said, "Is that what he was supposed to do? I think he forgot." His afro was getting a little longer, and today he wore a T-shirt with a nerd-cool graphic of wolves and dragons.

My eyes narrowed at James, but he reached into his pocket and fanned out white ticket stubs. "Very funny, Dev," he said. "You're risking my life and limb. Here they are. Although I think we may be the only people at this showing."

I started to speak, but Maddy laughed and said, "Wait, Lois, let me guess what you're going to say." She tossed her head to get a lock of hot-pink-streaked hair out of her face. Her T-shirt read Her Royal Shyness—it was, as always, for a fake band she made up, though only I knew that. But lately she hadn't been shy at all.

"Let's hear it, then," I said, crossing my arms.

"That's because people are barbarians," Maddy declared.

Anavi and Melody were talking to each other about something else. But I looked over to find Dante glancing back and forth as he followed our conversation. I felt a momentary pang for him, watching us quip at each other. Even after dating Maddy for months, he sometimes looked like he was standing outside a secret clubhouse.

I knew that feeling. In fact, I knew it much better than the feeling of being inside the clubhouse. I still understood being alone far better than I understood having good grades *and* a job that was a true calling *and* friends *and* a long-distance friend-who-was-more-than-a-friend. My family had moved to Metropolis at the beginning of the school year, and in the months since, it had become home sweet home, something I'd never experienced before. Soon we'd be out of school for the summer, free to spend every day working at the *Scoop*.

"People *are* barbarians," I said. Seeing "the true story of Nellie Bly" in little letters below the title on the marquee filled me with what could only be described as glee. "At least ones who don't appreciate Nellie. Everybody pay James back."

I passed James some money and so did the others. In exchange, he handed over our tickets. He didn't need the money, but it was the principle of the thing. James's family had lost some of their wealth to legal fees for his dad, but they were starting to recover. His dad was running in the emergency mayoral election set for next month, the former bogus corruption conviction against him expunged (thanks to us and the story we'd managed to get six months ago).

We proceeded into the theater, and Anavi noticed me eyeing the concession stand. "Would you like to split an assortment of refreshments?" she asked.

Trust Anavi to use a word like refreshments instead of snacks—she was a former spelling bee champ. "If you're talking about the giant tub of popcorn I'm about to buy, then yes," I said.

The others got candy and drinks too, and then we made our way down the grand aisles. Sure, it wasn't a stadium-seating theater, but it was the nicest one I'd ever been in. There was a vaulted ceiling with mosaic detail, and velvet lined the walls and the seats.

Maddy selected a row halfway down. When Dante started to go in first, she stopped him. "Girls in this row, and you boys can sit behind us," she said.

He raised his eyebrows. Was it me or had her tone been strained?

Usually Maddy and Dante were on the same wavelength; it was the kind of sweet that bordered on nausea-inducing—not that I could talk, given the way I was with SmallvilleGuy.

Dante stepped back around Maddy with a shrug and dropped a kiss on her cheek.

James watched all this, then moved aside to let Dante in the boys' row. Months ago, James had revealed to me that he had developed the world's largest crush on Maddy. She'd long carried a torch for him, but she had just met Dante. So I'd talked James into not doing anything about his feelings for Maddy. Wrong timing. I had no idea whether he continued to pine, and his expression told me nothing.

We sat down. I took a spot between Maddy and Anavi and almost dropped the popcorn when my phone buzzed in my pocket. "Hold this," I said to Maddy, thrusting the salty, buttery deliciousness at her so I could get to my phone.

Given that all my Metropolis friends were around me, there was only one person this could be.

SmallvilleGuy: *Did you make it?*

SkepticGirl1: *Yes. It hasn't started yet. Wish you were here.*

SmallvilleGuy: *Me too. Always. I wanted to let you know I won't be able to meet later in the game—Bess needs some TLC. Vet's coming over.*

"Oh no," I muttered.

"What?" Maddy asked, and I glanced over at her.

"Oh, just Bess the cow's pregnancy," I explained. "She's having a tough one."

Maddy bit her lip, obviously to keep in laughter.

"I'm ignoring you," I said.

SkepticGirl1: *Crossing my fingers. We'll talk tomorrow?*

SmallvilleGuy: *Miss you until then. xo*

"I'd make fun of you, but that expression on your face is too cute," Maddy said, shoveling a handful of popcorn into her mouth.

"I'm keeping my silence on this one," Anavi said.

Melody leaned over from Anavi's other side. "You still haven't met this guy in person?"

"Shhh," I said, grateful for the dimming of the theater lights. I retrieved the popcorn from Maddy. "The movie's starting."

"Saved by the cinema," Devin said behind me.

No, we hadn't met yet. And I still didn't know his actual name. But I felt like we knew everything else about each other—everything else that mattered. We'd gotten closer and closer over the past months. Which meant the physical distance between us was sometimes downright painful.

The movie proved to be perfectly cast and was heart-thumpingly exciting. I knew Nellie made it safely out of every situation to write her exposés. But I still held my breath when she was being examined by the doctors so she could infiltrate Blackwell Island for her famous story, which revealed the terrible conditions in which the facility's mentally ill patients lived. When she posed as a factory girl, my heart swelled with sadness at the exploitation she observed.

I felt almost dazed when we emerged into the night two and a half hours later. "Please give that movie every Oscar," I said. "If any of you didn't like it, don't tell me."

Everyone laughed. "It was great," Maddy said, lifting her hand to push back a strand of hair just as Dante reached for her hand.

Weird.

"Anyone want to ride-share?" James asked.

The others demurred, but Devin nodded. "That'd be great. Lois?" he asked.

I should have said yes, but I wanted to walk to the subway alone. I needed time to process my thoughts. "I'll see you guys at school tomorrow."

We waved and I gave Maddy and Anavi a hug, then exchanged a nod with Melody. I saluted the boys, and as everyone split off into separate directions, I waited on the sidewalk's edge for honking, merging traffic to clear so I could cross.

Given how heavy it was, it'd be awhile. I didn't mind standing here, waiting, though. After that movie, I had things on my mind.

It had left me with a distinct craving. I wanted another *big* story. Nellie Bly didn't wait for them to come to her. The last six months had been good, and we'd done some important work. But none of it front-page-of-the-*Daily-Planet* level important.

Something I'd learned from the whole big story clearing the ex-Mayor was that the little stories mattered too. I wasn't above them. And I had needed to learn to be more patient.

But . . . bringing down the bad guys? Restoring a good guy's honor? Helping people? That was heady stuff.

I missed it.

And, okay, I enjoyed having my name on the front page of the *Daily Planet*. Little stories didn't end up there as often.

We'd been watching for jerky mad scientist type Dabney Donovan to resurface. The evil doctor had gotten away clean after helping set up James's dad and endangering Maddy's sister in the process. There'd been no leads. He avoided tech networks like the plague, preferring paper records. Devin set up searches for him online anyway, and he had a regular trawl looking for vacant buildings that shouldn't be draining power and other oddities. So far, nothing. We needed to find Donovan and figure out how to take him down.

Suddenly, I wished I was going to the office instead of home. Nellie had inspired me. We shouldn't be waiting around for Donovan to reemerge. I preferred to chase my stories, not the other way around.

Then there was the whole mess related to the person who went by the mysterious online handle TheInventor. He ran a message board called Strange Skies, catering to fans of weird, unexplained phenomena. It was where I had first encountered my online friend-who-was-more-than-a-friend, SmallvilleGuy.

Of my friends, Devin was the only one who knew most of this; he'd even met SmallvilleGuy in *Worlds War Three*, a real-sim holoset game Dev was super into. The game was also where SmallvilleGuy and I frequently hung out together these days.

I'd asked for Devin's help to track TheInventor's movements online, but he'd never been able to manage it. The last time he tried was a couple of months ago now.

What Devin didn't know was that I suspected TheInventor

of working with members of a secret government task force who were hunting for someone I owed my life to—a certain flying man. And Devin didn't know that I also suspected one of the people on said task force was my dad.

But I needed to make absolutely certain TheInventor was playing double agent before I pressed the issue with SmallvilleGuy. Because SmallvilleGuy trusted him. Completely. And SmallvilleGuy didn't trust easily.

I hated keeping secrets from SmallvilleGuy. This, despite the fact he continued to keep his real identity a secret from me.

But I hadn't told SmallvilleGuy what I thought might be happening. Not yet. Or why I preferred meeting in the game to chatting on software designed by TheInventor. Not until I had proof that TheInventor might be willing to put us in danger. Or until I had proof that he had already put us in danger.

The street finally calmed enough for me to chance crossing, and so I did.

When I made it to the other side, I looked back at the theater and noticed a boy staring straight at me. He was short and too skinny for his frame, shoulders and elbows jutting out beneath a faded T-shirt. He had floppy brown hair on the right side of his head and a smooth shave on the other.

He lifted his hand in a sarcastic beauty-queen-style wave.

A horn honked and distracted me for a split second, and when I turned my head back, he was gone. No sign of him anywhere on the block. He had just . . . vanished.

Great, I thought, *now I'm seeing things.*

I took out my phone and sent Devin a text. The least I could do tonight was pursue a lead on something.

Can you give tagging my Strange Skies pal TheInventor another shot? Maybe he's been lured into a false sense of security.

Typing the words, I thought maybe they also applied to me over the last few months. And I vowed: no more.

CHAPTER 2

After my last class the next day, I finished stowing my books in my locker and shut the door. I turned around and discovered Maddy standing behind me. Her T-shirt today was for Passive Attack. "So?" she asked.

I blew on my fingernails in a universal sign for success. "I aced that bio test. A-*plus*."

"Should make your dad happy—and Principal Butler." Maddy said it dryly. She was fully aware of how little I cared about the loathsome principal's regard for me.

James walked up and joined us. "Hey," he said, "I'm on my way to the *Scoop*. Anyone want to come along?"

I did want to, but I couldn't. I had an impromptu date with SmallvilleGuy—he'd said he had "significant news" and refused to divulge more. No way I could wait until after hitting the office with *that* kind of lead-up, desperate to find another big story or not. Besides, Devin had also sent me a text after lunch saying that he'd made progress on his task.

Maddy nodded to James. "Sure, I'm headed there too. I have an album to review."

"Great," James said. "Let's go."

"Don't worry about me," I said.

"Um . . . why?" James asked, hesitating.

"Not that we would," Maddy said. She considered. "Unless you were doing something crazy dangerous. So I guess that means we would."

"Haha, hilarious. Have I done anything crazy dangerous lately?" I answered the question before they could. "I have not."

It was the truth. Winter had passed in what most people would describe as calm but I would call boring. Well, *almost* boring. I could feel my cheeks getting a little hot. There was one person in my life who was the opposite of boring.

Always.

"I'm meeting up with Devin here about something, and then I have somewhere to be . . . I'm not coming by the office today. So go ahead without me."

"She has an online *date* with her mystery boy," Maddy said. "That's what she means."

"I could tell by her air of glazed euphoria," James said. He and Maddy grinned at each other.

"I need to hit my locker before we go," Maddy said.

I heard my name and turned to see Devin at the end of the hall near the main exit.

"That's my cue. I'll see you guys later." Leaving the others behind, I walked toward Devin.

Of my fellow *Scoop* staffers, Devin was more like me than James and Maddy were. Except unlike me, he had crazy good tech skills. I hoped he'd have some info on TheInventor.

"I got him this time," Devin said. He pushed open the door and held it for me. He had on a slouchy gray T, jeans, and cool sneakers. "Fifth time's the charm."

"You really think so?" I asked Devin as we left school. As usual, I wore jeans and my boots.

I kept my voice down, because we were still surrounded by our classmates. Not that anyone was listening. It was the post-last-bell exodus and no one was much in the mood to linger. School buses pulled away from the curb.

"I know so," Devin said. "And this worm's so sleek, he won't even notice it's there. It should capture his activity so we know who he's in contact with and what he's sharing."

"Excellent," I said.

"You going to tell me what we're looking for?"

"You'll know it when you see it," I told him. "We're looking for anything suspicious."

"That's . . . nonspecific," he said.

I shrugged. That was as specific as I was willing to get for the time being.

Devin was a good enough friend to agree to help me out without knowing the full story. We stopped on the sidewalk down the block from school, the post-bell exit traffic starting to thin out.

I almost did a double take when I spotted a guy on the other side of the street watching us. The thing was, he looked an awful lot like the boy outside the theater last night. Skinny, check. Floppy hair, check. But he turned away before I could get a good look at his face.

Weird. But it didn't seem possible the same guy from last night had turned up at school.

I shifted to face Devin. "You coming to the office?" he asked.

"Not tonight," I said, biting my lip against a smile.

"Oh, I get it. You have a date," he said, teasing.

"Sort of." Apparently I *was* that transparent. But I was also grinning.

"Go on," he said, serious again. "I'll ping you if I see anything . . . unusual."

I should have taken off, but I hesitated.

"What is it?" Devin asked.

"Just . . . speaking of unusual, any sign of Donovan lately?" I mentally crossed my fingers.

"Nada on that front," he said. "I'd have led with it if there was. Why?"

"He can't ghost forever," I said, hoping it was true. "I think we need to come up with a plan to track him down."

Devin nodded. "Okay, but why the sudden rush?"

"It's not sudden. I just feel like we've been a little lazy about it."

"If you say so," Devin said with a small frown.

"I do." I thought he might argue, and I didn't want to explain that Nellie Bly had opened my eyes anew to what I *should* be doing. So I waved. "See you."

He opened his mouth, but then just shook his head and lifted his hand in goodbye.

We headed off in separate directions, my boots thudding on the sidewalk as I hurried to catch the subway home. I wove through bodies on the sidewalk like a native Metropolitan.

"Ow!" Someone knocked into me hard, sending my breath out of my lungs and forcing me to the sidewalk. Dad's lesson about safe landings during his self-defense training was the only thing that kept me from catching myself with my hands and destroying my wrists. Instead, I redirected, and my butt collided hard with the concrete.

I looked up to see who'd knocked me over.

It was the boy who'd been watching me. And he was definitely the same one from yesterday. He paused on the sidewalk ahead, his head crooked back toward me. He was so thin that his cheeks had hollows.

He *winked* at me.

I blinked at him in stunned confusion. Then the backpack he wore caught my eye. It—unlike the rest of him—was in perfect condition. There was a symbol on the back, a round logo that struck me as familiar. I squinted to get a better look, and noticed another odd thing as he started to move away. His feet—they appeared to be coated in some kind of silver armor. Also in pristine condition.

Then he really took off.

I scrambled to my non-armored feet as the boy put on a burst of speed. It was some burst. Whatever the armor was, it did the opposite of weigh him down. He ran so fast he almost blurred as he dodged between people on the sidewalk.

The passersby reacted with startled steps back and exclamations. So I wasn't hallucinating this.

I went after him as fast I could, which wasn't anywhere near fast enough. The speed he used didn't seem . . . possible. *No one* ran that fast.

I lost sight of him as he hung a right at the corner. When I reached the end of the block, I turned and saw him at the next intersection. Then he was gone again, taking a hard left.

Was he *letting* me follow him?

"Not such a quick thinker, if you are," I said, jogging ahead.

When I reached the end of that block, though, I really had lost him. The next street was quieter, and I scanned it hard in case I was missing something. There were awnings over shops, some buildings that seemed unoccupied, and trees dotting the sidewalk. A repurposed payphone booth covered in mural art sat near the corner. There were only a few people out on the sidewalks.

None of them was the floppy-haired silver-foot with the backpack.

"Is everything all right?" a woman's voice asked. Outrageously glam, she stood next to the Don't Walk sign, seemingly comfortable in skyscraper heels and perfect makeup with her hair piled on top of her head and a high-necked dress that I'd bet cost a thousand dollars if it cost a penny. There was a musical lilt to her voice, an accent I couldn't place.

News story alert. He wasn't just leading me. He's a lead.

"Everything's perfect," I said.

"Glad to hear it," she said, then crossed the street, though the light hadn't changed yet.

I considered continuing up the street to see if I could find any trace of the rude speedy dude. I even gave it a few more steps. But he was nowhere to be seen. I was alone, and I was in a hurry to get home. Continuing this way would move me in the opposite direction.

Still, I unearthed my phone from the outside pocket of my messenger bag and tapped out a group chat to Devin, James, and Maddy: *Got a lead on a story. Let's talk at school.*

The boy had showed up and drawn my attention on purpose. I was sure of that. I had his scent now, and I wanted a closer look at that backpack decal. I also owed him for knocking me down.

And I had a feeling he'd be back soon enough.

★ ★ ★

I unlocked the front door of our brownstone and swung it open just as my phone buzzed. I fumbled for it—though I was almost certain it'd be SmallvilleGuy teasing me about being late, as usual—and barreled right into Dad.

"That's my girl," he said, catching my arms to steady me. "Always in a rush."

He wore his dress uniform and Lucy was behind him, also

in fancier clothes than normal. Where he was shiny medals and ribbons, she was sedate baby-goth in a black dress.

Mom came down the stairs and was wearing a dress too. Though hers wasn't fancy. In a slate gray sheath with a jacket over top, she was the height of professionalism. Her blond hair was smoothed back into a low ponytail.

"Where are you guys going?" I asked. It would be just my luck to have blanked on a family obligation.

Mom answered. "They're going to an airfield just outside the city for a reception. I'm going to teach my first class. Do I look okay?"

She stood for inspection, nerves apparent in the slight trembling of her arms as she held them out to each side of herself.

Oh, right. This was Mom's first night teaching at a local college. She'd picked up a double masters before she and Dad got married, intending to teach college classes on English and/or Art History. But we'd moved around too much for her to do more than pick up a session here and there over the years. She'd always longed for the front of a classroom.

Dad smiled at her. "You look great, *Professor* Lane, and you're going to do great."

"I hope so."

"Yeah, knock them dead, Mom," I said. "Or whatever the teaching version of 'Break a leg' is."

"I think it's just 'Break a leg,' sweetheart," Mom said, but she sounded less nervous. She shouldered her purse, and then glanced down at my clothes. Okay, so my jeans were a little the worse for my tumble on the street. "Are you okay?"

"Fine. I, um, tripped leaving school." It wasn't a complete falsehood.

Dad shook his head. "Try not to break anything while we're out."

"I'll be back in a couple of hours," Mom said, heading off any bickering between me and Dad.

"But lock up behind us anyway," Dad added.

As if I wouldn't have.

Things were strained between me and Dad these days. Well, more strained than usual. The weird undercurrent traced all the way back to my last big story. Whether it was my fault or his didn't really matter. We were both aware of it, but neither of us had mentioned it or tried to address it. We just sniped at each other more than usual. Christmas had been particularly awful. I guessed he thought the weirdness would eventually go away on its own and normalcy would make a triumphant return. I worried more that things between us wouldn't ever feel normal again.

The three of them left together, and, as directed, I locked the door behind them. My phone was buzzing again. And my stomach growled. But that could wait.

I checked my phone. It was SmallvilleGuy messaging me in our app.

SmallvilleGuy: *ETA soon, or did something come up? Or did you forget about me?;)*

SkepticGirl1: *Be right there. Race you to the game.*

SkepticGirl1: *(Never.)*

I bounded up the stairs and went straight to my desk. In smooth sequence, I picked my holoset out of my desk drawer and then tucked it over my ear with one hand while I stretched out my other arm to close and lock the door. A little paranoia never hurt anyone. Much.

I settled on my bed and pressed the button to power the holoset on, finally taking a breath. A spray of lights focrused into the familiar, if ever-changing, landscape of *Worlds War Three*. Currently there was a storm-gray sky with scudding orange clouds above Devin's newly reconstructed castle. The turreted tower known as the Lois Annex, where SmallvilleGuy and I usually hung out, loomed in front of me.

A pretty, red-scaled dragon flew overhead.

A familiar form split off from the dragon and flew down to land by my side. This was one person I'd never mistake for another, here in the game or anywhere. Lanky, with black hair and light green-tinged skin, he was my favorite resident glasses-wearing alien: SmallvilleGuy.

"I see how it is," I said with a fake pout. "I take a few extra seconds and I'm replaced by a dragon."

"Never," he said, grinning. "She doesn't have much personality, being computer-generated."

"I knew it." I kicked the ground with a bare foot. Devin had made my character in here an elf princess; I was pointy-eared, scantily clad, and shoeless. "You like me for my personality."

He laughed. He had a good laugh.

"That's why I like you too," I said.

Our eyes connected, and our gazes held.

I can't believe I say this stuff out loud now.

We'd still never stood across from each other like this in real life. The real-sim tech might fool our brains into feeling like this was actually happening, might make my heart beat harder in my chest and my palms feel sweaty. And our relationship *was* real. At least, I was almost certain it was. But this *place* was a simulation. That's what the sim part of the name was short for.

When SmallvilleGuy reached out and offered me his hand, I slipped mine into it. The sensation of my hand enveloped in his felt real enough that—as usual—my brain was utterly convinced.

"How's Bess?" I asked. First things first.

SmallvilleGuy smiled and swung my hand. "Better. Nellie Bly is refusing to leave her side."

Nellie—named for my hero—was no longer a dainty baby calf, but I still considered her the world's cutest adolescent cow. In a few more months, she'd have a little brother or sister.

"Good . . . Sooo, what's the big surprise?" I asked. "Can you turn into a dragon now?"

His last surprise for me had been that he could fly in the game and take me with him—which led to a kiss with our feet off the ground. Maybe this surprise would be kiss-worthy too.

"No," he said, suddenly shy and studying my fingers in his. "It's not about the game. It's a real-life thing."

"Oh?" My heart picked up speed. I hadn't expected something real-life big. I couldn't decode his expression.

"So . . ." he said. "My birthday's coming up in a couple of months."

He took a step, and I let him lead me across the grass toward the Lois Annex.

"You'll have to tell me when it is so I can, um, get you something." Though as I said it, I knew that was impossible. I didn't know his address. I couldn't send him anything. "Never mind," I blurted.

"No," he said, quick. "I'm not letting you off the hook. I definitely want that present."

He steered me through the arched entrance into our turret, and I placed my other hand in his, the two of us staring into each other's eyes again. I felt like I was floating before our feet even left the ground. He flew us up to a ledge with a bench and a window that overlooked the hillside. The dragon was still visible off in the distance, sailing through the gray sky.

"Um, okay," I said. "But . . . how?"

"Telling you this is more embarrassing than I imagined." He stared out the window, avoiding looking at me. "I feel a little goofy."

"You imagined telling me this? Whatever *this* is?" I gently hit his arm. "And you're feeling goofy? I love it already. Spill the details. You're murdering me with this suspense."

He turned to face me again, and my breath caught in my throat for a moment. I hoped he didn't notice. I didn't want to spoil whatever his surprise was. But he was looking at me with such intensity. It legitimately short-circuited my brain and my nervous system along with it.

"What is it?" I asked, breathless.

"My birthday's coming up in a couple of months, and my parents have, uh, noticed how into all things Metropolis I am," he said. "Since you moved there, especially. And you know I mentioned you to my mom a while back."

He paused. The pause lengthened.

"Still being murdered," I said. "Possibly dying here."

He smiled, a shyness to it. "They gave me a choice of what I wanted for my birthday. A new laptop—"

"Oh, that's great," I said, happy for him. He'd spent the money he'd been saving for a new computer on a holoset to help me out, and I felt guilty about that. Even though it had also produced the nice side effect of allowing us to meet in the game.

"As I was saying . . ." He smiled again, still nervous. Still shy. It made me like him even more. "They gave me a choice. A new laptop *or* a trip to Metropolis." He paused again. "I chose the trip."

I knew my eyes were wide. My mouth had dropped open. I closed it. "Does this mean . . ."

"It does," he said. "It means I'm coming to Metropolis and we finally get to see each other. Together, in real life."

"In real life." I echoed his words, too overwhelmed to find my own. Finally, I managed to ask, oh-so-articulately, "Really?"

"Really." He reached over and gathered my other hand in his again. I clung to his hands, as if to convince myself this was truly happening. "And there's more to the surprise. I'm going to tell you my name. It's—"

"No!" I blurted, before I could think better of it. "Don't tell me now."

He arched his brows, puzzled. Who could blame him? I'd asked him nightly for more than two years.

"It's just, I'd rather wait." I felt my lips curve into a smile. "I want you to tell me when we meet. For real."

Yes, I'd asked him over and over again for his name. I'd reassured him he could trust me. But now that it was a certainty, I wanted it to be when we were *really* across from each other. I needed to save some part of our meeting each other for truly *meeting*.

"Whatever you want," he said, at last. "But . . . I mean. You're sure?"

Tempting, but . . . if TheInventor was as tech savvy as I thought, he could have figured out some way to monitor us in here too. Sure, the task force had been keeping a low profile. We hadn't had any close calls in the past few months.

But I didn't want to risk it. In person was the safest way.

"I will probably hate myself later, because you know I'm a total snoop. But yes. I'm sure."

"Okay then." His thumb rubbed across my hand, back and forth. "You know what I'm not sure about?"

That we'll like each other in real life? Oh god, did that have to be my first thought? *What is wrong with me?*

"Enlighten me."

"That I can wait two more months."

My heart might as well have leapt out of my chest and landed at his feet. I leaned in to give him a quick kiss. I rested my avatar's forehead against his.

"It does seem like an awfully long time." We smiled at each other, our in-game faces close, our real-world bodies states apart.

For now.

"Oh, wow, I almost forgot," I said, pulling back. "I'm still determined to track down Donovan, but I think I found my next story on the way home. I ran into this guy who's super-fast."

That straightened him up. "What do you mean, super-fast?"

"Like he ran faster than any normal person should be able to. And actually, he ran into me. He knocked me down on the street." I leaned back against the stone wall. "And it was on purpose. I saw him last night outside the movie theater too. After he barreled into me he took off, but then he kept slowing down. It seemed like it was so I could follow him. He had some weird armor on his feet and a backpack with a logo on it. I couldn't make it out, though."

"Hold up." SmallvilleGuy blinked at me. "He knocked you down? Are you all right?"

He touched my arm carefully, like he could examine me for injuries even though we weren't anywhere close to each other.

"Stop worrying, worrier. He just knocked the wind out of

me, maybe a bruise or two on my—" I bit my lip before I could say something embarrassing. "Um. My back."

He reached up and touched my cheek.

"You still showed up to meet me after that?" He sounded surprised. "You didn't run straight to the *Scoop*?"

"No. I came here. And it was worth it." I wondered about something, though. "How fast can a regular person go, anyway?"

He didn't even hesitate. "About twenty-eight miles per hour—but that's not regular-person speed. That's a professional running record. Most people run eight miles per hour or so."

"Gold star for sports trivia," I said. "Anyway, you know I plan to go all out to find him."

He looked back to me. "Of course. But be careful, okay?"

"I'll do my best."

As usual, that was the only promise I could make and have any chance of keeping it.

CHAPTER 3

I chomped down on a bite of chewy bagel, hunching my shoulders to prevent being jostled by the other passengers on the subway train Monday morning. Maddy had woken me with a text first thing, saying she'd reserve our study room in the library so we could huddle before school to talk about this new story I'd happened on. I'd rushed out my front door with my bagel clutched in a napkin.

Determined to be on time, I'd even made a mental note of what she'd set as our next password: Harriet Tubman. Who, Maddy had informed me, held among her many other excellent accomplishments being a female spy during the Civil War. Maddy had developed a minor obsession for lady spies, which I heartily approved of.

I'd gone to see *Madwoman* again on Saturday and kept my

eyes peeled for the boy who'd knocked me down. No sign of him—not yet anyway. I hadn't slept well all weekend. Every night it took me forever to even close my eyes instead of staring at the ceiling. Imagining SmallvilleGuy coming here and what it would be like to breathe the same air and really look into his eyes was too distracting. What if that chemistry I thought of as "us" didn't exist in person?

When I finally did sleep, I'd dreamed about running down the stairs in Dabney Donovan's old lab headquarters, footsteps echoing behind me. I heard the last and only words Donovan ever said to me: "You will never see me again."

And my most frequent nightmare had reappeared right before I woke, the one where I watched, helpless, as the flying man tumbled from the sky.

The flying man had been my introduction to the concept that there were things in the world that defied explanation. Dad and I had spotted a giant rock tower when we were driving through Kansas late at night, and we'd gotten out to investigate—only to have it collapse.

We'd have died there, crushed by enormous boulders, if the flying man hadn't saved us. He'd managed to gather the rocks before they could hit, and then disappeared—faster than the boy I'd seen the day before, to be sure, and faster than the supposed limit of human speed. Neither Dad nor I mentioned it again after that night, but it had changed how both of us saw the world.

I'd posted on Strange Skies about it and SmallvilleGuy had

sent me a private message assuring me what I'd witnessed *was* real—though he couldn't say how he knew or tell me who he was.

Dad, on the other hand, had started a top-secret government search for the man we'd seen.

The train slowed, and I finished off the bagel and balled up my napkin. The sliding doors parted and I stepped off. School was four long blocks from this stop. I paused at a trash can, and a flash of motion snagged my attention.

A male figure darted past me and up the steps *fast*. Eerily fast, like that boy. His heels flashed with silver, just like his armor. He had a backpack slung over one shoulder again, too.

"Wait!" I called out, rushing between people to go after him.

His head ducked back in at the top of the stairwell. Floppy brown hair, hollow cheeks. Yep, it was him again.

He shot me a mocking grin. "How about you catch up instead?" he asked, and then was gone again.

People on the stairs frowned and grumbled, but got out of my way as I pounded up the steps. When I got to the sidewalk, he was fifty feet up the busy block, standing in wait. He waved at me with that same mocking grin.

This guy was not endearing himself to me.

I shouldered my messenger bag across my chest and launched into motion. I ran as hard as I could, weaving through the crowd. He stayed right where he was, a still point as I approached . . .

I was almost there, would reach him in moments. He hadn't moved. I considered slowing before I collided with him. Three more strides to go—and then he took off.

"Can't catch me," he called.

"What are you, the freaking gingerbread man?" I muttered, panting and surging forward again, with no hope of keeping up.

I was no expert, but he was definitely outpacing the average person's speed when he burst into movement. I couldn't be sure about whether he was faster than the upper end of the range. Because he was toying with me. He'd erupt into speed and put on a serious lead, then slow down again. He *was* letting me keep up with him. Just as he had the day before, right up until he'd decided to lose me.

Wait, I thought, my boots slapping the pavement hard as I slowed. He was leading me somewhere. Should I go along with that? I'd promised SmallvilleGuy I'd try for caution. My friends at the *Scoop* didn't know about this guy yet. Which meant no one would figure out for a while where I'd disappeared to, should I disappear.

But I didn't have to risk anything to keep going. I knew right where we were. School was just around the next corner.

"You're losing me," his sing-song voice called. It came from closer than I expected.

He'd run back to me, and stopped a few feet away. His backpack was still slung over a single shoulder. I lunged and grabbed the free strap at the same moment that he started to run again.

"Get off," he said.

"I'd rather not." I tightened my grip.

He grimaced and lunged away. His momentum went one way, mine the other—and I managed to pull his backpack off.

"Give that back," he said over his shoulder. He was moving slower now. Much slower. Slow enough for me to keep up.

"I don't think I feel like it," I said.

School came into view as I clutched the backpack and pursued him. It had to be after first bell by now—so much for not being late—but the sidewalk wasn't empty.

Then I saw something that made my breath catch.

Maddy, James, and Devin were out front. Maddy was on the ground, James helping her up. Devin was climbing to his feet, having been downed too apparently, and seemed to be asking a question of the three unfamiliar people standing across from them, two girls and a guy. Devin assumed a defensive crouch, his fists up.

One girl wore silver gloves that reminded me of speedy boy's armor. A second girl had some sort of silvery mask around her eyes, molded to her face like a second skin. The boy had . . . spiky silver wings extending from his shoulder blades. They were all too thin, just like the boy who'd come after me.

I might not have recognized them, but I knew trouble when I spotted it. Whatever was going on here, well, it was trouble and then some.

"You want this back?" I asked the boy, speeding toward my

friends. "You tell me what this is about. Who are you? What are you up to?"

We reached the others.

"Lois!" Maddy said and held out a hand to me.

I stopped just in front of her, a friend and a shield, and held the boy's backpack up high. The vantage finally gave me a better look at the logo on it.

The art style was interestingly detailed. The elements of the logo for Donovan's lab—which was called Ismenios after the dragon that fought Cadmus—were present, the dragon and warrior facing off against each other. There was no name and the illustration style was different, but that didn't matter.

The logo was enough to send me to an immediate conclusion. This *must* have something to do with mad scientist creep Dabney Donovan.

Good. I've been looking for you.

"Give that back," the silver-footed boy said, joining his trio of friends.

"Not likely," I said, unzipping the backpack with my free hand. It was remarkably light. "Wonder what's in here."

The girl with the silver armor molded over her hands stepped in front of speedy boy protectively, and then came toward me. She was average height, curly brown hair. She could have been pictured next to *ordinary* in the dictionary—if not for her armored mitts. I'd never seen anything like that metal . . . if it was metal.

James appeared at my side. "Look out. She's strong."

"She can't be that strong." There were no bulging biceps to

be seen beneath her loose, faded T-shirt when her hand came up to grab the backpack.

"What are you—" I started.

She lifted the backpack, and with it, my feet off the ground. I grappled inside the black canvas and came out with a folder. Remarkably Donovan-like. I'd seen plenty of folders like this—plain, manila folders—in the filing cabinets at his old office.

The girl plucked the backpack away from me, and James and Maddy caught me before I fell.

"Okay, maybe she is," I said, disconcerted. "Deceiving looks, et cetera. I think it's the armor."

Maddy said, "Are you all right?"

"I'll live." I waved them off with my prize, the folder I'd liberated.

The crazy strong girl tossed the backpack to speedy, who pulled it back on. He used both straps this time.

But he didn't ask for the folder back. And none of the others seemed inclined to try to take it. From what I could tell, it had been the only thing inside too.

Interesting.

A boy who could run faster than he should be able to. A girl who was stronger than seemed possible. I narrowed my eyes at the remaining two teens, a dark-skinned girl with a silver eye-mask and street clothes and a boy with weird spikes jutting up from his shoulders.

They all had that same lean, hungry vibe about them as the first guy. Their clothes were frayed at the edges.

Yet they all had some kind of high-tech armor on, too,

which seemingly gave them their abilities. And they had some sort of connection to Donovan. I felt not only like the universe was giving me a gift, but that it was exactly the gift I'd been waiting for.

Might as well be up front about things. "Who are you and what do you want with us? Donovan sent you," I said. "Why?"

The girl with the gloves spoke up. "It's not about who we are or what we want. You made enemies, Lois Lane."

I glanced at my friends. "Yeah, we know. Dabney Donovan. Where is he? He's not someone you want to mess around with. No matter what he's told you."

The girl frowned, and I'd swear there was a confused cast to her squint.

"I don't know what you think," the strong girl said. "Or care. We love our parents."

What?

"I love mine too," I said, "but that's a weird thing to say right now."

The girl spoke again. "They rescued us. They made us powerful."

"They who?" I asked. Was Donovan working with someone else again, another patron like Boss Moxie? "If Donovan's involved, it won't last. Whatever it is he did to you, there *will* be consequences, side effects to that gear you're wearing. There always are when Donovan's involved."

"Trust us on that," Maddy added.

Speedy boy laughed then. "Sounds like you've got more enemies than you know, and no clue what you're talking about. We don't know any Donovan, we're here because we're Typhon."

That was a surprise.

Such a surprise, I didn't believe him, though I made a mental note of the word.

"Yeah, right." I tightened my grip on the folder. I hoped it had something in it besides his homework.

The door to the school opened, and the four of them looked at each other. "Bye now," the boy said. "We'll be seeing you soon."

The boy with the spiky wings embraced the strong girl. I gaped as the silver appendages on his shoulders pumped and he flew away with her. The other two ran, disappearing quickly around the corner.

I hesitated. Go after them or not?

And then I heard the worst possible voice to hear at a time like this . . . or at any time, frankly.

"Why, if it isn't my favorite reporting staff," Principal Butler said. "You're all late to school. And Ms. Lane, I do believe this is enough accumulated tardies to send you back to detention. Maybe you can convince me to overlook it, if you can explain what you're all doing out here."

I shuddered at the thought. Detention was as boring as boring got. Worse, it would get Dad on my back again. Plus, the *Scoop*ers and I had a lot of business to discuss now. Serious business.

I tucked the folder into my messenger bag to keep Butler from getting his hands on it.

He walked down the steps to join us on the sidewalk. The fabric of his suit picked up a silver glint in the sunlight. Combined with his hair, he was peak Principal Shark today. He smiled, coolly, baring his sharky teeth.

Maddy rubbed her arm. "I, um, I got knocked down," she said, speaking up. Her T-shirt today was for Riot Patrol. "Some guy and his friends attacked me. These three were just helping me."

"Yeah," Devin chimed in. "I saw the whole thing."

"Me too," James said. "Some random kids—I don't think they go to school here."

"No, I don't think they do either," I said. Maybe Butler could be useful in some way. "You'd better alert security to be on the lookout for them. They might try to sneak in."

"Are you working on a new story?" Principal Butler asked, sounding eager and interested.

"We're always working on a story," I said.

This answer seemed to offend him. His lips pursed. "I presume this isn't a game, Ms. Lane. James, at least, is trustworthy."

I gave an affronted gasp. "You wound me."

I wanted to roll my eyes. Maddy rolled hers, but only I could see that. Her face was still pale.

What had happened before I got here? I'd be dying until I could find out.

Also, dying to figure out what Dabney Donovan was doing that had given those teens powers with that silvery armor—and why they didn't respond to his name. Why would they risk being seen out in the open this way? Risk challenging us directly? Why had they let me keep the folder?

"Can we have a second to talk in private?" I asked. We were on moderately improved terms with Butler—no more Monday meetings for me—but this was a long shot on my part.

Butler's lips curled into an indulgent smile. "Of course. After school's out," he said, "you can have as many as you want."

So no collective confab, then. He waved toward the steps and the entry doors. "If no one needs to visit the nurse, then you'd best get on to class."

There was no getting around it. We nodded and marched to his orders. He'd let me off without detention, so I knew better than to argue. I made like a good little soldier.

As soon as I could slip my phone from my bag, I sent a text to Maddy, James, and Devin.

Let's regroup at the Scoop offices after school. We should ride over together in case they come back.

They surreptitiously checked their phones, and Maddy gave me a thumbs-up.

* * *

I wasn't able to examine the contents of the folder until third period. Even then I had to conceal it within the pages of my notebook to avoid getting busted. I wanted to begin formulating a plan before my friends and I met up after school.

My gut told me that guy's wings were a new kind of flying mechanism, which wasn't so hard to believe given the various powers the others had. I hadn't seen any wings in Kansas, but then I hadn't seen much of my flying man at all. Still, I felt certain this was something else, something different.

I didn't know what to expect in the folder, but it certainly wasn't what I found.

The two items on top were hard copy clippings, neatly scissored out of the newspaper. They were my own stories that had run in the *Daily Planet*. A select compendium. And my name in the bylines was underlined in black marker.

The first major story I'd done, on Advanced Research Labs, Inc. CEO Steve "Dirtbag" Jenkins and his research experiment on the Warheads. Then the story about James's ex-mayor dad, the then-current mayor, and Boss Moxie.

I hadn't been able to write about Donovan's role in framing James's dad by making a clone of him, because it would have put Maddy's sister in danger. She'd been used in the cloning experiment, linked up with the double, who was now voluntarily in jail and who everyone else thought was James's dad's secret twin.

There was also a story by someone else: a profile of my dad and his military service. Another story detailed rumors about more funding being set aside for military research into advanced technology.

I slid that aside and went cold.

There was a picture of me, taken as I walked up a street. The background was as blurred as I was in focus, so it could have been on the way to school or home. It could have been taken anywhere, anytime. I shivered.

A hand landed on my shoulder. "Lois?"

I flinched, then gave a chagrined smile to Anavi, who stood next to me.

"Are you okay?" she asked. Anavi and I had been friends since my story on the Warheads. She had been the one targeted by the Warheads in the first place.

"Um, sure," I said.

Even though she didn't try to look at what was on my desk, I shut my notebook on the contents of the folder. No need to involve her in whatever this was or remind her of bad things in the past.

"I was concerned by your immobility," she said.

I frowned.

She paused. Then, "The bell rang, and everyone left except you. And me."

"Oh," I said, rising from the desk. "Thanks, lost in thought."

In worries, more like. What did it all mean? The fact the kid had this intel on him and I'd been able to get it from him? Had he *let* me steal it? If not, why hadn't he asked for it back?

He'd whined for the return of the backpack itself.

I needed to know if the others had said anything else to my friends that would illuminate the situation. The word that kid had used to describe them meant nada to me.

I slipped my phone out and typed a quick message into the chat app to SmallvilleGuy: *Does the word Typhon ring any bells for you?*

He wasn't in the app and probably wouldn't log in again

until after school. I put my phone away. Anavi watched me with amusement.

"You must be in preparations for an article," she said.

"Seems that way. Don't tell Butler—he was salivating about it this morning."

"We're not confidantes, so no problem. And in case you forgot, Nellie Bly, it's lunch period," Anavi said as we emerged into the crowded hallway.

"Good, I'm starving," I said, but it was a lie.

For once, the only thing I was hungry for was knowledge. And finally taking down Donovan. That too.

CHAPTER 4

I'd sent a text to Taxi Jack at the beginning of last period. So my trusty favorite cabbie and his many-ringed fingers waved at us from the curb as we fled the scene of school after last bell.

I surveyed the crowd of departing students around us, but saw no sign of the silver-armored misfits who'd attacked us earlier. That metal hadn't resembled anything I'd ever seen or heard about. In fact, all I could say for sure is that it was metallic-*looking*. The way it had molded like a skin over feet and faces and hands, and even the way those spiky wings had moved so easily, meant it was flexible, though. Almost as if it was molten, though it clearly wasn't. Otherwise at least one of us would've been burned. I wondered if anyone had touched it.

James opened the back door of the cab for Maddy and

Devin. Then he got in too, leaving me to climb into the front seat.

"How's it going, Jack?" I asked.

"You tell me—we headed somewhere dangerous today? What's up?" Taxi Jack asked, the eagerness in his voice surprising.

I could relate, but . . . "Can you just take us to the Daily Planet Building?"

"'Course." He shook his head and levered the car out of park. "But you're losing your edge."

"My edge is razor-sharp," I volleyed back.

No one in the backseat weighed in. Traitors.

I still wasn't sure how to handle the contents of the folder. My friends should know what had been inside. I also knew they'd be concerned for my safety if I told them. Well, more concerned than usual.

That always proved inconvenient. I didn't want to risk outright lying though, not when they'd been targeted too.

"Uh-oh," Devin said. "Lois is being a little too quiet. Think she's figuring out how to manage us into letting her take point?"

"Definitely," Maddy said.

James couldn't resist chiming in too. "It's her way."

"I'm not *that* predictable," I said.

Taxi Jack made a disbelieving grunt, which I chose to ignore.

The thing was, even though they'd attacked all of us, my byline had been the only one underlined in the folder. My stories were the only ones included, even if the others had done additional reporting to help. Sure, there'd been four of them like there were four of us and they'd come after the others too. But that boy had come after me *first*. Not to mention the story about my *dad*. And not to mention the picture of me on the street.

It had to mean something.

On the other hand, Donovan was plenty smart enough to figure out that the best way to manipulate me was to put people I cared about in danger. That didn't mean I would risk them getting hurt for some vendetta against me. Where were these teenagers even from, that they'd spoken about being rescued? How had they gotten hooked up with Donovan?

Taxi Jack wove effortlessly through traffic.

"There are so many Loose Lips threads about spring formal season," James said. "I'm wondering if we should do a story."

I snorted, and scooted to face the backseat. "James, maybe you should volunteer to take someone shopping. An exposé on the horrors of dress hunting."

"You know," Maddy said, "it's not a half-bad idea." James shot her a skeptical eyebrow raise, and she said, "Well, for *someone* to do it. How to find something affordable and flattering, you know."

That sounded like Maddy was giving the dance real thought. It never occurred to me to do social stuff like that, not unless we *were* covering it. It's not as if I could take a date with SmallvilleGuy so far away.

"Wait, are any of you going to the spring formal?" I asked.

Devin said, "I already asked Katrina Long. We're keeping it casual."

"And you, you're going with Dante?" I asked Maddy.

She shrugged. "I guess so. We haven't talked about it."

Huh. I visualized one of the posters in the hallway at school. We were talking about something less than two weeks away . . . was it weird they hadn't made plans yet?

"What about you, James?" Maddy asked.

James shook his head, and if I wasn't wrong, there was an embarrassed pink tint to his cheeks. "I don't know if I'll go," he said. "There's, um, no one I really want to ask."

We pulled up at the curb in front of the Daily Planet Building, and so the time for dance talk was over. James practically leaped out of the car, Maddy piling out after him. I started to take out my wallet, but Devin said, "I got this one," and paid Jack.

As he accepted the cash, Taxi Jack shot me a kind look and said, "Take care you don't cut yourself with that sharp edge. A dance would do you good."

Then he screeched away into traffic. "Let's go," I said, giving a sarcastic twirl as we crossed the concrete plaza to the revolving doors of the Daily Planet Building.

The thrill of working in this building, with its iconic globe on top, would never fade. Some of the older, professional *Planet* reporters—even besides our editor Perry White—recognized us now, and we got friendly nods as we made our way through the gleaming lobby, all the way over to the grim, gray elevators down to our basement office.

So what if we were headquartered in the Morgue alongside the paper copies of the moldering archive? That didn't bother me anymore. Being part of the *Daily Scoop* meant we were also part of the *Daily Planet*.

We navigated the dim hallway, past the familiar row of framed front pages screaming about disasters and big news events. One more recently hung was the story with which we'd taken down mobster Moxie "Boss" Mannheim and cleared James's dad's name.

Tension built inside me. I didn't like feeling behind the curve. This story was mine. I *was* going to get Donovan.

But I still couldn't figure it out. The group had come after us, provoked us. They'd said they'd be seeing us again soon.

They were stronger than us. Faster. One could fly. I still didn't know what powers the fourth girl had—the one who'd apparently come after Devin.

James opened the office door and flipped on the lights, illuminating the room that held our four giant, ancient desks and rows of file drawers against the walls. Meanwhile, I logged into the chat app. There was a message from a few minutes earlier, a response to my Typhon query.

SmallvilleGuy: *Nothing. Let me see if I can track it down. Everything okay?*

SkepticGirl1: *Peachy-ish. Fill you in later.*

Researching the term was one less thing I had to worry about for now. I could always count on SmallvilleGuy to have my back.

Devin walked over and snagged his chair, rolling it into the middle area of the office between our desks. James and Maddy followed suit with their own.

I stood, crossing my arms. They'd accused me of plotting to manage them, but I was getting the distinct impression they had made a plan about how to handle me.

"What's going on?" I asked.

Devin strode over and grabbed my chair, then wheeled it over to the others. "You said we'd regroup, so we're regrouping. Whatever scheming is going to happen, we'll do together."

"We're all involved in this," Maddy said. "You think it's got something to do with Donovan."

I eased into the chair. "Fine. Tell me what happened to you guys this morning before I got there."

Maddy, James, and Devin exchanged a glance.

"Yes?" I asked.

"Shouldn't we ask you to tell us what you saw on the way home Friday first?" Maddy said. "I mean, chronologically. We're assuming it's related."

"Touché," I said, "it is and I will, along with what happened to me this morning. But I want to hear your impressions without them being biased by mine."

"Okay, I guess," James said. Devin and Maddy nodded.

They'd freak about the articles and that photo of me.

I was convinced it was Donovan. He loved paper records, and he hated me. But why would he be trying to lure me or any of us into coming after him? I couldn't puzzle it out. Maybe knowing what the other members of the silver squad had done would help.

"You can go first," Maddy said to James.

"I was going to school like always," James said. "Dad was heading into the campaign office, so I rode partway in his car. They let me out a couple of blocks away, and I was early, so I wasn't in any rush."

"I wonder what it's like to be early," I mused.

"You'll never know," Maddy said.

"When I got close to school, I saw a scuffle out front," James went on. "Then I realized it was Maddy and that winged guy." He paused. "I know we've seen some crazy things, but I can't believe I just said that *I* saw a winged guy."

"At least we all saw it too?" I said. James didn't know about my experience with the flying man years ago, so he had no idea I'd had a similar experience with far fewer witnesses.

Perry always says a good journalist trusts their gut, then finds the proof to back it up.

"We all saw it, and we saw some crazy stuff from the others," Devin said. He mimed zipping his lips and throwing away a key. "I know, I know, I'm waiting my turn."

James went on. "So, I saw a winged guy standing over Maddy, and she was kicking at him."

"Good job." I held up my hand for a high-five and she slapped it. She'd taught me a trick the other week for always connecting with the other person's hand: looking at their elbow. It was a high-five game changer.

"She could have been hurt," James said.

"She wasn't," I said.

Maddy leaned forward with her elbows on her knees. "It seemed to freak him out, honestly, that I was fighting back."

"Hmm," I said, "the others didn't seem freaked out. Not too freaked out, anyway."

James interrupted. "Then I called out to Maddy, but before I could go over there, that girl picked me up with those silver hands of hers and carried me there." He rolled up his sleeve to show an angry, darkening bruise on his forearm.

Maddy gasped. "James!"

He soaked in Maddy's concern. "It hurt. She wasn't gentle about it."

"You'll live," I told James. Was Maddy's concern for James friendly or something more? That wasn't my real question. My real question was whether something was up with her and Dante. (Was she still happy with him? Or was something going on between them? That was a conversation for me to have with her later. In private.) "What did her hands feel like?"

"Cold. Not stiff, though," James said. "Whatever was on them was flexible. She moved them like regular hands. Just very, very strong regular hands."

"Do you think it was metal?" I asked.

He considered. "Not any kind I've ever felt before. But . . . maybe."

"And she deliberately carried you over to Devin and Maddy?" I asked.

"Yeah, she did," Devin answered. "I saw her grab him, before I got distracted by the girl who came after me. I was walking up from the other direction when mask girl started shooting these eye-beams at me. I know how it sounds. I pretended it was some kind of laser game, because there were still a few people around—and I had to dodge to stay clear of them."

So that was her special thing. Laser eyes. Great. "But you could?" I pressed. "Dodge?"

"Only because she wasn't trying too hard. Or maybe isn't that good at using her eye lasers? I did feel them once, though. It was like a wave of heat pushing me where she wanted me to go."

"Let me guess," I said. "She wanted to push you to where James and Maddy were. The fast guy was watching me after the movie the other night. And he knocked into me twice— first on Friday, then again this morning. He led me to school."

"You were going there anyway, though," Maddy said.

"Obviously they wanted to mess with all of us." I thought of that photograph of me. They'd wanted to mess with me *more*. That guy had known where to pick me up all three times.

"What is it?" Devin asked.

They were getting far too perceptive, my friends.

"The guy had articles in his backpack," I said. "In the folder I got."

I wasn't going to conceal *everything*. I opened up my messenger bag and passed over the folder. They flipped through what I'd left inside it.

I'd taken out the picture of me. And I'd taken out our article about Steve Jenkins and Advanced Research Labs, Inc. But I'd left the military stuff. Except for the profile of Dad.

"These are articles about military research," James said. "Why would he be carrying them?"

"Who do we know who keeps paper records?" I asked. "That logo, it had the elements of the Ismenios logo in it. That was our dragon and warrior."

"True," Maddy said thoughtfully. "But they looked different. I'm not sure it's him."

This I hadn't expected at all. "Why not? Because of the art style?"

"Why would he come back? At us? It doesn't make sense," she said. "And they seemed to like whoever did this to them. I can't imagine anyone liking Donovan."

"You've got a point there." I shuddered just thinking of him and his creepy research techniques. "But who else could it be?"

"I'm not convinced either way," Devin said. "They didn't seem to recognize his name. And as far as I'm concerned, figuring out who's behind this is step two—especially if it's Donovan. We need to find out where the new test subjects came from. They looked like they were our age, and there was something sad about them . . ."

Rudely mocking, but yes, sad too. I knew exactly what he meant. Trust Devin to pick up on the same thing as me. "You're right. They were too skinny. Their clothes weren't in great shape. Maybe we should start by checking missing kid reports," I said. "Someone has to be looking for at least one of them."

Devin wheeled away to mouse his computer to life. "I can do that."

I tugged on my lip, thinking about how else we might be able to track them down. A series of actions unfolded. "Maddy, do you think Dante could whip up some flyers with their faces from your description? We could split up and take those around a few neighborhoods after school tomorrow."

And hope not to encounter anyone we couldn't handle.

Maddy hesitated, but said, "I'll text him."

So my sixth sense was right. Something *was* up with her and paradise boy.

"I volunteer to write some posts on Loose Lips, for schools around town," I said, starting to roll back to my desk.

I'd also be thinking about how to connect this to Donovan. How to nail him. Finally.

James moved back toward his own desk in his high-backed chair. "What should I do?"

I didn't get a chance to answer, though, because our boss chose that moment to storm in. Perry entered like a thundercloud, slamming the door behind him so hard the glass rattled. He sported one of his usual trendy knock-off suits, and his tie was loose around his neck.

I now recognized that as a warning. A loose tie meant he was in a mood.

"Was that just for the effect?" I asked. "Or were you hoping to shatter the door?"

"Do I do anything just for the effect?" he returned in one of his "end of my rope" tones.

"I'm going to refrain from giving an answer you won't like," I said.

"Smart move." He paced, noticing our chairs were still semi-gathered. "Am I breaking up a staff meeting?" Without waiting for a response, he said, "Perfect timing. Huddle back in."

Devin stopped typing and wheeled back over to us. Perry kept pacing. "I'm down here because I have an assignment. Actually, this is great. I can have the newsroom send those calls down to your phones. This will be good training. You can learn how to weed out the best information when there's a flood of cockamamie reports coming in." He shook his head. "Yes, that's it. This will be excellent training."

The others looked to me. I was the closest thing we had to a Perry whisperer. Which wasn't very close at all.

I had a sneaking suspicion that we were about to be cursed, not rewarded.

"Um, Mr. White?" I interrupted his pacing.

He pivoted and trained a dead stare on me.

"I mean, Perry."

"Yes?" he asked.

"What are you talking about?"

"Oh," he said, flapping a hand around. "Right. We've been getting inundated with calls about 'strange sightings' around the city. All afternoon. Fast people in silver shoes or some nonsense like that. Loonies claiming to see silver-winged boys or girls lifting cars and then taking off. It's madness, of course. There's no truth to any of it, obviously. The photos people are sending in must be some kind of optical illusion or pranks. Costumes, maybe. The police have a statement saying they're investigating it as a public disturbance—no harm's been done yet. *But* someone has to run it down and explain it anyway. And that someone is all of you."

"You're sure there's nothing to it?" I asked, bracing for an explosive response.

"People get hurt when they believe in things that are phony. There's a danger to it. So run it down," Perry said neutrally. "But I don't want the *Planet* turning into the *Weekly Weird News* or that irresponsible parasite Loose Lips. Bring me the real truth, not a bunch of crazy rumors about bat boys or flying people."

"Will do," I said without looking at the others.

Not that I thought for a second he wanted the real truth on this one.

CHAPTER 5

After Perry left, the four of us exchanged wary looks. Devin and Maddy got to work without further comment. James looked to me. "What should I do?"

"You want to be in charge of the deluge of calls when they start coming?" I asked. "You could try to get a location for each sighting."

Devin gave every appearance of having become oblivious to the world around him, typing fast. But he turned his head and said, "Good thinking—then I can plot them on a city map."

"On the plus side, at least you don't have to worry about dress shopping for the time being," I said.

"Point," James said.

I made my way over to my desk. We obviously couldn't do the assignment Perry had given us—not exactly—but we couldn't exactly *not* do it either.

I pulled out my laptop, logged on to the *Planet's* wi-fi network, and started searching for a list of other high schools in the greater Metropolis area. Each one would have a dedicated open thread on Loose Lips. Neither Perry nor our parent company were fans of the Metropolis-based site and its approach to "news gathering," i.e., a free-for-all of unsourced allegations with the most salacious highlighted on its homepage. But people *used* it. Lots of people. Gossipy people. And that's what I needed.

I searched the school threads out so I could write my posts.

Five minutes later on the dot—apparently just enough time for Perry to get upstairs and give his command to the reception desks in news—our phones started to ring. They were old-school desk lines and quickly became as loud as an orchestra in the middle of a *very* annoying symphony.

I heard James answer, *"Daily Planet . . ."* He raised his voice to be heard over the noise. "Slow down, ma'am. Now . . . what can we do for you?"

Maddy called over to him. "Let me finish sending this message to Dante, and I can help out."

"This one look familiar to you guys?" Devin asked.

He had paused on one mug shot with two snapshots scanned beside it in the missing teens database. We all gathered and squinted, the obnoxious *bringggg*-ing echoing around us. The boy in the shots had a slight resemblance to the speedy guy, but it wasn't him.

"I don't think so," I said.

"Yeah, me neither on closer look," he said, and clicked to advance to the next entry.

When I got back to my desk, I picked up my screaming phone handset, said "Call back" into it, then left the receiver off the hook. Devin picked his up and did the same, sans the command I'd given. The symphony quieted to a semi-manageable chorus of rings, in between which Maddy and James talked to the callers.

I made my first post on a thread for a high school halfway across town, on the edge of Suicide Slum. My Loose Lips account wasn't the same name I used on Strange Skies; it was one I used elsewhere online.

Posted by GirlFriday1 at 4:15 p.m.: The grapevine is buzzing with reports of teenagers committing incredible acts all over town while wearing silver costumes or accessories. Do you know anything about this? Have any teenagers at your school suddenly developed gifts you can't explain? Have any gone missing? PM me with a solid tip and I'll be in touch.

I added the message to each school thread on the boards, then hesitated. This intersected with Strange Skies in a way that made it a no-brainer to post there too. Just in case. I'd have to be more specific about the location, so I massaged it a bit to make it sound like I was just interested from afar. I hadn't posted on the site in ages.

Posted by SkepticGirl1 at 4:22 p.m.: The Metropolis grapevine is buzzing with reports of weird teenagers with silver armor of some kind committing incredible acts all over the city. Anyone heard about this? Anything to share?

It was vague enough that I thought it safe to risk hitting the post button.

My phone buzzed in my pocket.

SmallvilleGuy: *I have some info for you. You want it now?*

I hesitated. James and Maddy were both talking to people on the phone and scribbling notes.

SkepticGirl1: *I'll probably head home in a half an hour. Meet you in the game in 45 mins?*

SmallvilleGuy: *Sure. Question first—did you see that speedy guy again?*

I frowned. My whole idea to leave early was in hope that he might try to tackle me again. I *would* figure out what was going on here.

SkepticGirl1: *Yeah, and there are more of them. I'll tell you all about it. Why?*

SmallvilleGuy: *I had a feeling—the Loose Lips home page has a few eyewitness reports that sounded familiar. Maybe you should take a cab home?*

SkepticGirl1: *I'm not afraid of them.*

SmallvilleGuy: *So you've figured out what their deal is? There's no threat?*

"Lois?" Maddy asked, holding a phone receiver to her shoulder. "Did you just growl?"

"Of course not," I said. It must have just slipped out. I messaged SmallvilleGuy back.

SkepticGirl1: *I'll summon Taxi Jack. Again.*

SmallvilleGuy: *Thank you. <3*

I'd also risk running out of allowance money early this month, but oh well. Trying to outsmart Donovan and track him down qualified as a special occasion.

★ ★ ★

I arrived home at the same time as Mom, and I could tell from her slacks and tucked-in shirt that she'd come from campus. She tried the door first and found it locked, then fished out her key.

"Did you have class tonight?" I asked. "I thought it was only Tuesday and Friday nights."

"And office hours today and Wednesdays. I share a closet-sized space with three other professors," Mom said. She paused before she opened the door. "One of them is a total bore—talking to him reminds me of your face whenever Principal Butler comes up."

"Condolences," I said.

She laughed and let us inside.

"But you're liking it?" I asked, curious. She'd been so excited and nervous, and secretly I'd been afraid the actual experience of being at the front of the classroom would disappoint. Or that the students would prove to be obnoxious cretins.

"I love it. It's nice to feel useful. To somebody besides you guys, I mean. Not that that's not nice too," she said. "I don't have any regrets about waiting to do this."

I touched her arm. "Mom, I know exactly what you mean. I'm not offended. It's awesome. Would it be weird if I came to watch you teach sometime?"

"Yes," she said. Then, "But you could sit in the back."

"Deal." I started for the stairs.

"Dinner in half an hour," she said, tossing down her bag and heading for the kitchen. "Tell your sister."

"Aye, aye."

When I got to the landing, Lucy's door was open, a rarity. She wasn't wearing her holoset and hanging out with her unicorn friends, either. Instead she had a tablet on her lap. She must've borrowed it from Mom.

I tapped on the doorframe. "Dinner'll be ready in a little while."

"Okay," she said. She hesitated a moment, then waved me in.

I wasn't going to have much time left to talk to SmallvilleGuy at this rate, but Lucy was my sister. And sister time was important. I stepped in and shut the door behind me.

"What's up?" I asked.

She held up her tablet, and I could tell whatever she was showing me was some kind of mock-up of cockpit controls.

"You know how you said I'd find what I'm meant to do?" she asked.

I nodded. "You have plenty of time."

"Well, I don't need it. I think I'm supposed to be a pilot." She was practically wiggling. "The planes the other night were so cool. This game simulates some of the flying."

I sat down beside her, squinting at the console graphic. It was nice to see *her* excited too, but I worried. "Was this Dad's idea?"

She laid the tablet face down. "No. It was mine."

"Are you sure?"

That earned an outright scowl. "The airplanes were amazing. I talked to a guy about what flying is like and . . . it sounds like the best thing in the world. I want to learn how to do that."

"Then why stop with Earth? I think you should consider being an astronaut."

She stared at me for a moment, and then a smile bloomed on her face. "Oh my god. *Space*," she said. "The training's the same, I bet, at least at first. I'd still get to learn to fly planes."

She picked up the tablet and started scrolling around on it again, pulling up a search page. I stood and she didn't even notice.

"You're welcome," I said. "Best big sister ever."

"Sorry, thanks, Lois," Lucy said. She still didn't look up.

I grinned as I left her room. It was weird but in the most wonderful way to be part of a household of ladies who were following their dreams. Or at least figuring their dreams out.

My new dream was catching whoever had taken that picture of me, whoever had sent those armored mean girls and guys after my friends.

And me.

Donovan, you're going down, and so is whoever you're working with.

I locked the door to my room behind me and retrieved the holoset from my desk. The bedroom fell away as I sat down and switched it on, the game landscape surging to life in its place. I'd entered *Worlds War Three* right beside our turret, under a bright pink and purple sky.

SmallvilleGuy took my arm as soon as my avatar entered the scene. "I saw your post on Strange Skies," he said as I looked up into his concerned face. "You weren't worried? I thought you didn't trust TheInventor."

He wasn't wrong about that. I couldn't quite meet his eyes, not while I was spying on someone he considered a friend. "I kept it as non-specific as I could."

"You mentioned Metropolis," he said.

"Your handle has your hometown in it," I said. "So there. Lots of people live in both these places. It'll be fine."

Although there weren't *that* many people in Smallville, there were enough I couldn't track him down with the information I had. Not without serious effort, anyway, and I would never have intruded that way without permission. And, I realized, I didn't need to anymore. He was going to tell me. In person, before I knew it.

By silent agreement, we entered our turret, where we had more privacy. "I guess that's fair enough," he said. "I still don't feel like we have anything to fear from TheInventor. But I trust your judgment."

Were those the most romantic words ever uttered? No, but they were good ones to hear.

"That makes one of us," I said, only half meaning it. For the most part, I did trust my own judgment. But I was more than capable of screwing up. Just, sometimes, I forgot about that in my quest to move forward.

"What's wrong?" he asked. The shadows inside the turret fell over us, hiding his expression.

"I kept something back from my friends. I'm not sure I should've."

I filled him in on our encounters with the shiny, powered teens, how they'd herded us to school. Unlike with my fellow *Scoop*ers, I told him everything that had been in the folder. He froze when I mentioned the, um, surveillance photo of me on the street.

"I don't like this at all," he said. "You *should* tell the others. You're obviously in danger, if whoever's doing this is fixated on you like this."

"But so are they," I said. "These guys didn't just target me. And if I tell Maddy, James, and Devin, they'll worry about me and it'll distract them. We need to chase our leads. Don't you agree that it's best if we can wrap this up quickly?"

"I don't agree that you should risk your safety," he said. "But I also know that you are smart and can handle whatever comes at you."

Maybe *those* were the most romantic words that had ever been uttered.

"I hope so," I said, offering him my hands. He took them in his and we practically floated to our little ledge with the bench. We both sat down.

"I just have this gut feeling it has to be Donovan," I said. "He's involved. Who else could do this kind of advanced science without making it easier to run down? Who would come after *me*? But Maddy disagrees. She says it's not him, because these silvered types seem to *like* whoever did this to them. Or at least not be creeped out by the person. That's not Donovan's M.O."

"He sounds awful, so it's hard to argue with that." SmallvilleGuy shrugged. "I don't see any way to be certain at this point. Do you want to hear where Typhon comes from?"

"You say the sweetest things. Enlighten me." I was glad for the subject change.

"More mythology," he said.

"I mentioned the logo, didn't I? It's the same as Ismenios's almost. More mythology could point to Donovan."

"Or could point elsewhere, but it's worth noting," he said. "Typhon and Echidna were an infamous couple in Greek mythology—they were parents to a number of monsters. The Hydra was one of their offspring," he said, ticking it off on his finger, "along with Cerberus, the three-headed dog who guards Hades, a dragon, the Chimera—"

"I get it. A lot of monsters. Who knew I'd have to become a mythology expert to go after bad guys?"

"A lot, yes. And the fiercest ones. Typhon was a giant monster thing himself and nearly impossible to defeat in battle. He eventually got taken down by Zeus, working with the warrior Cadmus and another god."

"I'll remind you here that Donovan's company name is Ismenios, the enemy of Cadmus."

"I'll give you that does seem like a clue," he said. "Echidna was half beautiful woman, half snake-serpent, and she outlived Typhon. She was eventually killed too."

"Funny," I said, rolling my eyes. "That they'd use Typhon as a name for something, like Echidna wasn't the mother of the monsters. Like she didn't outlive him. That has Donovan written all over it."

SmallvilleGuy didn't say anything. I studied his light green profile.

"What?" I prodded. "Your silence is speaking volumes."

He hesitated. Then he asked, "You should gather the facts before you make up your mind, shouldn't you?"

I nearly growled again, but only because he was right. "You and Perry," I said, "will be the death of my sanity."

"I hope not," he said, smiling at me and reaching out to take my hand.

"Anyway, thanks for the mythological intel. We're trying to find out who the people who approached us are first," I said. "We figure someone has to miss them. But what I'm really looking forward to is hunting down the monster who's playing with us."

With me, I thought, but didn't say.

"Playing with the whole city, sounds like," SmallvilleGuy said. "I don't like that these guys are being seen out and about. Even if they're not doing anything harmful except being seen."

"Neither does Perry. He assigned us to find out the truth of these sightings. If he even believes they're happening."

But something in SmallvilleGuy's words stuck with me like an echo—the whole city part. "You know who I bet is still in the loop on anything happening to the whole city. Boss Moxie."

He snorted. "Too bad you put him in prison."

"Maybe not," I said.

"Lois, what are you thinking?" he asked.

"I'm thinking about checking in on visitor protocols at Stryker Island. What better source of intel than a crime kingpin who has nothing to do but gossip?" I asked.

"You said you'd be careful."

"No, I didn't." I grinned at him. "I said that I'd do my best."

CHAPTER 6

I logged on to Strange Skies when I got up the next morning, and skimmed the replies to my thread. They were all links to sketchy reports posted elsewhere online. Nothing firsthand. Based on what was being posted, it seemed that no one had *directly* experienced the powers the silvery armor gave these guys except for us.

Then I saw I had a PM. It was a message from our "friend" TheInventor, sent at 11:30 the night before. I hesitated, almost afraid to open it.

When the government task force had been using Strange Skies to post phony sightings, trying to flush out the real flying man, I had overheard something my dad said that made me believe he had a source at the site itself. And my guess was TheInventor, despite the fact that he'd helped us get rid of the government spies the first time, and despite the fact that SmallvilleGuy trusted him.

It was a gut feeling. Here was hoping Devin turned up some truth to support it.

I clicked the link to open the message.

Thought you might be interested in this, it said, with a link to a post on Loose Lips. I clicked through, unsettled.

Posted by Maya50 at 4:45pm: I don't even know what I saw, but I did manage to take a video with my phone. Looks real to me, but I don't know — I watched this guy running around two little kids in the park. They thought he was a delight. I did not. Too weird.

The video showed speedy guy running so fast he was a blur, to the sounds of two delighted kids in Centennial Park. It was short, and he took off by the end of it.

Not earthshattering, the kind of thing I'd seen with my own eyes. Definitely not enough to convince Perry.

But the most troubling part was the context of the post. TheInventor had sent me to a reply to one of the threads I had posted on Loose Lips—not Strange Skies—which wasn't comforting in the least. I should never have used such similar wording on both sites. This meant that he'd connected GirlFriday1 to me, and it meant that he was keeping an eye on me, too—at least online. He'd probably figured out that I lived in Metropolis. My posts on Loose Lips hadn't taken pains to hide that.

This wasn't good.

* * *

My commute was on the jumpy side. I kept checking

behind me on the subway, looking both ways twice at every cross street. I reasoned that now that I was on high alert, I'd be better prepared if I had to defend myself.

I just hoped I was right about that.

But so far, so good. I'd left a little early, so I could stop to pick up a cheap phone I thought might come in handy. Since I lost access to Dad's cabinet, I'd been studying up on other uses for readily available technology. I'd also taken an interest in the research of people who called themselves "locksport enthusiasts," detailing how to best various locks and safes for fun; most of them weren't even criminals, a lot were cops, and they treated it as a game. Then I followed my phone's directions up the street toward the spot where Maddy suggested we meet.

Someone had apparently reserved *our* study room. The nerve. The librarian had texted to let her know just in case we were planning to use it.

Here was hoping one of my friends had come up with some good information overnight. I hadn't. The few PMs I'd gotten on Loose Lips had been of the gross or useless variety, people poking fun or looking for dates. No thanks. Except for the one public reply that TheInventor had also seen. I'd just sent him back a short, no-nonsense PM: *Thanks.*

Of course, I meant the opposite. I didn't like it that he'd connected my identity across the two platforms. I didn't like feeling like my every move was being scrutinized. Like someone might be watching me.

I especially didn't like the idea it was Dabney Donovan. Or, for that matter, the mysterious TheInventor. Based on the online chatter, it seemed that armored group had made their presence known for a couple of hours the day before, and not been spotted since. I had a feeling they wouldn't lie low for long. The police were reportedly continuing to look into the sightings as a public nuisance, but nothing more serious.

The aroma of sugar and icing when I opened the glass door at Maddy's designated address was all it took to convince me that Dough-Re-Me Donuts was an *excellent* substitute for the library. A case filled with colorful and regular glazed donuts dominated the space, and the employees had brightly dyed hair that seemed to match.

"Over here!" Maddy called out, She, Devin, and James were sitting at one of the small square tables. They had an open box of donuts and a cardboard thermos of coffee with a spare cup beside it.

"I love you," I said, reaching out for a red-frosted donut before I even bothered to sit.

Maddy grabbed my arm to stop me and asked, "Password?"

"Here?" I said.

She nodded, while James and Devin grinned, amused. Her T-shirt today sported the fake band name Get InFormation.

"Fine. Julia Child," I said.

"Now you may have a donut," she said.

I took one and the empty chair. And yes, I'd been surprised to learn the famous chef who loved French food had been a spy. Lesson: Never underestimate a woman. Or a chef.

Maddy sat back down and slid over a thick stack of photocopies.

"The librarian let me make these gratis this morning, to make up for giving up our room," she said. "No ten cents per page."

I leaned over to look at the renderings.

Dante had captured all four of the skinny silver armor gang remarkably well for never having seen them. The two girls and the two guys should all be recognizable from these sketches— at least, if we could find someone who knew them. The caption Maddy had added read: *Do you recognize these faces?* And gave our *Scoop* main phone number with James's extension.

"Your boyfriend is so talented," I said.

"Yep," she murmured, and sipped from her coffee cup.

I narrowed my eyes at her, and she was definitely avoiding meeting mine. I took a bite of my donut and then slid the handouts back.

"This means we can divide and conquer right after school," I said.

James open his mouth and I knew without a doubt he was going to volunteer to be Maddy's partner. But I wanted to talk to her about whether something was up with her and Dante. So I said, "Maddy and I will take the schools on the west side. You two cover the south, then we'll reconvene at the office. Okay?"

James looked disappointed, but he nodded. Maddy, if I wasn't wrong, seemed downright relieved.

"Anything useful?" I asked. "In the calls?"

James reached out for a glazed donut. "There must be something about my voice that encourages people to go on . . . and on . . ."

I said, "It's those politician genes you've got."

"Yes, that must be it," James said. "Or the fact I didn't hang up on people."

I shrugged innocently. "Anything else?"

Devin put his elbows on the table. "I plotted in coordinates, but they were pretty evenly scattered. I can show you the map at the *Scoop* later."

"I got nothing from my message board posts either," I said. "But I had a couple more ideas last night after I got home." I rummaged in my bag and pulled out the small prepaid phone I picked up on my way to school. I held it out to Devin, and he accepted it.

"You got me a phone?" he said, squinting. "You shouldn't have?"

"It's not for you. Not exactly." I crossed my fingers he could make my idea work. "Can you figure out a way that, if they show up again, we can plant it on one of them, and we can track them using it? I read an article about GPS signals."

He turned the phone over in his hands, and checked something in the sim port. "With a little fiddling around, should be able to," he said. "I'll work on it at lunch."

"Excellent," I said.

Maddy never missed a thing. "You said you had idea*s*. Plural. What else?"

"Oh," I said.

I *had* said I had ideas. Maybe I shouldn't have. On the other hand . . .

"Well, I was just thinking about who might have heard if someone was up to no good . . . You know, a source who would be really plugged in, one of our last connections to Donovan . . ." They'd never guess, and I figured they'd be skeptical too. I selected another donut, regular glazed, and considered it before taking a bite.

"Who?" Maddy's brow furrowed.

So did James's. "My dad won't know anything about this," he said.

"No, not him." I decided to play it as no big deal. "Boss Moxie."

There was absolute silence for a second, and then Devin burst out laughing.

I gave him the look I reserved for catcallers. My dad jokingly referred to it as my death ray glare.

"Sorry," Devin said, but he was still laughing. "You're serious."

"It's Lois," James said with a genuinely affectionate smile. "Of course she's serious. Why and how would he talk to you?" he asked me.

"You laugh, but I did a little research. It's a long shot—"

"I'd think so," Maddy said, and then she *and* Devin were both giggling loudly. The people at the nearest table gave us dirty looks.

"It's not funny," I said. "If anyone knows something who isn't directly involved, there's a fair bet it's Moxie. You know he still has spies all over the city. He considers it his." Though it wasn't. It was *ours*. The city belonged to everyone who lived here.

"So," James said, and at least he had a straight face,

"how are you planning to go about this? Oh, I know—hire a skywriter?"

"No, I'm going to call Stryker's Island and ask to be added to his visitor's list." I took a satisfying bite of my glazed donut.

"Oh, that's all," James said.

"No sweat," Maddy added.

"Come on, you know you want to mock me some more too," I said to Devin.

"I'm sure he'll be falling all over himself to see you," Devin said.

"Very mature. I'm beginning to feel a little ganged up on." But I couldn't help smiling. "Look, I know it's a long shot, but hey, you never make the ones you don't take."

"Truer words," Maddy said.

She picked up a donut of her own and we tapped them together in a sugary version of cheers.

* * *

After school, armed with our bags full of flyers, Maddy and I climbed up the steps of the subway stop closest to the first neighborhood we were canvassing, on the edge of Centennial Park. I was attempting to conserve what cash I had left for the inevitable emergency cab rides we'd need.

I'd chosen this section of the city in part because of the video TheInventor had forwarded. There was a possibility—slim, but it existed—that he was just trying to be helpful.

"What are we going to tell Perry if he sees these?" Maddy asked as we exited onto the sidewalk. The high wall that fenced in this side of the park was visible up ahead. "Do we mention we ran into the people everyone is reporting seeing?"

"I don't think so. We can say we based the sketches on eyewitness accounts and we haven't confirmed anything yet," I said. "Until we have."

"But . . . then we'd tell him the truth?" she asked.

"If we had proof—this is a little more believable, isn't it? It's not mind control. It's not a clone. It's something he will be able to *see*. There's a reason they say seeing is believing."

"I think Perry might have to be lifted into the air by the winged guy to believe," she said.

"Or pummeled by the strong girl. You may be right." I had the same worry; Perry was so sensible, so fact-based, and the kind of facts we'd tended to find lately didn't square with the status quo of reality. I paused to take some flyers out of my bag and Maddy did the same. "First school should be up here on the left."

"I brought tape," Maddy said.

"Good thinking." We waited for a walk sign, and I figured it was as good a time as any to bring up the weirdness I'd picked up on around her beau. "So, Dante's pretty cool to help us out with this."

"Yep," Maddy said.

Clearly I was going to have to break out the investigative journalism techniques, aka be direct.

"Are you fighting with him?" I asked. "Are you breaking up? Talk to me. What's going on? I thought you two had the perfect relationship. He worships you, you really, really like him."

There was a lengthy silence in return. An awkwardly lengthy one.

Oh no. Maybe I'd gotten too cocky. I was still relatively new to this friend business. Had I screwed up even asking? Should I have waited for her to offer up details?

"Wait," I stopped walking and turned to her. "Should I not be asking this? I waited until we were alone. I just wanted to know what's up. Things have seemed . . . weird. The not knowing if you were going to the dance yet. The different rows at the movie. The general vibe has been weird." I raked a hand through my hair, then waved my free hand around. "I can't get your back and tell you he sucks unless I know that's what I'm supposed to do."

Maddy shook her stack of handouts back and forth. "He doesn't suck. And it's fine to ask. It's just . . . I'm not sure how to answer. I don't know what to say. That's why I didn't bring it up. I've never had a, you know, boyfriend before. Maybe it's normal for feelings to change. After a while. It's been six months. That's a long time."

That didn't sound good. "So you feel different now?"

Maddy looked at me, and now there was relief in her eyes. She kept her voice down, but she started talking. "It's like . . . I used to get nervous around him, and then I didn't, and it was cool. We were just comfortable together. It would have gotten exhausting, right? If I'd always been nervous around him. But now I don't feel comfortable anymore." A group of girls approached us as they left the school, and she flashed a flyer at them. "Any of these faces look familiar?"

They squinted and shook their heads no. "Thanks," she said, and we moved on up the sidewalk.

"So you're not comfortable with him anymore?" I asked, not willing to drop it.

"No, I am. But then I'm not," she said. "I'm not explaining this very well. It's like, when we first got together, there was this sort of invisible wall between us. I always wanted to reach through it, climb over it, get around it."

I nodded. I knew that feeling well. "But?"

"These days it feels like it's still there and I *want* it to be. I'm happier that it's there. He hasn't changed, but I may have. I used to feel like we knew each other, but now I feel like he doesn't really know me at all. And maybe I don't know him either. What do you think?"

I thought I was utterly useless in this situation. "I've gone on like, one date, and my boyfriend lives in a video game. We're going to meet each other at some point, but . . ." The details of that could wait. This was about her. "I don't know what to tell you."

"Yeah, I don't know what to tell me either." She threw her shoulders back. Her eyeliner made little wings at the corners of her eyes, and the right side was smudged. "It'll work out or it won't, right? This'll pass or it won't. We have a story to get."

I considered bringing up James, asking if she still thought about him in a way that might play a role in this new distance between her and Dante. If she wanted him to play one. I'd never mentioned to her that James's feelings for her had changed. Should I have? But James's confession was six months ago. I had no idea if he felt the same now. Best to stay out of it.

So I decided to go with her subject change instead. We had a job to do. "There is news to be gathered," I agreed. "You're singing my song."

We circulated outside the school's basketball and tennis courts—no luck getting a hit—and posted a few flyers on the walls outside, then headed several blocks south. My feet were screaming by the time we finished with our third school. No one had recognized anyone yet.

"Maybe we should be showing pictures of Donovan," I grumbled. I pulled out my phone and checked it. There was one message from SmallvilleGuy that said: *Any luck?*

SkepticGirl1: *Nada so far. We're canvassing.*

SmallvilleGuy: *I'll save you the time you'd spend on this part: no posts about any new sightings this afternoon. I've been watching Loose Lips.*

I considered what Maddy had said, about the wall between her and Dante. If there was ever one between me and SmallvilleGuy, I'd fly over it. Figuratively speaking.

SkepticGirl1: *You are officially the best.*

SmallvilleGuy: *I know.*

I grinned.

SkepticGirl1: *Cocky. Talk to you later.*

SmallvilleGuy: *Actually you are officially the best. Can't wait. Good luck on your search.*

When I stowed my phone again, I glanced over to find

Maddy shaking her head. "I wonder if I'll ever have a smile like the one you're wearing right now. Your mystery boy must be something. Is your favorite cow doing okay?"

I knew I should mention that he wasn't going to *stay* a mystery, that he was coming here soon enough. But there were two months between now and then, and I didn't want to rub in how happy I was that we'd defined our relationship as, well, a relationship. Not right after we'd been discussing her issues with Dante.

Besides, I spotted something up ahead that felt like the equivalent of a lightbulb going off over my head. The sign identified the single-story brick building as the West Side Metropolis Youth Homeless Shelter.

"Bess is much improved, thank you," I said and pointed. "Let's try up here."

"You think . . ." Maddy said.

"It's worth going in," I said. "These are the kind of places that help kids whose parents don't always report them missing."

Just saying the words made me angry and covered in sympathetic chills at the same time. I might not always get along with Dad, but I had zero doubt that he'd try to look out for me until his dying day no matter what I did and no matter how much he disagreed with it. Whether I wanted it or approved of his methods or not.

Having a family who cared about you was the ultimate in good luck, and even bad-luck-cursed me knew it.

CHAPTER 7

There were two painfully thin boys a couple of years younger than us sitting on the sidewalk as we approached.

The smallest almost flinched away when I bent to show him the flyer. "Any of these guys look familiar to you?" I asked as gently as I could.

He didn't say a word. Instead he went pale, and shook his head.

"I'm sorry if I scared you," I said. "We're not here for anything bad. We're just looking for them to help them. We're, uh, not cops."

The other kid let out a guffaw. "Figured," he said, "since cops are older. But, y'know, people—even cute girls—asking questions is never good."

"I beg to differ," I said. "Asking questions is a number-one good in my world."

The front door of the shelter swung open. "Boys, who you talking to?"

The asker was a kind-faced older man who had a steel-straight spine. Despite the kind face, I wouldn't toy with someone who had such serious posture. I'd been around enough soldiers to recognize someone who ran a tight ship.

I straightened and walked to the door. I held the flyers in one arm and offered him my other hand. A firm handshake should go a long way with someone who had posture like that. "Lois Lane, from the *Daily Scoop*."

He blinked, but accepted the handshake. "A little young to be a reporter, aren't you?"

"Apparently not," I said. "This is Maddy. We're looking for these four teenagers—we think they may need help. Do you mind looking at the flyer?"

"I guess not," he said. "Jeffrey here; the kids call me Mr. Jeffrey."

He held out his hand and motioned us inside.

The corridor inside was cool, the air conditioning on full tilt, and the citrus-chemical smell meant someone worked hard to keep the place as clean as possible. The building was old, but well kept. There was a wall of taped-up artwork, drawings and paintings, some with ages marking them as the work of the very young, but others more sophisticated, missing ages as the artists got too cool to want to include that info. Voices in conversation could be heard up the hall.

It wasn't a home, but at least it seemed like a good place. A safe one.

Mr. Jeffrey accepted a flyer from Maddy and held it up to a light. "I can't say they jump out at me as familiar right away," he said, continuing to consider.

I took the opportunity to walk along and peruse the row of artwork, and stopped in front of one that hit me like a mythological lightning bolt from Zeus. The style was the same as the logo on the fast kid's backpack. There was a woman, and above her, a winged creature—a dragon, I realized on closer look. But that wasn't the part that had stopped me in my tracks. No, it was the woman depicted in the drawing. It took me a second to realize why she was familiar.

She wore a fancy long dress and teetering heels, her hair coiled sleekly on top of her head. It was the same woman I'd seen on the street corner after my first encounter with the silver speed demon. The one who'd asked me if I was all right with that strange lilt to her voice. I'd have bet my life on it.

I pulled down the art. There didn't seem to be a signature.

"Excuse me!" Jeffrey said, thrusting the flyer back to Maddy. "What are you doing?"

I held the piece up where he could see. "Who did this? Is the artist still here?"

"Wait a second," he said. "Show me your pictures again."

Maddy handed the flyer back to him, watching me wide-eyed.

After a moment, his finger hovered over the girl with brown hair. The one who had seemed capital-O-Ordinary. "Her face is a little off," he said. "But she does favor the girl who made this drawing. Reya. Talented."

"Is she still here?" I asked.

"Disappeared a month or so ago," he said. "I thought maybe her parents had found her. I try to hope for the best when our kids go missing."

"I don't blame you," I said.

I imagined it was far better to be optimistic, to proceed assuming wherever you could that you had cared enough, that you'd made a difference, that you would again. Dwelling on the worst was no way to live.

"Do you know who the woman is?"

His eyes went back to the drawing, then to me. "When people donate to us anonymously, our bylaws prevent us from saying anything that might identify them. We don't even keep names on file, assuming we have them. Which we often don't."

Aha. I read that loud and clear. She'd made an anonymous donation, left no details we could pry into.

"Any idea where Reya was from originally?" Maddy chimed in.

"Afraid not."

"Reya—will you spell the name for me?" I asked. "Can we leave a flyer up here, just in case someone else has seen her?"

Maddy handed him one to write the name on, then another when he nodded. "I'll ask the kids to let me know if they see her around," he said. "This number's good?"

"Yes, but ask for Lois," I said.

Maddy made a face, but hey, I didn't want a real lead getting lost in James's deluge of calls transferred from upstairs. On second thought . . .

"Here's my direct number. Just call me," I said, scribbling it and my name on another of the flyers and handing it over. "Do you mind if I take the art? We want to help her. I promise."

"I guess so," he said, after the briefest hesitation.

"Call anytime if you think of something else," I said. "You've been very helpful."

"Good luck," he said.

I laughed. Good luck was not something I had. Ever. But we did have our first actual lead on who one of the armor-sporting gang was. Maddy and I made our way back to the door.

"Wait!" Mr. Jeffrey called out before we were quite gone. "I remember—Reya was close with a boy. They were from the same neighborhood, I think. He would never spend the night here. He might be one of your others. I didn't ever see him up close. But his name was Todd. She told me he was like a brother—not one, but like one."

Make that a lead on two of them.

"Floppy hair?" I asked. "On just the one side?"

He nodded.

"You're a hero," I said, and meant every word.

Once we got outside, I looked at Maddy. "I'm thinking we narrow our search for the others to other homeless shelters. You want to shoot James and Devin a text to that effect, and that we're headed back?"

"Who would do this, recruit homeless teens into their lab experiment?" Maddy said, shaking her head with disgust. She pulled out her phone and started to tap out the message.

"You know who I think it is," I told her. I held up the drawing. "I took this because I've seen this woman. Maybe they do have new 'parents.' Maybe it's her and Donovan."

"Who is she?" Maddy asked.

"I have absolutely no idea. Yet."

★ ★ ★

The boys had beat us back to the office. James was dutifully on his desk phone when we waltzed in, probably following up on messages from way after hours the day before. And Devin was at his giant desk with its two monitors. His head swiveled between them, and he was typing and frowning, frowning and typing, as he consulted them. He didn't even notice our entrance.

Maddy and I waved, and James waved back. She went to her desk, and I to mine.

I'd skimmed through the home page of Loose Lips on my phone on our way back and, just as SmallvilleGuy had said, the only new posts about people seeing weird stuff referred to things that had happened the day before. Our silver-armor gang seemed to have remained out of sight today.

The whole thing made me uneasy. What were they up to?

And who was that woman?

I didn't like not having the full story, or having to just wait for our attackers to pop back up. I was eager to debrief the boys more fully, see if they'd gotten any information we could use. But first, I had a phone call to make.

The information I'd read online about Stryker's Island visiting requests had recommended using a landline instead of a cell phone. So I went to my desk, pulled out my notepad, and dialed the number.

"Visitor relations." The woman on the other end was no-nonsense, with a voice that was impossible to read.

"Um, I'm a journalist—"

"We don't permit media into the facility except by prisoner or administration request. I can transfer you to the PR department—"

"Hang on. I'd like to be added to Moxie Mannheim's visitor list," I said as confidently as possible after the two of us competed to interrupt each other.

No-nonsense paused. "Has he requested a visit from you?"

"Uh, no, I'm calling to ask that he permit me to visit him."

A moment of silence. "Name."

"Lois Lane," I said.

"Are you a minor?"

"Yes. I'm sixteen."

"Address and phone number."

I rattled them off.

"Lois Lane, sixteen years old, Metropolis resident, requesting to be added to Moxie Mannheim's visitor list." She read back my phone number.

"That's right. When, uh, can I expect to hear?"

"You'll hear if it's approved."

And click.

Maddy was watching me when I replaced the receiver. "You gave it a shot," she said, her giant headphones around her neck.

"We'll see what happens."

Why *would* Moxie Mannheim agree to see me? Maybe he was curious about the girl who'd sent him up the river. I hoped so.

Devin looked over at me, and I could tell by his somber expression that something was up. "Dev, what is it?"

"You want to step out into the hall?" he asked, finishing up copying something down from the monitor in front of him. Then he stared at me.

"What's this?" Maddy asked.

"Uh, it's private stuff," Devin said.

There could be no doubt what it was about. Or, rather, who. TheInventor. But Maddy didn't know that, and she raised her eyebrows.

My palms started to get clammy. That look on Devin's face was no good. I was afraid.

"Private stuff of mine. I asked Devin to do me a favor," I said, hearing how thin my voice was. I channeled bluster that belonged to a different moment. "You fill in James on what we found out."

James and Maddy exchanged a glance, but didn't object.

If Devin's news couldn't wait, I was certain I wouldn't be too thrilled about whatever it was. I followed him out into the hallway. It was darker than our office; they'd turned half of the ceiling fluorescent panels off as a cost-savings measure. We were the only ones regularly down here.

"What'd he do?" I asked.

Devin's face stayed grim. "You were right that I'd know it when I saw it."

He handed me the piece of paper he'd been writing on. It was a list of usernames I recognized from Strange Skies, along with cities or states. But I gasped when I focused in enough to read it. There on the first line:

SmallvilleGuy – Smallville or region, Kansas

My vision swam, and his username was all I could see.

"Explain," I said, my whole body going cold. I tore my eyes away from the page. "What is this?"

"It's a list this dude sent to someone in the government," Devin said. "Defense department, I think, or maybe military. I wasn't about to breach those firewalls to find out. Lois, he didn't even try to hide it. I think he *wanted* us to see. And I'm getting nothing now. He disabled the worm."

I gaped at Devin, then put two and two together. After that private message to me, it made sense. "He figured out we were spying on him. This is retaliation."

"Looks that way." Devin frowned. "The context that went with that list was a list of Strange Skies users of likely interest and the cities he thinks they live in. The response from the government contact was an enthusiastic thanks for reopening communications. That was all I could see."

"This is bad." I didn't know what to do first, where to go. I paced a few steps and doubled back, thinking. Then the answer hit me. "I have to go home."

"Okay. But did you read the whole list?" he asked.

"No, I've seen what I need." I started to walk past him.

"Read the whole list."

I skimmed down the full list, seven names total, not sure what had been so urgent until I reached the last line.

SkepticGirl1 – Metropolis

My blood froze.

"I have to go."

I started past him again, and he gently took my arm. "You want your stuff?"

"Oh, yeah," I nodded. My thoughts were spinning a million miles an hour.

SmallvilleGuy was number one on the list. And there was my name at the end. Who knew what else TheInventor might pony up to the military? And now we wouldn't be tipped off about it. He must have sent me that link to the Loose Lips post to get my paranoia started. He'd known that we'd discover this.

This was a disaster in the making.

When we came back into the office, James and Maddy peered over at us. Maddy got up. "What'd you do to Lois?"

Devin said, "Nothing, but she has to leave."

"I do." I slung my messenger bag strap over my shoulder, my brain stuck in overdrive. I texted Taxi Jack and asked him to pick me up outside. He responded immediately: *Be right there.*

"We'll talk tomorrow," I said.

"Okay," Maddy said, frowning in concern. "Text if you need anything."

"We're all here for you," James put in.

"Thanks, guys," I said. "Right now, I just need . . . to get home."

I needed to figure out how to prevent the catastrophe my snooping might have brought down on us. I didn't know SmallvilleGuy's reasons for holding his identity so close or exactly what his connection to the flying man was. But I knew someone snooping around his hometown wasn't good news. He had something to hide, and I trusted his reasons. He wouldn't take this well.

And then there was the idea of Dad looking for SkepticGirl1, aka me, and discovering that I hadn't kept quiet about what we'd seen in Kansas that night.

I was in too much of a hurry to wait for our uber-slow elevator, so I found the stairwell door and pounded up to the lobby. Stopping myself from running to the doors wasn't easy, but I managed to just walk extremely fast to them.

Where I stopped. Through the glass, I saw a boy waiting outside. I recognized his haircut right away. The boy Jeffrey had said was named Todd. He was leaning against the wall of the building next door, along the path I typically took to the curb. A girl stood beside him, and since her hands weren't silver I realized she must be the laser vision girl—the fact she wore oversized sunglasses that hid her eyes was enough to confirm it.

Gotcha. I dug out my phone and texted Devin: *Do you have the cell I gave you before ready? Can you bring it to the lobby ASAP? Typhon duo out front.*

No one, not even Speedy Todd, was going to stop me from getting home to deal with my emergency. But I could risk a brief, hopefully profitable delay.

Devin, with Maddy and James in tow, appeared in the lobby a couple of minutes later. I stepped back to avoid us being spotted and pointed to where the boy and girl lounged. A flash of Todd's silver foot was visible as he shifted against the wall.

"I'll get the phone on him. You guys stay in here." I held out my hand to Devin, palm open.

He put the phone in it, but then said, "I think someone else should go with you. There are two of them and only one of you."

Maddy nodded and said, "I can."

"No, I should," James said.

"No, none of you should. You guys will be right here if anything goes wrong. Just grab a security guard. I'll . . . flash you a peace sign if I need help."

James narrowed his eyes. "Why a peace sign?"

"I don't know, because it's the first thing I thought of." I made sure the phone was on, then turned. "I don't want to start a war, I want to help these guys. Here I go."

I shoved open the door and started on my usual route across the concrete plaza toward the curb, trying to appear as normal as possible. On cue, Todd peeled away from the wall and burst toward me with uncanny quickness. He had his backpack on again.

I jerked my head back in pretend shock, but when he got close—

I dove for him. Grabbed hold of his arm.

The force of his movement pulled me with him for a moment, before he stopped. "Let go, and we'll let you follow us. But only you," he said. "Alone."

I was tempted, despite this being a clear trap. What would Nellie Bly do?

The girl with the sunglasses had caught up with us, and now she took them off. "Just come with us," she said, her voice quiet, thin. I saw a faint glow from her eyes, the silver mask molded around them like skin.

"I'll have to pass for now," I said, grabbing Todd tighter with my free hand. He started to grapple with me in an attempt to get loose. I glanced at the Daily Planet Building, but no one was running out.

Good job, guys.

I managed to let him twist away, to a perfect angle for me to grab for the backpack's zipper and shove the phone into the inside pocket. The girl lingered to the side, the boy's body blocking her view of what I'd done. We only needed them not to discover it right away.

"Get off," he said, and pulled away.

A blaring honk sounded. Then another: *Honk! Honk!*

I spotted Taxi Jack at the curb, and then he escalated

the honking, leaning on the horn so it became a constant blare.

"Catch you next time, Todd," I said, and he shot me a confused look. I hesitated, and then turned to the girl. "What's your name? I know you're not Reya." I watched to see how it landed.

"No, I'm Sunny," she said, confused.

Todd had paused, taken aback. "You don't know us. Not any of us," he said.

Then he took the girl's—Sunny's—hand and darted away, across the plaza. They disappeared into the sidewalk traffic. Apparently they'd given up on luring me along for now.

I had all their first names except the winged guy's. Wherever they were headed, they'd report we had found out information about the group.

Tell away. Maybe Donovan will escalate into doing something really stupid.

Jack eased off the horn, and I aimed a subtle—I hoped, in case any of the other silvery teens were hidden nearby— thumbs-up toward the front doors of the Daily Planet Building.

Mission accomplished, I booked it and climbed into the backseat of the taxi.

"New boyfriend?" Taxi Jack asked, and I could tell he was concerned. As always, his worrying about me was sweet.

"New story," I said. "Getting my edge back. Home, please? As fast as you can get me there?"

"No problem." Taxi Jack levered the car into drive and turned his head to find a break in the steady flow of cars.

I pulled out my phone and sent a group text to Maddy, James, and Devin: *Wait for me before you try to track them down. Got it? We'll do it tomorrow. Together.*

Devin sent back: *It'll take a while for me to get the data anyway.*

I nodded and tapped out another message: *The masked girl is named Sunny. Maybe try to see if the name turns up a hit? Maddy has two more.*

My phone dinged with a solo message from Maddy that said: *Good luck with whatever had you looking so worried. Here if you need to talk.*

Having friends was weird . . . but in a good way.

Taxi Jack broke into my train of thought. "I'm just glad to hear you're not dating that guy."

"Please," I said. "Like I'd ever."

No, the only person I wanted to date was in potentially grave danger, depending on his reasons for extreme secrecy. And I was the only person who could warn him.

I hesitated, then sent another message. Even though for all I knew TheInventor could see it, since he'd designed this chat app, along with our computer chat software, and Strange Skies.

SkepticGirl1: *I need to talk to you in the game. On my way home now. It's important.*

CHAPTER 8

As I stepped out of the taxi onto the sidewalk in front of my house, my phone buzzed. I figured it was a message from SmallvilleGuy, but then it rang.

I didn't recognize the number. I clicked to answer, a thousand possibilities of who it might be racing through my mind—some DoD official, TheInventor, Dabney Donovan, or one of the Typhon crew. "Hello?"

"Is this Miss Lane?"

I recognized the voice as the no-nonsense woman from the prison. Was she calling to tell me Boss Moxie had turned me down? It hadn't sounded like anyone would bother.

"Speaking." Instead of going inside, I stepped to the edge of the sidewalk in front of our brownstone. "Do you need more information or something?"

"No," she said. "Moxie Mannheim approved your addition to the visitor log and requests you come on Saturday at eleven a.m. You'll need to bring a photo ID and an adult companion."

I took that in. He'd said yes. But . . . "An adult companion?"

"You're under eighteen, so you must be accompanied by someone who isn't a minor. They will also need photo ID. Thank you."

And click.

The woman never wasted time, that much was certain.

So Boss Moxie would see me, and apparently *really* wanted to, judging by how quickly that call back had come. But . . . an adult. I couldn't take Mom and I definitely couldn't take Dad. Obviously.

It would have to be Perry.

I could tell him it was as a potential source on running down the weird sightings. He wouldn't be happy we hadn't tracked down the silver kids yet, even if the attention on them had quieted. That was temporary. I could feel it.

But I'd deal with convincing him later. For now, I had more pressing business to conduct.

I stashed my phone, hurried over to the front door, and let myself inside. My plan was to sneak upstairs and get my holoset on before anyone even realized I was home.

"Lois? That you? Dinner's ready," Dad said. He appeared in the doorway to the kitchen.

So much for my plan.

He was in running clothes, and Mom leaned over beside him. "I didn't know if you'd be home or not," she said.

I was about to make my excuses and say I wasn't hungry. But as I moved forward I spotted Lucy, already at the table. "It's a good thing you are, because Dad's about to abandon us again. Who knows when you'll see him next," Lucy said.

I frowned, and so did Dad. Mom said to me, "Dad has to travel for work again this week."

I sensed where this was heading. I pulled out a chair and sat across from Lucy. Dad joined us, with Mom sitting down last.

"Where are you off to?" I asked, as casually as possible. Which wasn't very.

"Kansas first," he said. "Then maybe Pennsylvania. Just depends."

"For?" I asked.

Mom passed the salad to Lucy, who took an entire three leaves as usual.

"Classified," Dad said. "But here's crossing fingers I'll be back by early next week."

"Yeah," I said, accepting the bowl from Lucy. But there was no way I could eat. Not right now. So I passed it on to Dad.

"I came home from the office early because my stomach's upset," I said.

Lucy goggled at me. "You're not hungry? I didn't think that was possible."

"You think you've got a bug?" Dad asked. His eyes crinkled at the edges with concern. "Even a cast-iron stomach like yours can't fight them off forever."

"Maybe. Also, thanks for the compliment." I got up. "That's

what they call me—old cast-iron stomach. Do you mind if I go lie down? I'll try to eat something later."

Mom and Dad both nodded. "Take it easy, sweetheart," Mom said, concerned.

I wasn't faking feeling weak. I was facing absolute disaster. That would make anyone feel a little queasy.

But I had an idea how to prevent it.

The thought of running my plan past SmallvilleGuy made me feel even queasier. I *should* tell him how I found out about the list. He'd want to know.

That might distract from the more obvious problem though, which was the fact the list existed at all.

I trudged upstairs to my room and prayed he'd be waiting in the game.

I sank down on the bed, put on my holoset, closed my eyes, and then opened them as I pressed the button to power it up.

In front of me was a twilit night, stars glowing a million different colors. It wasn't usually late in the game's universe at this time of day, so I worried I'd hit the wrong coordinates. But then SmallvilleGuy stepped into view, a shadow clarifying into a familiar form.

"Thank god," I said.

He rushed forward. "Lois, what's wrong?"

I let myself exhale with relief. The worst hadn't happened yet. We could still get out of this.

"It's my dad," I said. "That task force we think he's on? Well, I think they're sending him and who knows who else to look for the flying man or people who know about him again.

There's, ah, a list from Strange Skies, handles and cities. You're first on it. I'm last."

He stiffened. "How do you know?"

Thinking of what Dad had said, I crossed my fingers behind my back. I *hated* not telling him everything, but it still felt necessary. I needed to figure out how to control my own damage. I'd imply finding out about it a different way than I had . . .

"Dad is headed to Kansas again. To Smallville."

He dragged a hand through his hair and began to pace, clearly as panicked as I'd felt when I saw that list. He obviously couldn't remain still either. In his case, it was like he had to keep moving or all the excess energy would explode out of him. I could relate.

"I have an idea how we can head off the worst. He doesn't know where in Smallville. You're careful about your IP address?" I asked.

He'd told me as much when he gave me the secure (supposedly) chat software from TheInventor for our computers. "Yes," he said. "TheInventor showed me how to spoof it. Everything that goes through my phone or computer just traces back to the school."

I took a second to marvel at how smart he was. How careful. *And you've jeopardized that.*

"Good, that's good," I said. "Then maybe my idea will work. Talk to your parents, explain as much as you can. I know you need to keep your identity secret—for whatever reason— at least from my dad and his task force. Tell them to move up your trip to Metropolis. Leave tomorrow."

"I don't know if they'll go for it . . ." he said, but he didn't outright reject the idea. He stopped pacing and looked at me.

"If you know anything about the flying man, you can't risk being there," I said. "Not with my dad poking around."

He just stood there, visibly thinking it over. I didn't move. I couldn't.

The multi-colored stars above us twinkled like eerie fairy lights.

"I'll talk to my parents," he said finally. And then he moved closer, taking my hands in his. "On the plus side, if I can convince them . . . I'll be happy not to have to wait a second longer than I have to in order to see you. For real."

My cheeks went up in flame. "Um, ditto," I managed. I felt even worse for concealing my part in creating this situation.

"I should tell TheInventor too," he said.

"No." I shook my head. "He wasn't on the list."

"But it was all Strange Skies people?" he asked.

I had to nod.

"I'll tell him. He'll want to know," SmallvilleGuy said.

I didn't try to convince him not to. It might be for the best. My bugging TheInventor had obviously ticked him off; he needed to keep trusting SmallvilleGuy.

Assuming he ever had.

"Okay," I said.

"I'd better go—big conversations to have." He reached up and touched my cheek. I leaned into it, the touch of his hand steadying. "I'll report back."

As always, he waited for me to leave the game first. I

reached up and pressed off my holoset, removed it from my ear. My phone was buzzing over on my desk, and I got up slowly, shaking off the lagging otherworldly feeling that the holoset always left behind.

It was a group message from Devin: *I have an area where the phone stopped transmitting. Google maps doesn't look promising tho.*

I responded: *It's a place to start looking tomorrow.*

With nothing else productive to do, I spent some time searching the names "Reya" and "Sunny" and "Todd" combined with "Metropolis," but only turned up random hits about other people.

Finally, I lay down and, as occasionally happened, my body realized it was actually exhausted. And so I fell asleep, still waiting to hear how SmallvilleGuy's talk with his parents had gone.

CHAPTER 9

I checked my phone as soon as I woke up. There was a message in the chat app.

SmallvilleGuy: *They're thinking it over. Will report back when there's a verdict.*

SmallvilleGuy: *Take care today. <3*

His little old-school heart made my real heart seem to do a backflip in my chest, as always. But I was certain I would spend the day worrying that his parents would ultimately decide to say no.

★ ★ ★

When I arrived at school, I knew I was running late to our meet-up. But I had to crack a smile at the sight of Maddy, James, and Devin actively waiting for me in front of my locker.

They were chatting among themselves, shutting out the hallway hordes.

We'd agreed via text on a quick huddle at my locker before first period. I'd been running too late for a library meeting and, alas, I'd been informed that Dough-Re-Me was too pricey to hit daily. Not that I wouldn't have been too late for that too.

They were so deep in conversation, I managed to sneak up without any of them noticing.

"Boo!" I inserted myself between James and Devin.

"Finally," James said, pretending like I hadn't startled him. I'd seen that little jump he made.

"Nice entrance," Devin added. He must have caught James's jump too. "Everything okay?"

"Ask again later. The verdict should be in soon." I met Maddy's eyes. Her T-shirt today was for Great Wall of Denial. "I'd tell you, but it's complicated. Don't worry."

She gave me a small nod. "You have any news?"

The hall was crowded, so I leaned in to officially join the confab. The four of us put our heads together.

"Well, I guess it's news that I'll be going to see Boss Moxie this weekend," I said.

That got a reaction. All three of their heads reared back, jaws falling open.

I smiled. "Never doubt me."

Although I still think it came too easy.

The first bell rang, which meant we had five minutes to wrap this up before the second one signaled the start of first period.

"Other than my bombshell, where are we? Did you turn up any info from the names?" I asked.

"Nothing," Devin said. "Which means—"

"The parents likely didn't report them missing." Unbearably sad to contemplate. And these poor kids whose families had either driven them away or left them to the world's whims were mixed up with one of Donovan's schemes.

Devin nodded. "I do have something else from the phone though." He pulled up a map app and showed us the street and block where he'd lost the phone's signal—never for it to return.

"It's not far from here," I said. "I think it's around where Todd, the speedy guy, smashed into me the first time."

"Should we give them nicknames?" Maddy asked. "'Speedy guy' isn't very catchy. And neither is Todd. 'Smash' has potential."

"No. We are not giving them nicknames. They are not pets." I leaned back against my locker. The hallway traffic was clearing out. "Mad, you told them about the drawing?"

"She did," James answered for her. "The woman sounds like someone who'd be at a fundraiser for Dad."

I stood up straight. "Wait a second. Are you saying you know her?"

"Sorry, no," he said. "'Sounds like,' generically."

Devin motioned for us to huddle back in, swiping across his phone screen. "The thing I find interesting is I checked this against our sightings—which, remember, were spread out around the city. Look at this."

"You're going to have to interpret it," I said. "I don't speak fluent mapese."

"Because that's not a language," Devin said. "You should know how to read a map."

"I know how to read a map. Just not how to read this fancy one you've made."

James started to laugh at our bickering, until I shot him a scowl. "You can't read it either and you know it," I said.

James shrugged to concede the point. *Ha!*

"Try this," Devin said, swiping a couple more times and brandishing the phone at us.

"Oh, well, why didn't you do that to begin with?" I asked innocently.

The sightings popped now, bright red dots flung across Metropolis. There wasn't any pattern to them. Until you looked at the spot where Devin had placed a block-long X.

"They're pretty equally spread out around that point, aren't they?" Maddy asked.

"Yeah, they are," I said. "In fact, I bet the only sightings within the zone around the X are ours."

Devin said, "See, you *can* read a map." I fake-scowled at him.

"What are we talking about?" a loathsomely familiar voice asked. "It's almost time for class."

Principal Butler had chosen that moment to interrupt. Unfortunately, none of us had been paying enough attention to our surroundings to notice his approach.

"Mapping applications," I said brightly.

"Mapping applications," he said. His eyes narrowed in an expression that said he didn't believe me.

"Show him," I told Devin.

Devin sighed and held up his phone.

"That does seem to be a map," Principal Butler said. "What's it of?"

The four of us exchanged looks.

"Metropolis," Devin said at last.

"You guys can stop treating me like your enemy," Principal Butler said, straightening his tie. It was blue and shone with expense. "I did help you out with James's dad. And I told the security guards to watch out for unfamiliar people on campus the other day. I was just curious what you're working on now."

I held in a snort. Barely. We'd called in Principal Butler's help that time only out of desperation. Sure, he'd let me out of our otherwise-mandatory weekly meetings as a result, but I feared he . . . missed me. Or at least missed the excitement of being part of a big story.

I could relate, but he was still the worst.

"Oh *no*," I said, as if I was horrified. "We think of you as a friend. Because of just that."

The bell rang, cutting off whatever response he was about to make. His mouth hung open.

"We'd better get to class," I said, and patted his shoulder. "Tell Ronda hi."

Maddy did snort out loud then, but I didn't think Butler heard it. We made our way up the hall.

"Meet out front after school?" I asked.

★ ★ ★

School lasted *way* too long; it was a fact.

Staying focused during my classes when I knew we should be out there pursuing our lead—well, it wasn't easy. What if they moved headquarters after they found the phone? What if the guy had found the phone and tossed it before he ever got close to their base of operations? What would Perry's reaction be when I asked him to accompany me to Stryker's Island this weekend?

And the big one, the question to end all questions, the one that hovered in big neon letters inside my head: what were SmallvilleGuy's parents going to decide?

There was no word from him when school let out, and I didn't want to seem like I was obsessing. Even though he must *know* I was obsessing.

Besides, I had some people to locate. I'd suggested my friends meet me out front to prevent another huddle crash by Principal Butler. The others were already there waiting for me, along with Dante. Maddy had her hand in his, but she was gazing off up the street.

Dante had helped us out with the story about James's dad and in aiding Maddy's sister—and he had been completely sanguine about the fact there were beyond strange things going on in the world. He'd also painted an amazing wall-sized mural that featured, among others, the four of us as heroes. He was a good guy.

But Maddy's Great Wall of Denial T-shirt couldn't be good.

Not after our conversation the other day. She was getting practically poetic here, and I wondered if she meant her denial or Dante's. The wall being described as "great" didn't seem like a good omen.

The streets around school were crowded at this time of day (and at most times of day), busy with people running errands and going to and from home and offices. We had to stagger our group along the street to avoid gumming up the works. I ended up walking behind Devin with James at my side, Maddy and Dante right behind us.

I hadn't yet told them about the other part of getting the thumbs-up to see Boss Moxie—that I had to ask Perry to come with me. But now seemed as good a time as any.

So I took my phone out and scrolled to my contact for Perry. He answered right away. "Lane? This had better be good," he said.

"Hi, Perry. It is," I said. James gave me a wide-eyed look, and so did Devin, turning to do so. "We're having a little trouble really nailing what was going on with those sightings . . ."

"You don't say," Perry said.

"I thought I might cultivate Boss Moxie as a source. You know he must still have eyes on everything that goes on in the city," I continued.

Perry barked a *ha*. "Fat chance of him agreeing to that."

"Actually," I said, "he's put me on the visitation roster for eleven o'clock tomorrow morning. I need, uh, an adult to come along. Would you be able to join me?"

There was a long silence. I waited for his response.

"Of course," Perry said. "Interesting strategy, Lane. See you tomorrow at the ferry where the transport loads. Or before, if you manage to crack this story without his help. If it even is one."

"We're working on it," I said. "Thanks for coming with me."

Maddy and I high-fived, and I even managed not to drop the phone by employing the elbow trick. I slid my phone in my back pocket and gave them all a grin that was meant to be a lesson. "I don't think I got to fully crow about this earlier." I put my hand up to my ear. "Who's laughing now?"

James shook his head, blinking admiringly. "Wow."

"I hope Moxie's not seeing you to tell you he plans to take you out," Devin said.

Dante said, "He's not the type who would be sentimental that way. He'd just do it."

Dante knew what he was talking about. He lived at the edge of Suicide Slum, a neighborhood Boss Moxie had run—and kept down—for years. He and James both had firsthand experience the rest of us didn't, not quite, in terms of Moxie's impact. Though we'd been close enough to the crime boss to get the grim picture.

"We'll see," I said.

"I'm glad Perry will be there," Maddy said.

I started walking again, and so did the others. "Did you check the power grid and abandoned buildings database for this block yet?" I asked Devin.

"Of course. Nothing. Most of these buildings have

occupants," he said. "And none of these addresses are leaving a record of using more power than they should be."

We were getting close to the block, if I was right about where to go.

Devin said, "Look alive, guys."

"This is where he knocked me down the first time," I said.

"I still can't believe you let him get away with that," James said.

"Well, he was exceeding regular human speeds." I didn't like that he had gotten away with it either.

"We've learned our lesson, officially," Maddy said. "Plus, you can still retaliate. There's time."

"I appreciate the vote of confidence, oh ye of little faith," I said, and sped up.

Plus the corner where I'd seen that glam lady, and where I'd lost Todd, was right ahead.

"This is it," I said, stopping.

Devin pointed ahead of us. "And this is the block where the phone stopped transmitting."

The street was, once again, quiet. Awnings and a couple of empty storefronts, an apartment building and a couple of others that were nondescript, maybe business offices.

"I say we go up and down both sides, looking for anything unusual," I suggested.

Maddy asked, "Do we split up? Each group take a side?"

"No," I said, "we're not in a huge hurry. Let's stay together. We might get ambushed by our armor-wearing pals. Strength in numbers."

The only people on the sidewalks were dressed in comfortable clothes. No glam ladies to be seen. We started up the block, not seeing anything noteworthy—a little market, a flower shop. "We could go in and ask if any of these people have noticed anyone weird running around the neighborhood," Maddy said.

I looked at the other side of the street, up and down, then back at the one we were on. The building just ahead of us was a brownstone, fairly anonymous, with no particularly memorable details. It had caught my attention because it sported security cameras poking out from the upper floor, pointed at the street. No other building on either block had visible cameras like this.

"Too risky," I said.

No one responded, but I turned to see Maddy watching me. "Do you have a fever?" she asked. "*You* think asking questions is too risky?"

Right. They didn't know about the surveillance photo of me. Or Todd saying I could have an exclusive if I went with Sunny and him. They had no idea about the silver squad's fixation on me.

"I should have said not necessary," I clarified. "Yet."

"All right," Maddy said, a skeptical note in her voice.

Dante nudged her and said, "Usually you'd be telling her not to take unnecessary risks."

"You don't know everything about me," Maddy said.

Dante's smile vanished.

Before things could get more awkward, I said, "Up here,"

and started toward the building with the cameras. I'd never seen anything like them. They were sleek and black and reflective. Not like the silver armor, but fancier than the usual crappy surveillance camera. I pointed at one.

"I count four of them," Devin said. "You ever seen cameras like this before?"

I shook my head.

"That seems excessive for a brownstone," James said. "The neighborhood hardly seems crime-riddled."

I held up my phone and snapped some photos of the building. I could feel in my gut this was the right place. Or *a* right place, at least. "Can you guys tell if this is residential or a business? I sure can't."

There was no identifying signage. Not even the numbers of an address.

"It could be anything," Maddy said.

"Anything that has a *little* touch of paranoia," I agreed.

Another camera was mounted just over the front door, which was glass. No helpful Ismenios logo here.

But there was a buzzer and speaker beside it. And I wanted a look inside.

I walked over directly in front of the door and peered through the glass. What I saw was even odder. No furniture, no lighting fixtures. It was by all appearances unused.

"There's nothing in there. It's empty," I said.

"Maybe it's not the right spot, then," Devin said. "They probably found the phone and tossed it into a trash can on this block."

That was logical. There was no reason to think otherwise. The cameras could just be someone protecting an investment they wanted to rent later. But, for some reason, my senses were on high alert. I could *feel* this was the place.

Despite there being no real evidence.

I walked back toward the sidewalk where the others were waiting, but stopped before I reached them. I turned so the camera over the door had a clear angle on me.

"Lois?" Maddy said. "Isn't this a little . . . *nice* for Donovan's style? Seems like we're either in the wrong place, like Devin said, or it's not him."

"Probably," I said, and smiled straight into the camera above the door.

I both felt and heard the others move into position behind me. James questioned me this time. "Then what are you doing?"

Dante muttered, "I still don't like all this security."

"Let's just make sure no one's home," I said and stepped forward to press the buzzer.

We were quiet, waiting to see if there'd be a response. I wouldn't have been surprised if a voice welcomed us, or if the silver gang appeared out of nowhere and went for a full-throttle attack.

Instead there was nothing. No response at all.

But I couldn't shake the sensation of being watched. That could be left over from seeing myself in a surveillance photograph, *or* it could be my gut. The one I trusted without question.

I rang the buzzer again and leaned in to the speaker. "Lois Lane here, if anyone's home. I think you've been looking for me."

Watching me.

I considered asking for Reya. Or Sunny. Or Donovan himself. But we still weren't sure what was going on—and this might only be one location. We might be at the wrong place altogether, like the others clearly thought. My gut could be wrong.

It was also possible no one was home.

We certainly weren't *prepared* for a confrontation. Not really. Not without knowing more.

"I saw a light flashing in there just now, in that camera," Dante lifted his hand beside me and pointed at the door camera.

I eyed it and saw only the dead black reflection of the lens.

"Maybe we should go," James said. "Could be a security system we triggered. This seems like a dead end."

For once, I agreed. Except about the dead end part.

I took a step back to be plainly in the center of the camera's lens again. Then I waved. "Bye for now," I mouthed.

CHAPTER 10

We headed back to the nearest subway stop, pausing before we parted ways to say goodbye.

"Everybody be careful on your way home," I said. "Eyes peeled."

"You too," Maddy said.

Dante reached out a hand, offering it to her, and I saw that moment of hesitation before she took it. He saw it too, I was pretty sure. He was moving a little more stiffly than normal. He nodded to me, but his usual easy smile was nowhere to be seen.

I pulled Maddy into a quick hug, which meant they had to drop their grip on each other's hands anyway. I whispered into her ear. "Are you about to break up with him? If I'm right, call me later."

"Thanks for the assist, as always," I told Dante.

Maddy and Dante peeled off, with no attempt to hold hands again. I saluted Devin and James, who were going to share a taxi across town together.

Heading down the subway stairs, I signed into the chat app and sent SmallvilleGuy a message that I was on my way home.

I rode the train thinking over the weird intuition I had about that building—that Dabney Donovan was inside it—and yet how nothing we'd discovered quite resolved into a full picture. Why had the armor-wearers gone to so much trouble to be seen, to make clear they were baiting *me*, only to then go quietly to ground?

Finally, when I was almost home, walking up our street, my phone buzzed in my pocket with a new notification.

SmallvilleGuy: *I have news. Breaking news.*

I badly wanted to know what it was. Positive or negative, revelation or catastrophe. But I was still worried about TheInventor snooping on our comms using his software programs.

SkepticGirl1: *Almost home. Game in 15? Crossing my fingers.*

His response was short and hint-proof.

SmallvilleGuy: *k.*

I sped up, boots thudding on the sidewalk. I had to admit to myself that I now felt exposed whenever I was outside home or school or the Daily Planet Building. Like there was no way for me to know who was watching or plotting against me.

I didn't like that feeling. Fear didn't suit me.

I remembered Maddy saying that I had time to retaliate for being knocked down by the speedy guy. I preferred to think of it not as revenge, but as when I would get to shut down these threats, find the loathsome bad guys who thought it fine and dandy to use others as their pawns, drag them out of their hiding spot and into the fresh sunlight of newsprint.

No more skulking in shadows for Donovan. Not when we were done.

Mom and Dad were hanging out together on the couch when I came in. Or so it seemed. They got up right away, and it was clear they'd been waiting on me to get home.

Mom kissed my cheek. "We wanted to make sure you were here before we left."

She was in a pair of slacks and a crisp white button down. Dad was dressed similarly, sans his usual ribbons and medals.

"Where are you off to?" I asked. It seemed like I was home almost as much as they were these days.

"We're checking out an art exhibit opening on campus," Mom said. "Meeting some of my colleagues there."

I noticed Dad's suitcase packed and waiting by the front door. He followed my gaze to it. "I'm leaving when we get back; late flight tonight."

The words echoed. Late. Flight. Tonight. *Please, please, let SmallvilleGuy's news be good.*

"Too late for me to see you off?" I asked.

"Probably," he said. "You girls look after each other for me while I'm gone."

He glanced warmly from me to Mom. She'd been so happy and energized in the days since her teaching gig started. It hit me that Dad only dressed down to go out to functions when he wanted to downplay the whole "here comes the General" thing. Which meant he was *intentionally* dressed down to let Mom have the spotlight at this event.

Spontaneously, I gave him a hug. "See you when you get back." He tightened his arms around me.

The surprise on his face when we parted almost hurt. Was it that unusual for me to hug Dad? I might not always agree with him, but I knew he thought he was doing the right thing. He wouldn't do anything he believed was wrong.

"All right, off with you, excellent parents," I said. "Have fun."

Mom put her hand to my forehead. "No fever. It seems she's acting this way of her own free will."

"Ha," I said. "I can be grateful, can't I? About having good parents?"

They studied me and exchanged one of their patented looks, but this was the less-often seen positive version.

"I just can't believe it's right before I'm going to be gone. I suppose it'd be too much to expect this treatment when I get back," Dad said.

Depends on what happens while you're gone.

"Get out," I said. "You're ruining my tender feelings for you."

They laughed and headed for the door. "Lucy's already had supper," Mom said.

Dad added, "There's food in the fridge if you're hungry."

As soon as they shut the door, I hurried upstairs—past Lucy's closed door—and retrieved the holoset from my desk drawer. If SmallvilleGuy had noticed I basically never wanted to use our chat software these days, he hadn't remarked on it. Maybe he thought it was because the game made our meetings feel realer. It did, after all. That was definitely an added benefit. But it wasn't my only motivation.

The familiar nerves I felt whenever I was about to see him fluttered to life.

I powered up the holoset and the spray of lights took form in front of my face, resolving into a landscape. I gaped at the sight. Giant electric bolts split the sky overhead, sound effects crackling afterward so loudly my bones seemed to rattle with the force.

"Is this a meteor shower or something?" I asked no one in particular.

SmallvilleGuy stepped in front of me. "It's a lightning storm," he said, smiling down at me.

"Impressive phony weather."

He pulled me into a hug, and my whole body vibrated with warmth. "How did the reconnaissance go?" he asked.

"We found a building with a bunch of weird fancy cameras. Nothing to officially confirm it's our guys, though."

"And Perry's going with you this weekend?" he asked, releasing me.

I nodded.

My hopes sank. Why was he asking me about this stuff?

His parents must not have been convinced. My dad was going to show up in Smallville asking questions about flying men and . . . nothing good would come of it.

"What's wrong?" he said. "You look like I just said Nellie Bly is hideous."

"Don't even joke. She is the cutest creature on the planet." I thought of the picture he'd sent me of Nellie when she was just a baby calf, with his arm around her. It was a really good arm.

"Really," he said, "what's up? You seem upset."

"Why do I get the feeling you're stalling?" I asked, steeling myself so I could hide some of my disappointment. "Did your parents say no?"

"Why would you think that?" he asked with a little frown.

I waved toward the turret. I felt too exposed out here, and, as if to underscore that, I jumped when another lightning bolt cracked across the sky.

Once we were inside, I stuck to the shadows, where he wouldn't see anything I didn't want him to. "I assume, since you're just asking about my day and the usual, that the news is bad."

He looked at me for a second, face absolutely straight. Then he cracked a smile and threw back his head in a laugh.

"What's so funny?" I tried not to sound mad. Or hurt.

He straightened up and tugged me where the light from a sconce would show my face. The game's ability to capture emotion was something else. I fought hard to keep my expression neutral.

"I was asking because I always want to know how your day was," he said. "Not because I have bad news."

"Oh."

"In fact, I have good news."

I forced myself not to burst into song like some goofball in a musical. But I kind of wanted to. "You do?"

"My parents weren't thrilled," he said. "You know I can't fully explain why they worry so much . . ."

"I do," I said. "I know there's some connection between you and the flying man and that it has something to do with why your parents are so careful. Why they want you to be careful. Right?"

He nodded. "So they weren't thrilled about my receiving tip-offs that 'shady' people are coming to town looking for information about someone who can fly . . . They don't like the idea that I'm on anyone's radar in, uh, relation to this."

I started to protest that Dad wasn't exactly shady, but I let it pass. "Got it. Go on."

"So, they agreed to move up the trip and let me take a few days off school. Our neighbors are watching Bess, Shelby, cutest creature on the planet Nellie Bly, the whole farm. We're driving. Leaving tonight."

"Yeah?" I couldn't keep a little goofball from my voice.

"Yeah. So I'll see you Sunday."

I'll see you Sunday.

I would see him *Sunday.*

That was the day after tomorrow.

Sunday.

The calendar took on a whole new relevance. The concept of days filled with new meaning.

I was being a *complete* goofball. But, still, when I took his hands I only realized how hard I was squeezing them when he squeezed back. "Oops," I said, relaxing my death grip, "wouldn't want to crush your character's hands with my joy."

"I think I'll survive." He smiled again. "Your *joy?*"

My cheeks were burning red, hot as the lightning over the fake landscape outside. But his were pink too.

"Don't push it," I said. "Sap."

"Well, speaking of . . . I seem to remember a certain bet you lost that you've never made good on." He shook his head in disapproval.

SmallvilleGuy loved the Metropolis baseball team, and so to get him to worry less about the Strange Skies flying man postings, I'd bet him they would turn out to be nothing. I, of course, lost, when it turned out the government task force was behind them. But baseball season had been a long way off then.

He went on, "I believe you promised to dress as a real Monarchs fan."

I feigned outrage. "I would never shirk a bet! I have just been waiting for the right time."

He fidgeted. So he was nervous too. He was adorable. I *adored* him.

Boy, he *was* turning me into a sap.

He half-blurted, "My parents have tickets to see the Monarchs—they got one for you too. For Sunday."

I was meeting his parents on Sunday too? My knees felt weak. Parents—adults in general—weren't always my best audience. *Oh god.* What if they hated me?

What if *he* hated me?

"Don't freak out on me," he said. "This is going to be great."

"Yeah?" I asked. "You don't freak out either, then."

"Promise," he said. "Make sure you have the right clothes for the game. Everyone should know you're a fan just by looking. A superfan, in fact."

"You're pushing it again," I said.

But he must've known I loved it. He said, "I wish I didn't have to go . . . but for once, I can honestly say—I'll see you soon."

I might have been in a full swoon. Our lips met.

We'd see each other soon.

"Not soon enough," I murmured and felt embarrassed again despite myself.

He laughed that excellent laugh of his, which I would soon hear *in person*, and then waited for me to leave *Worlds* first.

"Sunday," he said as I reached up inside and outside the game to switch off my holoset.

"Sunday," I repeated to my bedroom, after I turned it off. "Sunday. Sunday. Sunday."

I made an unseemly squeal and bounced on the bed.

Sunday. Sunday. Sunday.

CHAPTER 11

I couldn't set aside my feeling that I was missing something about that security-camera-ed building—that all of us were. While I was getting dressed in jeans and a T-shirt with a spaceship on it, I considered a detour there on the way to school. But who was I kidding? I'd have had to get up way earlier for that. As it was, I ended up dashing to the subway and only made it to school on time because the train was pulling up as I arrived at the platform.

As I walked into school and headed to my locker, it was clear the first bell had already sounded by the flurry of people rushing to and entering classrooms. That meant my main goal for the morning would have to wait. I'd wanted to track down Maddy and find out how her date with Dante had gone. She hadn't called me, so that must have meant no breakup. But things had definitely seemed . . . off between them.

And since I couldn't read the expression of a text, I hadn't bothered to send one to ask. I was saving it for in person. Speaking of which, I opened my locker at the same moment my phone buzzed with a new message.

I chanced a look up and down the hall and spotted no Principal Butler, so I risked checking it.

SmallvilleGuy: *We're on the road—Dad decided we should see roadside attractions on the way.*

No, gah, I wanted him to *get here* already. A new message popped up before I could think of a non-pathetic way to convey the sentiment.

SmallvilleGuy: *We'll be there for our date on Sunday, no worries. I reminded him about the tickets. And I told him that it was cruel to make the trip longer. We compromised on one roadside attraction in each state, close to the highway. This morning's is Truckhenge in Topeka. I'll send you a pic. Everything okay there?*

Whew. I should have known we'd be on the same page. I just hoped we still were when he got here.

SkepticGirl1: *So far. I'm going to check out that building again after school.*

SmallvilleGuy: *You going to take someone with you?*

I wasn't planning on it.

SkepticGirl1: *Maybe. Gotta run to class. Don't get crushed by any falling trucks. ;)*

Were the next three days going to creep along with road progress reports? I was betting on yes.

I stowed my phone, grabbed the textbook at the top of the pile in my locker, and then closed the door.

I rushed toward first period with what I suspected was the world's goofiest smile on my face. But it vanished when Maddy appeared beside me. Her eyes were shiny, the rims slightly pink—she was holding back tears. Her T-shirt was a repeat, which hardly ever happened: Dangerous Ladies.

"Mad?" I asked. "What's wrong? Are you okay?"

"No, I'm a mess," she said, brushing a hand under her eye. "Obviously. Dante is the nicest guy. He asked me to tell him what's wrong again this morning and I'm—" she waved her hand to indicate her face, "—well, I wasn't able to say anything and then I almost started crying. He looked so worried. I just . . . what's wrong with me?"

"Nothing," I said, the one thing I was confident about. "Absolutely zero is wrong with you." I hesitated. I'd risk another tardy for my friend. "Do you want to go somewhere and talk about it?"

She shook her head. "It won't help. I still don't know what to do. I guess sometimes just being yourself feels really difficult. Is that a jerky thing to say? I know I have no reason to complain. Oh, my boyfriend is so nice. He wants us to get even more serious, but I'm not sure how I feel about him anymore. I think I just want to be my own person, on my own. But what if I don't feel that way after I break up with him? Woe is me."

We were alone in the hallway now, and the second bell sounded. I touched her shoulder.

"No. I know exactly what you mean. Sometimes it is hard to

be yourself, feeling like you always make the same mistakes."

Her shiny eyes widened. *"You've* felt this way?"

"Sure. When I came to school here I was determined to stay out of trouble."

That earned a half-smile. "You were?"

"I got over it." I touched her arm. "Anyway, you can't help how you feel. Does it help if I say you're still awesome? No matter how difficult this feels? No matter how it works out or doesn't?"

She paused and considered. Thoughtful Maddy, she would turn around every fact into many facets and consider each one. "Actually, yes, it does help. Okay, we'll talk later." She shoved me toward the classroom door. "I don't want to be the reason you get in trouble with Principle Loathsome again."

"You're amazing," I said, just for good measure, and went into class.

★ ★ ★

I hurried up the sidewalk after school, staying alert for any flashes of armor around me. It seemed odd that our Typhon pals were still lying low. Maybe we'd spooked them by finding out their names.

I'd claimed I had to run an errand before I went to the *Scoop*, which was sort of true. None of the others had challenged it, anyway.

When I reached the right block, I stopped at the corner and took a good look around. There was nothing different from our visit the day before. There was a light amount of foot traffic, and of course the same businesses. It was the same absolutely calm, normal Metropolis street. So why did the back of my neck prickle?

"Busted," Devin said, stepping up beside me.

I sighed. "Don't sneak up on me. I could have punched you or something."

"I'm shaking in my boots," he said. "What are we doing here?"

"I don't know." I pulled him back around the other corner so we could talk in safety. "What are *we* doing here?"

"Lois," he said. "Like we didn't all know what you were doing when you said you had an errand to run. I volunteered to be your backup. You obviously thought we were missing something yesterday."

Having friends had its positives. And its negatives. Like them being able to predict your actions in advance.

"Fair enough," I said. "You guys all seemed so sure this isn't the place. I feel like it is."

He tilted his head. "The same way you're convinced Donovan's involved even though it's not clear he is? Do you know something we don't?"

Yes. That this person's mostly after me.

"I'm just following a hunch," I said. "Like any good reporter."

"Okay," he said, "then what are we doing?"

Maybe it wasn't the worst thing to have backup. I wasn't sure if I'd planned to bang on the front door and try to get them to admit me solo—which Todd had made it sound like they would happily do—but I could at least hit the buzzer again.

"Let's just take another stroll by, see what we can see," I said.

"I like strolls," Devin said.

We swung back around the corner and up the sidewalk toward the building with the weird cameras.

"So, everything okay with that list? Should I be worried about you and our friend in the game?" Devin asked.

"He's coming here," I said.

Devin let out a whistle. "Wow, that's big," he said. "You nervous?"

"No." I huffed out air, blowing my bangs out of my eyes. "Except, yes, extremely."

We were a couple of buildings away from our destination. Devin said, "How could you not be? But hey, if you decide you don't like him . . . I'll ask you out."

I rolled my eyes at him. "You will not. Anyway, I'm more worried he'll decide he doesn't like me. Or what if we're just too awkward together in person? Or what if he's physically repulsed by some weird habit I don't even know I have . . .?"

"You really *are* nervous," Devin said. "I think the only weird habit you need to worry about is letting your imagination drive you crazy with scenarios like that."

"Easier said than done." I squinted at the building. So boring, except for those cameras. A few of the windows were tinted to keep out sunlight, but it was just a regular three-story brownstone otherwise. No signs of life. "Those cameras *are* strange, aren't they?"

Devin was quiet for a second. "I'm not encouraging your hunch, because this building seems unoccupied by all the signs. I rechecked the power grid and found nothing . . ." He frowned.

I crossed my arms. "But?"

"But I did a little research on security cameras and I didn't find anything like that commercially available," he said. "They're something new. Maybe custom."

"Hmmm," I said.

I walked closer to the front door, peered inside its tint-free glass again. Devin joined me this time.

"Still empty," he said. "Doesn't look like anything's been here in a while."

He was right. And yet . . .

I stepped back and rang the buzzer again, leaning on it for a long moment this time. Then I watched the camera where James had seen the little red light before.

This time there was nothing.

We waited for a couple of minutes, and there was . . . more nothing.

"Nobody's home," Devin said.

"Or nobody's inviting us in, at least. Okay," I said, "let's go to work. I'm giving up on this."

Devin looked at me, eyes narrowing in suspicion. "I almost believed that."

"I'm giving up on this for today," I amended.

After work and dinner, I decided I might as well do homework. I was still waiting for SmallvilleGuy's check-in—I could guess he didn't want his parents to see him obsessively on his phone.

I thought I was focusing on writing my short essay on Kate Chopin's *The Awakening* for English, but my phone was right in front of me on the desk. I had it in my hands almost as soon as it buzzed.

SmallvilleGuy: *Behold…*

He sent me a picture of some rickety trucks piled up in stacks and mounds of metal, and then another photo followed. This one was of boats sitting up on their ends, in a more deliberately placed henge fashion, surrounded by trees.

SkepticGirl1: *???*

SmallvilleGuy: *Our Missouri stop was Boathenge. And now we're in Illinois for the night, where we went to the birthplace of the hot dog on a stick for dinner.*

Another picture popped up, this one of old, formerly snazzy oversized letters that spelled out FOOD over a diner. I laughed as I tapped back a message.

SkepticGirl1: *Were they good at least?*

SmallvilleGuy: *They were, um, memorable. How was your day? Any progress on your story?*

SkepticGirl1: *Not really, and tomorrow I prep for interviewing Boss. No sign of our guys either.*

SkepticGirl1: *So what is your favorite of the sights so far?*

There was a pause, and I pictured him considering. Except, of course, when I pictured his face there wasn't anything to picture.

Soon there would be.

SmallvilleGuy: *Where we are now, because we're this much closer to Metropolis.*

My real eyes turned into heart-eyes, like the emoji. I settled for a simple response:

SkepticGirl1: *<3*

★ ★ ★

Friday's classes passed and there was still no sign of our attackers. I thought their absence left us all with a deep uneasiness. Maddy was maintaining the status quo with Dante, making up her mind. I wasn't going to push her to talk about it anymore.

Mom was teaching class, and so when I got home Lucy and I ordered a pizza. Dad, of course, was still off in Kansas searching for the flying man.

After scarfing some pepperoni slices, I spent the evening holed up in my room going through the *Planet*'s digital archives and reading every story I could find about Boss Moxie or in which he was quoted. He was slippery, so there wasn't as much as there could have been. But there was enough.

Interviews reporters had grabbed with him at one of the many real-estate meetings he attended. Reports on the failed sting operations to take down his crew over the years. And, of course, the stories that followed our scoop about his role in framing James's dad that finally got him sent to prison.

I decided my strategy would be to try to get him to warm up to me, then be as direct as I could. Reading between the lines, I had developed a theory that Boss hated when people played games with him . . . but loved when it was the other way around. I was confident I was right in thinking that he would know something. So many of his early quotes were along the lines of, "I've devoted my life to this city, and will continue to do so despite smears on my character."

Uh-huh. They weren't smears if they were true.

My phone buzzed near bedtime, and I picked it up, eager for today's photos.

SmallvilleGuy: *You still up? Sorry I didn't message sooner. We just stopped at a hotel.*

SkepticGirl1: *Yep. Report please. What'd you see today?*

SmallvilleGuy: *Good stuff—in Indiana we visited a place you would love.*

SkepticGirl1: *Oooh, what was it?*

SmallvilleGuy: *Rotary Jail Museum. It has the only working rotating jail cell in the country. It rotates in a circle so eight cells could be brought around to the door separately. Only one guard needed. From the 1800s.*

He sent a photo of a little cell with beige metal bars.

SkepticGirl1: *That is indeed cool. I bet I won't see anything like that tomorrow.*

SmallvilleGuy: *You ready for your big interview?*

SkepticGirl1: *Ready as I can be. What else from today?*

I waited and another photo popped up. It was a bronze deer statue complete with horns standing at the railing of a bridge in a city.

SmallvilleGuy: *Columbus, my fave because we only had to hop out of the car for this one. Tomorrow is our last day of driving, and then . . .*

SkepticGirl1: *Then you'll be here.*

We both typed in messages that popped up at the same time.

SmallvilleGuy: *I can't wait.*

SkepticGirl1: *I can't wait.*

I put my hands up to my face, then managed an answer.

SkepticGirl1: *Jinx. You owe me a Coke.*

SmallvilleGuy: *You got it. Good night, Lois.*

SkepticGirl1: *Night, soon-to-no-longer-be-a-mystery boy.*

Two more sleeps, and then Sunday, Sunday, *Sunday.*

CHAPTER 12

But before Sunday came Saturday, and my first ever visit to a prison. Obviously I couldn't tell Mom where I was going, so I planned to say to the *Scoop*. It was *Scoop* business after all.

I pulled on my leather jacket and, after a moment's hesitation, put Reya's drawing of the woman and the dragon in my bag. It might come in handy.

When I got downstairs, Mom was in the kitchen reading today's edition of the *Planet*—which she'd insisted on subscribing to, Dad's protests about the sensationalist media pressed aside by her allegiance to me and my employer. She looked at me over the top of it. "Where are you off to?"

"To commit journalistic enterprises," I said.

"Carry on," she said. "What time will you be back?"

Good question. I honestly had no idea.

"I'm, um, not sure. I'll text."

She shrugged. "Okay, well, have a good day, hon."

Why, yes, I did feel guilty as I left and as I navigated the subway. From the appointed stop, I followed my directions to the dock for the corrections department's ferry to Stryker's Island.

Perry was already there, and he waved as I walked up. The West River shone flat and gray in the sunlight. It emanated a smell like old laundry and fish guts that made it hard to appreciate looks-wise.

The ferryman—noteworthy for his captain's hat and friendly-walrus mustache—stood waiting on the dock beside the boat with a few other guards who apparently formed his crew. He held a clipboard and, when we approached, asked, "ID?"

I flashed my ID, and then nervously said, "This is my adult companion."

"I figured, Ms. Lane," the walrus-mustached man said, putting a check by my name and making Perry sign that I was under his supervision.

The ferry guy and his crew checked everyone against the list, marking them down or turning people who weren't on it away. Then he climbed over onto the deck of the dingy white boat, which had the corrections logo on the side.

"All visitors to Stryker's aboard!" he called.

There were about ten of us, a small contingent, who stepped over onto the wobbly deck. The boat was older, rough around the edges, with an enclosed cabin where we were made to sit on benches.

Perry and I got the front row, at least. And the boat had windows, so there was some view as we lumbered out across the water. The river was prettier with a buffer against the odor.

"At least on the way back we'll have a view of the city," Perry said.

"What? You don't like looming fortresses?"

Stryker's Island was already visible ahead. The prison was located on a literal island, between New Troy and Queensland Park. This, our mode of transport, was the only way for visitors to get there. A municipal ferry ran for employees only.

The prison was a towering structure, built high on the rocks of the island, getting larger as we approached. Not exactly a place that shouted "pleasant day trip."

"You know what you're going to ask Boss?" Perry asked.

"Of course," I said.

I had made notes and scrawled some questions in my notepad in case I froze up. But my main plan was to wing it, and use what I'd theorized about his nature. "I thought I might try to get him talking a bit first, see if he gives us anything else interesting."

Perry made an appreciative grunt. "I admit I'm shocked he agreed to see us. It would be great to get him as a source—but I want you to be ready for him to just be toying with us. I've covered him for a long time. He's not known for being friendly to journalists."

"Well, we're not known for being friendly to mobsters, so I think we'll get along with him just fine." But I nodded. "Message received. I don't expect him to be respectful."

"This should be an interesting day, no matter what happens." Perry leaned back against the seat. "What progress have you guys made on the other story? Do you think we should even do a story about those sightings at this point? Maybe it was just kids."

Mayday. Proceed with caution here too.

"I have a feeling we haven't heard the last of them. It'd be good to be prepared whenever they start up again."

"You think it's a group?" he asked, keying in on my use of "they."

This had a logical answer. "It has to be, multiple sightings at different locations at the same time."

"Right," he said, but nothing else.

I stared at the fortress-like prison, looming so large now that we could only take in part of it. We could see the wire fencing at the bottom, segueing to barred windows as the levels went up. Then there was the dock. It offered a single entry from the water, leading to an imposing sliding warehouse-like entrance.

The lack of exits and the barbed and shock-wave-capable high-tech fencing was smart, or inmates would constantly be trying to jump into that fishy, stinky water and swim away. The prison's website touted its lack of successful escapes. The fencing was supposedly the only high-tech innovation, besides thumb-keyed doors that prevented inmate substitutions or disappearances within the facility.

The website made these claims as proudly as a tourism board would. Which I supposed the Metropolis tourism group might: "Come visit! Don't worry about escapees from our world-class, grim prison out on the river! Most of the convicts there aren't even from here!"

"Remind me never to become a criminal," I said.

"I'm not worried." Perry grew serious after that, though. "It is good to see the consequences of putting people away. And of freeing them."

We were both thinking of James's dad, I knew. He'd been here. Through no fault of his own. We'd cleared his name. But Donovan was still out there . . .

A sense of responsibility sank onto my shoulders, and I knew I'd carry it with me inside.

The boat docked, and we disembarked along with the other visitors on the transport. We were being given somewhat privileged treatment, if I wasn't wrong. We had been seated at the front, and we were now ushered off first *and* maintained the first place in line.

The guard who'd been on the ferry stopped at the enormous mud-colored sliding door, then knocked on it with a thump against the thick metal. Someone inside levered it open with a loud cranking noise.

I saw that a solidly built woman was manning the other side of the door as it slid to reveal a broad entrance. Both visitors and supplies must use this same door—there was no reason for its size otherwise.

Several other guards stood farther back in a line. The space behind the door was cavernous, some fluorescents overhead giving everyone's complexions a waxy cast. The floor was plain concrete, and stacks of boxes were visible along one wall.

"This way," the guard from the boat said.

I looked at him and smiled as we entered. I didn't know what else to do.

"*You're* the ones here to see Mannheim?" he asked. "Not what I expected."

"Why?" I asked. "What do his regular visitors look like?"

The man sniffed. "Lawyers."

"Figures," Perry said to me as he steered us through the door.

The cavernous chamber had another door at the end, which led to a long, soul-crushingly repetitive hallway. Lights flickered overhead. The guard from the boat and the woman guard led us and the other visitors along the hall, turning to head past a cellblock (empty at present).

I couldn't imagine living in such a small space. Some cells had two bunks, some had four. So make that an even smaller space. The lights continued to flicker, giving the whole place a horror-movie vibe.

"They could use some updates," I muttered.

"Write a story," Perry said mildly. "Their budget gets cut every cycle."

"I'll petition James's dad."

"A subject it might be better not to mention during our interview," he said.

Another hallway, this one with doors that had nameplates with titles like "Vice President of Therapy," "Vice President of

Prisoner Relations," and "Vice President of Prisoner Facilities."
Apparently, if you were an administrator at Stryker's Island,
you eventually became a VP of something.

Finally, we approached a room with small tables and a glass
wall that allowed guards to monitor it. The sign beside it said:
Visitors' Lounge.

Yeah, some lounge. All luxury.

The guard opened the door, and we walked through it into
the lounge. It swung closed behind us. With our escort on the
other side.

"Perry," I said, turning to see the rest of the visitors and
guards standing on the other side of the glass. Our escort had
his hand up, explaining something to them. There was, however, a female guard already in the lounge with us.

Perry asked her, "Why aren't the others coming in now?"

"Mannheim asked to see you two alone. I just work here,"
she said.

And Mannheim was just supposed to be a prisoner.

"Lane, we can leave if you want," Perry said, ready to argue
the point. Clearly.

"No," I said. "I'm not afraid of him."

The guard looked at me with something that was half
"you poor girl" and half "if you mean that, then respect."
She pointed as a door at the other side of the room opened
and another guard brought in—handcuffed—Boss Moxie.
He looked exactly the same as he had on the outside.
From the thick neck up, anyway. The prison jumpsuit was
different.

He shuffled along, choosing a table for us. I shrugged to Perry and we crossed to take the chairs on the other side of the table.

Moxie was looking at me in a mocking way that made me want to put him away all over again.

"The famous Lois Lane," he said. "I was thrilled to get your request. It seems fitting to sit across from one who has gotten the better of you. For now."

"I wouldn't know," I said.

Perry coughed, and Moxie's eyes shifted to him. "There are two guards with us. You're perfectly safe with me," the inmate said.

"Forgive me for doubting." Perry and his sarcasm.

Mannheim frowned. On anyone else, it was a facial expression. On him, it managed to be a threat.

"It's so quiet here," I said, interrupting whatever was going on between those two. "Downright peaceful."

"Not usually," Mannheim said. "But I asked people to be nice for your visit. We want you to come back, after all."

No thanks, I thought. But who knew when we'd need him again?

"Thank you for seeing us." I pulled out my notebook. "I thought it would be good for us to chat. We do both care about Metropolis. It's something we have in common."

He smiled, but it didn't touch his eyes. He just stared at me, my notebook, my pen in hand. I willed my hand not to shake, and felt grateful when it obeyed.

I'd forgotten somehow, or maybe never understood,

because I'd been able to stay away from him . . . This was a very dangerous man. Still. Even in here.

Yes, that's why you came.

"Yes, yes, it is," he said finally. "My city, going to the weeds with me not there."

"I wouldn't go that far," I said.

Perry coughed again.

"Do you need a candy or a drop of some kind?" Mannheim asked him. "You really shouldn't bring germs into such confined quarters."

"I am not sick," Perry said.

"He's high-strung," I muttered, a wink to Moxie. I chanced a glance at Perry and knew from the scowl he shot back that I would pay for this later. But it was a technique I'd learned from him—to build a rapport with a hostile interviewee. Make them trust you. Make them want to talk.

"I can see that." Mannheim finally relaxed, or at least pretended to. "What made you come?"

"There were . . ." I paused, glancing at Perry again. Why hadn't I realized this would be hard with him here? I couldn't give away anything *extra*. What if Mannheim decided to start talking about clones and mad science? I'd have to just do the best I could and hope he went along with me. "There have been reports of people doing strange things around the city. I wondered if you knew anything about that."

"Strange things," he said. "Interesting choice of words. For a writer, not very descriptive. Is there anything truly strange for a great city? Hasn't Metropolis seen it all before in her centuries of existence?"

Perry watched me.

I kept my voice even. "Not unless she's seen people lifting cars like they weigh nothing and flying with silver wings, and running faster than anyone can with silver feet. Not unless she's seen that."

"Had people *claiming* to see that, anyway," Perry said.

Mannheim's eyes darted between me and Perry, then he chuckled. "Ah, I should have guessed that's why you wanted to come. Those stories, about children like you—no wonder you're interested in them."

"I'm not a child," I said. "I'm here because I think there's a story there. I think someone is trying to make some sort of move on your city, but I don't know to what end."

I wanted to throw up at calling Metropolis his city, but it was necessary. It would help gain his trust, let him feel he was in charge of whatever game he was playing. I kept my attention on him.

"You *are* a child," he said. "You shouldn't be in such a hurry to grow up. Grown-up problems are complicated. Tell her, Mr. White."

"Some are, and others are simple. Like matters of guilt and innocence," Perry said casually.

Ah, there's *my boss.*

Maybe I was being too nice after all. It seemed I'd recovered my own, um, moxie, during their exchange. "It is true that people seem to get caught when they're up to no good in

Metropolis these days," I said. "It makes me feel good about my city. Maybe whoever's behind these appearances is just that much slicker than the others, though, the ones who got busted."

I gave him my most innocent smile, the one that made Dad crazy.

"Doubtful," Moxie said, putting his elbows on the table. "There's a new player in town—old money, and I do mean old." He paused like that was important, though I had no clue why. "Name's Erica Alexandra del Portenza."

I lifted a finger to interrupt, wanting to make sure I got the name down right.

He smiled. "You need me to spell it? I heard you're not so good with that."

From where? I wanted to blurt, but that was obviously what he wanted. I pushed over the pad and gave him the pen, which made Perry shift nervously. He didn't intervene, though.

Moxie scribbled down a name and slid the paper back to me, extending the pen. When I reached over to take it, he pulled it back. "I have another one," I said.

With another chuckle, he gave it back to me. "She's some kind of Contessa, acts like a queen. Dresses like one too, from what I've heard. Italian. She's the real brains in the operation, not that the others know it. They think she's just controlling the purse strings."

"What others?" Perry said.

"Hold that thought," I told him.

I bent down and rummaged in my bag, glad I'd tucked in

the folded-up art before I left home. One of the guards started to come over and Moxie raised a hand to keep him back. Where had that guy been when Moxie was insulting my spelling ability?

I found the paper I'd taken off the wall of the homeless shelter and held it up. "This her?" I asked.

"Being where I am, I haven't met her myself," he said, scrutinizing it. "But this fits the description. I had no idea you were also an artist."

"I'm not. I think one of the people who were spotted around town drew it." Perry cleared his throat, but he didn't speak. So I asked his question from earlier, "What others did you mean?"

"Now, now, what good's a journalist who has to rely on a little birdie for all her information?"

Less a little birdie and more like a canary who runs the coal mine.

"Is, uh, Donovan involved?" I asked. Direct, just like I'd planned.

Perry raised his eyebrows, but again, he didn't speak.

"He's not the only one," Moxie said. "But they do know of you. *Everyone* wants to know the enchanting Ms. Lane, get her on their side. I can see why."

The man was a bully. A bully who'd elevated himself to a high-level position, but a bully just the same. No amount of flattery would change how I saw *him*.

"We have what we came for." I pushed back from the table. He'd confirmed my suspicions and given us a new lead. To try to get anything more would be pushing it. "I'm ready to go."

"I couldn't resist myself when they told me you wanted to visit," Moxie continued, as if I hadn't spoken. "After all, you put me in here, and you're just a girl."

I had to work hard not to grit my teeth. "I'd rather be 'just a girl'—which is a great thing to be, by the way—than anything like you."

Moxie shot me a smile that appeared to be in admiration. He made no move to get up, but he said, "The Contessa, I'm told she likes funding pet projects and that she's hard to pin down. Good luck tracking her."

"I never rely on luck," I said.

Which was true. I couldn't afford to. Not when mine was the worst.

"It was a pleasure meeting you, Ms. Lane," Moxie said. He tipped an imaginary cap to Perry. "Until next time."

"If there is one," I said.

And I promptly thought, *I hope it's next century.*

CHAPTER 13

Perry had been right about the view on the way back. Approaching Metropolis by water was our reward for going to see that gross old lion in his unwilling den.

Well, that and a name for the glam lady who'd been standing out on the street, apparently waiting for a look at me. She'd asked me if everything was okay. I'd ask her the same once we finally tracked her down.

"I take it you're running down that lead," Perry said. "And why do I feel like there was more going on in that conversation than I was aware of?"

"You're a smart guy," I said. "Pretty sure he just wanted you to think that."

Until we had proof, I couldn't bring Perry onto team "conspiracies are real, and so are clones, flying men, and mind control experiments—so far." He was too good a reporter. He'd demand to see the receipts.

Which meant we had to go get them.

"I'll have something for you soon," I told Perry.

I fished my phone out of my bag and typed out a group text that said: *Confirmation Donovan's part of this, maybe someone else. And definitely a woman named Erica Alexandra del Portenza. She's a Countess or Contessa or something. Devin, maybe see what you can find on her?*

Perry tapped his fingers on the seat, gazing out in front of us. "All I'll say is this," he said. "If you think you're right about more sightings on the way, then make sure that story's ready ASAP. We are *not* getting scooped by Loose Lips. Message received?"

"Loud and clear."

★ ★ ★

With nothing else to do later that night (except envision SmallvilleGuy and his parents' car somewhere on the highway approaching the city), I spent an hour unfruitfully googling the Contessa's name. There was nada that I could find. I hoped Devin was having better success than I was. He had ways of teasing information out of thin air and private databases, after all.

My phone buzzed with a text and I slid it over to read. Speaking of Devin, the new message was from him.

I'm not finding anything.

I sighed, and shot a message back.

Me neither. Do you think Boss Moxie made up the name?

Devin took a minute or so to respond.

It's possible. But I'm not ready to give up yet. I was thinking about how we had to use paper records to find Moxie. You want to come with me to the Metropolis Public Library tomorrow?

I had to meet SmallvilleGuy at the ballpark in the late afternoon, so something to keep me occupied before would be nice. I didn't want to cut the timing close, though. *Is it open?*

Devin shot back: *Every day of the week.*

I responded: *Can we do it early? I have a thing tomorrow.*

Sure, Devin typed back. *See you there at . . .* A few seconds passed . . . *10 (that's when it opens on Sundays).*

I spent a little time clicking around on Strange Skies, looking for recent posts by TheInventor. There weren't many—instead, he was the all-seeing force in the background. I closed the tab, realizing that if he *was* in fact all-seeing, he might be seeing me trying to find him.

You're being paranoid, even for you. It was true, there was no way he could know what I was looking for. He might be able to track my online activity—at least on his site—if he wanted to. But no matter what else he might see or know, he couldn't see inside my brain.

Some small comfort there. I decided I might as well catch up on my homework and then maybe do some more locksport reading.

Mom poked her head in around bedtime, and said, "Lois Lane, doing—" She stepped over to see which textbook I had open. It was biology, thankfully, not a locksport diagram. "Bio homework on a Saturday night. I'd never have believed it."

Well, I did go interview a mobster earlier in the day. "I am virtue personified," I said instead.

She rolled her eyes. "Let's not go overboard," she said, but then she hesitated. "Everything's all right, isn't it? With you? I feel like I never ask."

Where was this coming from? "Yeah, everything's great," I said.

If only Dad wasn't out there hunting for the flying man and I could crack this story and bring Donovan down. Then things would be great.

Meeting SmallvilleGuy tomorrow, though—hopefully that would be great.

"Okay, well, I'm always here if you need to talk," she said, then kissed my forehead.

Clearly I'd been acting weird. I would have to do better or my parents would be prying into my business. They might anyway, once Dad worked his way down to the bottom of the list of Strange Skies posters and found SkepticGirl1.

I'd worry about burning that bridge down when we got to it.

In the meantime, I finished up my bio homework, set my alarm for eight o'clock the next morning, and flipped off the light.

Then I turned it back on and logged into our chat app. SmallvilleGuy was supposed to let me know when they made it to town.

I lay there, still awake, when my phone got the message.

SmallvilleGuy: *We're here.*

SkepticGirl1: *Yay! Today's report?*

SmallvilleGuy: *First, how was Boss Moxie?*

I bit my lip and typed a response.

SkepticGirl1: *Gross, but surprisingly helpful. Now photos please!*

SmallvilleGuy: *Okay okay . . . First we have Big Jim, the metal cowboy of Bentleyville, Pennsylvania.*

And, in fact, that was exactly what the photo showed. A giant metal cowboy, with a pistol pointing up at his side and a funny mustache.

SkepticGirl1: *That is in fact a giant metal cowboy. Anything else?*

SmallvilleGuy: *How about the World's Largest Tooth? In Princeton, New Jersey.*

I cracked up.

A photo popped onto my screen. Of a giant molar.

SkepticGirl1: *And now you're here.*

SmallvilleGuy: *First we stopped at a museum on Staten Island with art made mostly out of mufflers and car parts. But yes, now we're here.*

SkepticGirl1: *You must be tired. I'll let you go. And I'll see you soon.*

SmallvilleGuy: *Sweetest dreams. See you tomorrow.*

I smiled and held the phone to my heart and hoped impossible things I'd never say out loud. Then I sent back a short reply.

SkepticGirl1: *Night.*

★ ★ ★

The Metropolis Public Library was a massive and impressive old building not far from the courthouse downtown. I hadn't seen it before, and so I couldn't help taking a moment for a good awestruck gape at it.

The three stone levels were grand, covered in ornate carved sculptures, gods and goddesses, strange creatures and gargoyles. The front was dominated by massive columns. Stone stairs led up to it and on either side of them sat two matching mythological creatures. They had the heads of eagles and the back ends of . . . horses? They sat, relaxed, like guardians of the place.

"Hippogriffs," Devin said, stepping up beside me. "Their names are Sue and Aliza."

"The hippogriffs are named Sue and Aliza? Not some grand mythological names?"

"They're named for the sculptor's nieces," he said.

"And you know all this how?"

Devin put a hand to the back of his neck, a little embarrassed. "My mom brought me here a lot when I was a kid."

I smiled. "Is this where your love for your griffin army comes from?"

"Maybe," Devin said. "A little. Griffins and hippogriffs must be like cousins, don't you think?"

It suddenly made all the sense in the world to me that he loved amassing his in-game creatures so much.

"Must be," I said. "Ready to track down a mysterious Contessa?"

He laced his fingers together and pressed them out to crack his knuckles. "More than."

It was funny that this had been his idea *and* that he was so into it. I'd practically tricked him into our excursion to sift through stacks of paper at the Hall of Records when we'd been after Moxie. Data was data, though, I guessed. He loved it.

"How was it seeing Moxie up close and personal?" he asked as we took the stairs up.

I mock-shuddered.

"That fun?" he asked.

"He's a gross old bully. But he was helpful . . ." I said. "I still don't understand why."

"Yeah, me neither."

We reached the entrance and, unlike at city hall, the security here was old school. We showed the guard the inside of our bags and breezed on into a stunning marble hallway. "Whoa," I said.

It was impressive. I was impressed.

"You see why I love coming here?" Devin asked.

"Uh, yeah," I said. "Most of the towns where we've lived, I loved the libraries, but they were small compared to this. They were like the one at school. Metropolis is officially the best."

A swell of love for the city filled me.

"You are hilarious," Devin said. "Let's go up to the reference desk. We need an expert."

The woman at the desk was poring over a ledger with some sort of fancy handheld gadget when we got there. Behind her were rows and rows of desks with reading lights, the tall ceiling ornately designed and the walls hung with massive oil paintings.

She glanced up and spotted us. She had cool glasses and wore a head scarf. A pencil poked out one side, where she'd tucked it between glasses and scarf.

"Devin!" she said and stood. She gave me an interested look as we approached. "And friend?"

"This is Lois Lane," Devin said. "We work together at the *Scoop*. Lois, this is Neema, the baddest and smartest librarian in the world. Don't make her mad."

She patted the side of her head. "He's not wrong," she said.

"Good," I said, liking her instantly. "We came because we could use some help with a story."

Devin jumped in. "We hit a snag researching. We have a name, but can't seem to track down anything about the person. No hits anywhere."

"She's an Italian countess, if that helps." I pulled out my notepad and flipped through it to the page where Moxie had noted the name.

"You've checked all the online sources?" Neema asked, then shook her head. "Of course you have." She plucked the paper from my hand. "If she has a title, we should be in luck. Italian, you say?" She was already walking.

Devin and I followed, rushing to keep up with her. She led us through a wooden door and along a corridor that proved to be a back way into an enormous room filled with stacks. The bookshelves stretched high around the edges of the room.

Without a hitch in her step or even slowing, she snagged a tall ladder against one of the shelves and steered it over. Then she began to climb.

I was wide-eyed when I turned to Devin. "I think I want to be her best friend."

He nodded. He'd seen this prowess at work before. "I know what you mean."

"Aha!" We heard an exclamation above us.

Neema started back down to us, a volume held under one of her arms. When she got back down to the bottom, she leapt off the ladder and revealed the cover of an obviously old leather-bound book. *The Great Families of Rome (Antiquity to 1948)*.

"Some things," Neema said, as she went to a table and placed the book on it, "never make it into the digital space. Or, at least, they haven't yet."

She held the paper with the Contessa's name on it above the book, and then squinted and flipped to the last few pages. An index arranged by year from oldest to newest, I realized.

"Hmmm," she said, in an unpromising way, as she scanned the columns looking for the name.

Devin and I exchanged a look. "What is it?" I asked.

"A lot of the old titles faded away around this period, when they stopped being anything but courtesy titles. I was sure it'd be in here," she said. "We'll just go back further."

We weren't doing much of anything except watching her flip through the book, but I stayed quiet. Another negative grunt, and she went back another section of pages. This went on until she was near the middle of the book.

What were the odds we would need to go back so far? The disappointment of a dead end began to build.

"Here it is," she said, placing her finger on the page. "I know you were losing hope, but I'm amazing."

"No kidding," I said.

Devin and I leaned over to see the line she indicated. There was the name, in Latin, then translated to Erica Alexandra. The deal-sealer was the title. Named Contessa of Portenza.

"No count listed," Neema said. "And no family tree or record of the lineage related to the title beyond this. She must have done someone important a big favor. It's possible she was from a family with older ties, but once the Italian nobility started there were prohibitions on how far back you could claim." Her forehead wrinkled. "Why are you guys doing a story on someone who was around in the 1600s?"

"That's a good question. You think she's using a fake name?" I asked Devin.

"That seems the likeliest option," he said. "Or maybe the family hid their tracks and chose that name because they dig it?"

"Do you know anything else about this woman?" Neema asked, closing the book and handing me the paper.

"We think she's a business investor," I said. "We can guess that she tries not to leave much of a paper trail."

Neema tapped her lip, thinking. Then she said, "I have a

possibility—it'll take a lot of wading through, but we do have some business journal collections in Periodicals, things that never got digitized."

My hopes sank. I checked my phone—I wasn't in danger of being late to the baseball game yet, but I would be if this took much longer. And I needed time to be nervous and agonize over what to wear. "That sounds time-consuming."

"Oh, right," Devin said. "Your thing. Why don't you go on and I can stay and wade through the journals?"

"Seriously? You don't mind?" This really was a transformation.

He had that embarrassed air again. "It's like a treasure hunt. If the Contessa's mentioned anywhere, I'll find it."

Neema beamed at him. "I'll show you where to get started. Bye, Lois—nice to meet you."

So I left, wondering how in the world this story just kept getting weirder. There had to be a development that would help us understand what was going on at some point, didn't there?

"Good luck," I told Devin. "I think we need it."

CHAPTER 14

The time I had allotted for getting ready was spent bouncing around the house like a big ball of nerves. Which I was.

SmallvilleGuy was *here*. In Metropolis. And in a little while, I'd be meeting him.

In person.

Every time before this that I thought I'd die of impatience—or worry—was a false alarm. This had to be it, the big one. The fit of impatient worry that killed me.

Finding it impossible to be still, I headed downstairs to grab a soda. Mom was in the living room grading a batch of short essays when I came down. She'd been there the last time I made the trip too. "Lois," she said, "you seem at loose ends—you want to catch a movie this afternoon? Lucy said she was in."

"Oh," I said, about-facing to, um, face her. "I can't. I have plans."

She raised her eyebrows.

"I'm going to a baseball game," I said, trying not to seem like I was hiding anything or like it was a big deal. "A favor to a friend."

"Which team?" she asked.

"The Monarchs." I was unable to keep the hint of a smile off my lips.

She gave me an odd look and said, "Have fun. Maybe the sports gene your dad was so disappointed you were born without will kick in after all."

"Don't hold your breath."

She went back to the paper she was marking up. "I won't."

I hadn't lied to her, not really. What I'd said was mostly true.

Just . . . it was a very big deal. And this wasn't just any friend.

I took my soda upstairs and got dressed for the game. I checked my phone for the time. I knew I needed to leave in the next fifteen minutes, if not sooner.

Instead of hurrying, I set my phone on the sink and stood in my bathroom in front of the mirror. I tugged nervously at the hem of the T-shirt I'd ordered shortly after I lost the bet (but had been too chicken to take the promised selfie in). It was dark navy, with the words Metropolis Monarchs in big, light-blue letters outlined in white. A little baseball man pointing his finger and wearing a crown was at the far end, and I assumed he was the mascot.

Right. A baseball king. The *Monarchs*. I finally got it.

Were my jeans and boots too regular? Should I be dressing up? But this was how I usually dressed—except for the costume shirt.

My phone vibrated across the porcelain with a new message in our chat app. I picked it up and swiped to see what it said.

SmallvilleGuy: *Have you left yet? We're on our way to the park.*

I sighed. *No, I haven't left yet, I'm staring at myself in the mirror like a big nervous wuss.* Obviously, I couldn't type the truth back.

SkepticGirl1: *On my way out the door. See you soon.*

I hesitated, took a breath that did nothing to calm my nerves, and sent one more text.

SkepticGirl1: *How will I recognize you?*

There was the immediate flare of the little dots that meant he was responding, and I clutched the phone waiting to see what he'd say.

SmallvilleGuy: *Don't worry—I'll find you.*

SmallvilleGuy: *And stop freaking out.*

SmallvilleGuy: *I can't wait to see you.*

I laughed and shook my head. This was comfortable, talking *this* way, pixels on a screen. Where he couldn't behold my sheer dorky nervousness. It was cowardly to fear change, to fear making this real, but . . . I had to admit to myself that I was afraid of just that.

A little.

A lot.

He was important to me.

What if meeting in real life screwed *us* up?

It hadn't happened yet, though, and so I shot back a flip response.

SkepticGirl1: *YOU'RE probably freaking out.*

I waited to see if he'd respond to that. He did.

SmallvilleGuy: *A little, tbh. Let's get this part over with.*

I smiled at the phone again, then gave my hair a nervous swipe. I'd had bangs cut since I'd posted a picture online. What if I looked cuter before?

Lois Lane, stop it, you know he doesn't care if you have bangs or not.

I put on my leather jacket and zipped it up, so as to avoid questions about my newfound sportswear love.

"Break a leg," I told my reflection. *And try not to get your heart broken.* "Stupid heart."

And then I headed out to meet my more-than-best-friend.

* * *

There were a lot of baseball fans in Metropolis. It was a big city and there were a lot of everything fans in Metropolis, so this should have been obvious to me. And yet, I was overwhelmed by the throng of people gathered and milling around outside the stadium. The game was still a good half hour from starting, but SmallvilleGuy had suggested we arrive early to give us time to find each other and get settled into our seats.

I tried not to seem like I was looking for someone, but I failed miserably. Several people turned away after I studied their section of the crowd too hard. I should have asked for a physical description. Who was I even trying to find—an alien with green skin and glasses, dressed in a Go Monarchs costume?

The idea of his avatar appearing in this crowd made me smile.

My phone buzzed in my pocket.

SmallvilleGuy: *Look to your right.*

My pulse sped up, and I tried to not appear like a full-blown madwoman as I slipped it back into my pocket and turned . . .

And completely lost the ability to breathe, be casual, or think. Right on cue.

My SmallvilleGuy stood about six feet away, his hand lifted in a wave. He had on a Monarchs baseball cap and a Monarchs T-shirt that was not exactly the same as mine (thankfully), and . . . he had the nicest face I'd ever seen.

I stared at him.

Tall, black hair, non-green skin, a strong jawline, black-rimmed glasses . . . and muscles. Not gross bodybuilder muscles, but more muscles than I'd expected.

Farm boy, I reminded myself.

He awkwardly lowered his hand, and I realized I'd been standing there gaping at him.

Oh god. Please let the Earth swallow me.

I moved toward him, pretending I was not freaking out. I pasted on a smile.

"Um, hey," I said, when I was a couple of feet away. I stopped before I walked right into him. Part of me wanted to. "I think you're looking for me. I'm, uh, Lois."

He blinked at me behind his glasses for a second. With his blue eyes. His very blue eyes.

Then he smiled at me. My heart curled up into a ball of happiness. The crowd around us ceased to exist.

"Lois Lane, I'd know you anywhere," he said. "I'm SmallvilleGuy, aka . . ."

Good voice too. I held my breath like a dope and he had to know it. I couldn't help it.

"Clark Kent."

"Clark Kent," I said, possibly the most pleasant words to ever cross my tongue. "It's not the *worst* name."

I'd been joking—it was a *great* name, a *perfect* name—but his eyes went wide with surprise.

"I was being funny," I said. "I like it. It suits you."

"Oh, right," he said.

Please, Earth, swallow me.

He smiled at me again.

Or maybe not. Maybe let me suffer.

"Your outfit's missing something," he said.

"I didn't have any cleats." I'd checked online about what

kind of shoes baseball players wore. I seriously was missing the sports gene.

"No, silly," he said. "You need a hat. Here, take mine."

Before I could protest—not that I would've—he removed his Monarchs cap and stepped nearer to me. He paused suddenly and asked, "Is this okay?"

I found myself unable to speak, so I nodded.

He settled the cap gently on my head. I would have told him my deepest darkest secrets in that moment. His face came close to mine and I thought we might be about to kiss . . .

In real life . . .

I closed my eyes . . .

"Perfect," he said.

I opened them.

"Ah. Haha, I'll take your word for it," I said.

I was the biggest dope in dopeville.

"You changed your hair," he said.

"You noticed." I couldn't help smiling.

But instead of taking the moment to kiss me, he held up two tickets. "We should probably get inside. My parents will be wondering if we got lost."

I accepted the ticket he gave me. "Yes, go inside. Watch sports ball," I said.

He laughed, and there it was. A little piece of *us*, joking with each other. Maybe this wouldn't be a disaster. If I could stop being the most awkward human who had ever lived.

And his parents. *Oh god. Will I live through today?*

"Lois . . . did you just ask if you'd live through today?" Clark asked me.

Clark. Asked. Me. Clark. I knew his name.

"Of course not, Clark," I said. "That would be so embarrassing. I'd only ask something like that if I was totally freaking out."

"Right."

We smiled at each other and joined the ticket-holder line.

CHAPTER 15

We made it through the ticket line and into the stadium without my inserting foot into mouth again, through some sort of miracle. Now we paused at the top of the aisle in the section where his parents were already seated.

The field stretched out beneath us, and in the stands there were all the things I'd expected to see at a baseball game—hot dogs, beer vendors, foam fingers.

"Where are we?" I asked, wondering why we weren't going down the steps to our seats.

Clark stepped up next to me. *Clark*. Would I ever get used to knowing his name? He peered down at the tickets.

"My parents can be . . . intense, sometimes," he said. "They're a little protective."

"You're talking to the girl whose dad is a general," I said. "I get it."

Though he was hardly making me feel better about meeting them.

"I know." He raked a hand through his hair, the gesture familiar from the time we'd spent together in *Worlds*. But so much better to see in person.

I kinda wanted to run my hand through his hair too. And, boom, my cheeks heated with the embarrassing line of my thoughts.

"It's just," he said, apparently not noticing my flushed face, "they may interrogate you. I asked them not to, but . . ."

"Clark," I said, "I'm pretty good at interrogating people myself. It'll be fine."

If only I actually felt that way.

Someone behind us cleared their throat. "Excuse me," a man in a full Monarchs costume with a foam finger on one hand and a beer in the other said.

"Sorry," I said, and touched Clark's bare arm. It was like an electric shock. We looked at each other, and then the guy obnoxiously stepped around us.

I smiled again, for real, my hand still on his forearm. "Do I make you nervous?"

Who was I and how had I made that sound so confident?

"Don't ask questions you already know the answer to," he said. "You're too good a journalist for that."

I laughed, delighted, and stepped away. "Where are our seats? I'm ready to face the Kent Inquisition."

"Right this way," he said, gesturing for me to go first. Then, close to my ear, "Famous last words."

I grinned, and was still grinning when he said, "This is our row."

I spotted two empty seats next to a couple a few seats from the end, and I let Clark take the lead into the row. We were near the bottom of the second section from the field.

"Good seats," I said.

"You have no idea if that's true," he said over his shoulder.

"Busted."

Then we reached his parents.

They stood up to let us slip past them. I shimmied past with a tentative smile, stopping on Clark's other side and turning to face them. His mom was around the same age as mine, maybe a few years older. She had warm brown hair and lines at the corner of her eyes that suited her, like they were from sun and a life she'd enjoyed. The flannel shirt that was over her Monarch's T was well worn. Clark's dad had similar lines around his eyes, plus darker brown hair and a plaid shirt that managed to neither match nor clash with his wife's. Clark didn't favor either of them, except they all radiated the same kind of, well, goodness.

Clark glanced from me to them. "Mom, Dad, this is Lois Lane, my . . . um . . ." he paused, and I willed him just to say girlfriend. But his cheeks had gone a light pink and I knew I'd have done the same thing, not been brave enough to say the word out loud yet.

Sharing the same space was too new.

"Lois, we're so pleased to meet you," his mother said, rescuing him. "You can call me Martha."

His dad removed his cap. "And I'm Jonathan."

I hesitated, my hand going up to the cap on my own head.

Jonathan laughed. "No, the man takes off his cap, you can leave yours where it is."

I took it off anyway. "That hardly seems fair," I said, waving it in the air, unsure what to do.

"She's got you there, Jonathan," Martha said. She added, "Looks like Clark's cap to me."

Annnd like that, I was blushing again, worse than Clark. "He, um, loaned it to me."

"Forcibly," he said. "Lois doesn't know anything about sports."

"We'll just have to teach her," Jonathan said, kindly, and moved back into his seat.

Martha did the same, and I sat down in the seat on Clark's far side. A buffer for which I was grateful.

I gripped the side of my seat so hard I thought I might break it. "Did I pass?" I murmured.

"So far, so good," Clark said. "But you don't have to worry about passing. Now, tell me about yesterday. I want the long version."

"Here?" I asked, looking around.

There were people on all sides of us. People who mostly weren't paying attention to us, including Martha and Jonathan, who were chatting with each other. (I suspected just to postpone any planned interrogation.) The players were in the dugout but the game hadn't started yet. Music blared out across the field.

"I don't think we're being spied on," he said. "Just keep your voice down."

So, as quietly as I could, I related the trip out to see Boss Moxie, the revelation about the Contessa's title being *very* old, and the confirmation that Donovan was involved. It was amazing what a difference it made, to switch to talking about the story. I didn't feel nervous anymore. Our conversation flowed easily. He listened, breaking in when he had a question.

Things settled into a rhythm that was almost comfortable. Except for when I looked at him and remembered he was *right here* and then I felt like I might throw up out of excitement and nerves and the force of reality.

"You still haven't told them about the pictures of you? The stories?" he asked when I'd wrapped up.

"I will, when the right time comes," I said, feeling guilty.

"Speaking of telling, TheInventor's reaction to the news about the list was weird," Clark said.

My skin chilled. "How so?"

"This isn't going to make any sense, but I got the feeling he was shocked but not surprised."

I shook my head. "It doesn't. What did he say?"

"He was completely thrown, but only for a minute. Then he said he'd do some looking into it."

Shocked that Clark had found out about it, more like. But I couldn't say that. The time hadn't been right to tell him about my suspicions and where the list had come from—and this certainly wasn't it.

Proof came when an announcer's voice boomed out above the park, and Clark stood to clap as his team was announced. My knees felt a little weak, the glow of our conversation dimmed by the secrets I was keeping. So I stayed put.

My mistake.

Martha leaned over behind Clark. "It really is so good to meet you, Lois. You seem like a serious person for your age. Clark said as much."

"I am," I said, trying to relax. "My mom used to tell me I act like everyone's problems are mine."

Martha nodded. "Clark's the same way. Your family's close to the city?"

"Right in Metropolis, about twenty minutes away from here by subway," I said. "We moved around a lot growing up. It's nice to have somewhere that feels like home."

Clark turned his head to catch my eye, and I smiled, letting him know I was okay. So far, this interrogation was on the lighter side.

"I wondered if maybe we could have dinner with your folks, meet them, while we're here in town," Martha said.

Argh. I saw Clark's posture go stiff.

"My dad's away on, um, business," I said.

"That's fine—your mom and, is there anyone else? Siblings?" she asked.

"My little sister, Lucy." I did not like the direction this was going, but what could I do? The train was officially speeding toward me, and I was caught on the tracks.

"We'd love to meet them. Wouldn't we, Clark?"

Clark finally eased back into his seat, so he was between me and his mother. "You may as well give her your mom's phone number," he said. "She won't take no for an answer. Believe me, I've been up against her."

I searched for a way out. I could clamber through the aisle above ours and bolt from the park. I could fake my own death and never reemerge. I could . . .

Clark's eyes sparkled. I could tell he was imagining the various escape scenarios playing out in my mind.

"He's right, you know," Martha said. Her smile took any bite out of it.

I could . . . hand over my mom's number. Which is what I did, scribbling it on a piece of paper from my notebook and handing it to her. "Could you maybe wait until tomorrow to call her?"

Martha accepted the piece of paper and gazed at me with brown eyes that I discovered could be as sharp as they were warm. I had zero doubt that she knew the time request was so I could explain to my mother they were even here. At last, she said, "Sure. I'll wait."

I collapsed back in my seat. "That was exhausting," I said to Clark under my breath.

"I warned you." He smiled at me, though. Even his teeth were good. "I can't wait to meet Lucy. And bribe her to tell me all your secrets."

I pushed his shoulder. "Mean." Also, "She'd tell you for free. The brat."

His laugh flowed out of him like a melody. And at that thought I knew I'd gone full sap.

I didn't even care.

His left hand was stretched out along his leg, pretty close to mine. I caught his eye and laid my own hand on the seat palm up next to my leg. I didn't dare breathe or say anything except to hope—

He reached over and took it in his. Boy, was I glad to be alive. *Thank you, Earth, for not swallowing me before this happened.*

My stupid heart beat fast enough to travel a mile a minute, faster than speedy Todd could run. I pretended to watch the game, but my thoughts were as wrapped up in his hand holding mine as my fingers were. It was hard to think about anything else.

This was fine, because despite Jonathan and Clark's valiant and occasional attempts to explain to me what was happening on the field, I was mostly soaking up the afternoon. I liked all of it—the park and the loud music and thunderous applause when the home team hit the ball, the warm sun shining on my arms and the way Clark's cap shaded my face from it, the delicious smell of hot dogs in the air *and* the one I ate. After which Clark held my hand again, and I caught Martha nudging Jonathan while they smiled like protective but happy parents at the sight.

But the thing I liked best about baseball, I decided, was that the games lasted *forever.*

At least, so it seemed. The ninth inning rolled around—even

I knew that was the last one—and there was a crackling hit. The score was tied, but this might give the Monarchs that last point they needed to win. Clark was on his feet instantly, and I was caught up enough to jump up too.

The ball soared toward our section of the stands, moving fast and—wait, it was coming right for *us*! For me!

I ducked, put my hands in front of my face, and waited for the impact.

When the people in the stands around us burst into applause, I lowered them. To find Clark clutching the ball in his hand, and extending it to me. "For you," he said, with the best smile that had ever existed.

He was officially cuter than Nellie Bly.

The people had stopped clapping, but still went "awwww" when I accepted it and held it to my heart, beaming. "Cute kids," the man behind us said to Martha and Jonathan. Then he added, "A pair of star-cross'd lovers, if ever I've seen one. Sorry, I have a thing for Shakespeare."

I fell back into my seat. Clark eased back into his. I could guess that Clark was as mortified as I was, but I still had the baseball he'd saved me from.

Now it was my turn to save him.

"Should I bite my thumb at thee, sir?" I asked the man. "'Star-cross'd' is from *Romeo and Juliet*, right? Not my favorite Shakespeare—and star-crossed means they're doomed." Clark was looking at me with an awestruck expression. "But it is better than *Macbeth*. Clark can't stand *Macbeth*."

"Is that so?" the man replied.

"No heroes," Clark explained.

"You're right about the reference, I just meant you make a cute couple," the Shakespeare fan said. "A-plus to both of you."

I stashed the ball—my new most-prized possession—in my bag, and then offered Clark my hand again. He took it without hesitation.

"You know, they call baseball the thinking man's sport," I said to him, when everyone else had returned to the business of watching the last of the game.

"Did you google 'quotes about baseball,' Lois Lane?" he asked.

"As the great Yogi Berra once said, 'Baseball is ninety percent mental and the other half is physical,'" I said, instead of answering directly. "I was afraid there might be a lull. But the Shakespeare I just have a good memory for."

"Lucky me," he said.

The Monarchs did win, but I was sad the game was over. "You're sure we shouldn't bring you home?" Jonathan asked when we reached the outside of the park.

"I'll be fine," I said. "It's not far."

"I'll call your mother tomorrow," Martha said.

Like I'd forget.

"Can we have one quick minute?" Clark asked them. They both nodded.

He led me a few feet away. Nervousness suddenly descended between us again.

"Did you have a good time?" he asked.

"I love watching the sports ball, very exciting," I said. "Yes, I did. Thank you."

"I'll see you tomorrow, won't I?" he asked. "After school? I wondered if I could come by the *Scoop*."

"We might have a lead to chase down, but I'll text you. We'll make a plan."

"Sounds good," he said.

"Sure does," I said.

We looked at each other. Then we both leaned in and . . .

I smacked my forehead right into his glasses, practically knocking them off his face. When I pulled back, my lips collided with his nose.

"Oh no, I'm so sorry." I scrambled to try and straighten his glasses at the same time he did, just as we both broke up with laughter.

It was too awkward to try the kiss again—especially with his parents standing nearby. I settled for taking off his cap and returning it to his head.

He brushed my cheek with his hand. "See you tomorrow?"

"Definitely," I said. "See you. With eyes that I have. And since I didn't break your glasses, you'll be able to see me, even."

"Bye, Lo." He raised his hand.

"Bye," I said, and turned to leave. I refused to check and see if Martha and Jonathan were laughing at the most awkward real-life attempt at a kiss ever. That would be just my luck.

But then, right this second, my luck felt remarkably good for a change.

CHAPTER 16

I was still walking on cloud nine, practically floating, when I reached the last block before home. Even the prospect of telling my mom that the mother of a boy I liked who lived in another state would be calling her so they could come for dinner didn't dent my bubble of happiness.

Even the way I'd fumbled our kiss didn't. Because there was *almost* a kiss. Which meant there *would* be a kiss at some point. Tomorrow?

Meeting each other in person did not seem to have ruined everything. I checked to make sure no one was around and did a little un-me-like whirl on the sidewalk. And when I completed my turn, two people appeared who burst my bubble entirely.

The boy with the silver wings landed in front of me,

carrying the brown-haired girl, Reya, the one with the silvery strong hands.

I slipped my phone out of my pocket in case I needed to call for help, then waited to see what their move would be.

"Hey guys, out for a stroll?" I asked. Not my best, but I'd been distracted. I should've known better than to be walking around all wrapped up in my thoughts and not paying attention. "Come to confess all and ask for my help?"

The boy set Reya on the sidewalk. He didn't say anything, but she stretched her silver armored hands out in a way that could only be described as menacing.

"I have no problem with you," I said, talking fast. "I know the Contessa and Donovan did this to you. What I don't know is why, and how to help you get away from them. I want to bring them down, for good."

Reya stalked closer, and my brain told me to run. But my instincts said otherwise, so I stood my ground. I looked past her, and asked the boy, "What's your name?" I looked back at her. "I know you're Reya."

"He's Jamie," she said. "We're here because you made Todd all worried and sad again. How *did* you know my name?"

Todd must have some hidden charms for her to feel so loyal to him.

"Mr. Jeffrey said you two are close, that he's like your brother." She'd stopped a couple of feet away. I dug in my bag for the sketch and held it up. "You're a talented artist."

Seeing the sketch hit her like a blow. She even took a step back. Then she moved forward and snatched it from my hand.

"I shouldn't have drawn that. It was stupid, *I* was stupid. But I'm not anymore—and I can't draw anymore anyway." Her fingers flexed and the paper tore. "We don't *need* your help." But when she stopped talking, she didn't move.

She hesitated, like she wasn't sure what to do next. Her eyes went to the crumpled drawing and I saw sadness there too.

"Are you sure about that?" I asked, as gently as I could.

The boy behind her—Jamie—was trying to mind his own business, gazing off into the sky. I wondered what his deal was.

"Are both of you *sure* you don't need help?" I asked.

"I'm fine," he said, smiling at me. "Never better. No tortured soul here. I've got nowhere else to go."

"Neither do we," Reya said. "Todd can't ever go back home, which means we don't *have* homes anymore." She tilted her head closer to me and lowered her voice for the next part. "But Lois Lane . . ."

I worried it might be a trap, but I leaned in to hear what she had to say.

"The people who saved us, they want you too," she told me. "If you don't want to be part of this . . . or to need help yourself, then I'd stay far, far away. Get out of town. Hope they forget about you." She paused. "Or just come with us. Maybe we can be friends."

So there was good in Reya. She wouldn't be warning me otherwise, and her worry for Todd was plain. Leaving home because a friend couldn't go back was a serious commitment.

And Jamie saying he had nowhere else to go fit to. I didn't know about the other girl, Sunny, but I could guess she was in the same boat.

Donovan and the Contessa had given the four of them something like a home. Of course they wouldn't think they needed help. To them, it must seem like help had already arrived.

"I would like to be your friend," I said. "It may feel like things are good for you now, that you're safe, but it won't last. They're using you."

She didn't make a move to leave, so I waited. I had a feeling she might say something more.

"I think we could have been friends, if we'd met before." She didn't bother denying my points. "They won't give up on getting you. You're part of their plan."

I shrugged. "And I won't give up on taking them down. That's *my* plan. I won't give up on helping you guys either. Remember that."

"It doesn't matter," she said. "They're getting tired of waiting. But they want you to come to them. They will make us force you to, eventually."

I smiled, though I didn't feel even a hint of happiness about this situation. "Then *they* don't know me very well. I'm not great at doing what I'm told."

"They understand you better than you think," she said, and turned on her heel. She spoke to me, her head crooked over her shoulder. "The next time we meet, we won't be friends. At least not yet."

Jamie held out his arms and she jumped into them. His small silver wings beat, once, twice, and they were far overhead.

My hands were shaking. Whatever the bad guys had planned, it was definitely aimed at me. It was definitely coming soon.

And I still didn't know how to stop it.

* * *

I rushed the rest of the way home, half-expecting speedy Todd to show up, or maybe even Donovan himself. He and the lady with the high heels and the title, who liked "pet projects," they wanted me to come to them.

Pretending I wasn't tempted to march straight there wouldn't do any good, but I recognized there was something else going on here. I'd be playing right into their hands. I had to figure out what they wanted me *for* first. Which wouldn't be easy to do, given that I'd held back the full contents of the folder from Devin, James, and Maddy. Here was hoping Devin had turned up something more useful this afternoon.

I let myself inside our front door and relaxed against it with a breath. Only then did I realize the lights were on and I wasn't alone in the living room.

Mom had a cup of tea and was curled up with a book on the couch. "Sports that scary?" she asked, a hint of legitimate concern in her voice.

Lucy was on the other end of the couch with Mom's tablet, and she didn't look up from whatever cockpit swiping game she had underway.

"There were some, uh, weird people up the street," I said. "Spooked me a little."

I can't draw anymore anyway, Reya had said. The Contessa and Donovan had plucked that girl out of a homeless shelter with her friend Todd, who was practically her brother, and taken away the talent she had. They'd made her strong, but they seemed to have taken away most of her strength.

She wasn't fighting them, that much was certain. But she had come to see me—because I'd upset Todd.

She was right. We probably would've been friends under other circumstances.

"Are they still there?" Mom set down her tea and got up. "Should we call the police?"

I eased away from the door. "This is Metropolis, Mom. I don't think 'weird people' raise an eyebrow for the cops."

"Fair point." She touched my shoulder. "Did you have a good time?"

I needed to get upstairs and fill the others in on what had happened, or at least as much of it as I dared to. But . . . I might as well get this over with.

"So, you know when I said before that I was meeting a friend at the game?" I studied my boots, then chanced a glance at her.

Mom's expression had grown measured. "Yes."

"That was true, but it was a long-distance friend—remember, the guy who called on the phone that one time because we play the game together?"

"The one who scared your dad and me half to death, you mean?"

"Um, yes," I said. "That was entirely my fault. You'll like him. I promise. He's nice, dependable, smart." My extolling his virtues did not seem to be softening her up. "*Anyway,* he and his parents are visiting Metropolis. His mom and dad were there the whole time at the baseball game, so don't freak out or anything. They run a farm. They're so nice. And his mom, um, she'd like to meet you, and so she may call you tomorrow. I think they want to go to dinner. Or have dinner. We don't have to, obviously—"

"Lois."

One little name that could communicate so much, depending upon who was saying it and in what tone. I knew I should have stopped talking before I did. I stood and awaited her verdict.

It hadn't really crossed my mind that she might protest not just this, but everything about the situation. Mom could forbid me from seeing Clark again while he was here in town.

If she wanted to keep me from sneaking out, she would. She could be as tough as Dad, and even tougher when she perceived a threat to one of her daughters.

Never underestimate a woman. I knew it to be true.

Lucy, meanwhile, was gaping at us. She tossed her tablet aside and shouted, "You *do* have a boyfriend!" And then she started to cackle.

I stuck my tongue out at her. Which was perhaps not mature but seemed a fitting response.

Mom's lips ticked up on one side, a sign she was battling a laugh too. She controlled it and stayed wary.

"Mom," I pleaded, "you don't need to lose it over this. You'll like them. He's a really good guy."

"I don't like that you lied to me," she said. "Is this why you've been acting weird? Worrying me?"

"I didn't exactly lie." But I nodded. Was I helping myself here?

"Avoided the full truth, then," she said.

"I'm sorry," I blurted. "I was nervous and . . . I'm sorry."

She sighed. "I knew you were nervous about something. Lois, you went up and down the stairs ten times in an hour today. I'll attempt to keep an open mind." She pursed her lips. "Your dad's not going to love missing this. The first boy you bring home."

The one bright spot in this conversation. "Do you have to tell him? Can't we just . . . wait?"

"I do have to tell him," she said. "It's part of the marriage deal, and if you really like this boy, he's going to find out sooner or later. But I'll hold off until after I talk to the boy's mother. She sounds sensible at least."

"She is." Were we going to regret introducing Martha and Ella? Probably for the rest of our days.

"What's his name?" she asked.

"Clark Kent." I inadvertently broke into a grin as I said it.

She shook her head at me.

I gave her a peck on the cheek. "Thanks, Mom. I . . . I don't always think so rationally about this stuff. I should've told you."

And then . . . I lingered. This situation called for delicacy. If she wanted me to tell her about him, I'd have to. I eyed the stairs, but wondered if I should take a seat on the couch to hang out with them.

"Did you guys go to the movies?" I asked, testing.

"We did," Mom said. "Not that you care. I'll get my first impression of this Clark Kent from meeting him. Now go. I can tell you're dying to get upstairs for some reason."

"*Scoop* business! Good night!" I said, and I raced up the steps.

I heard Lucy make kissing noises and the two of them laughing behind me. I barely cared—as long as they didn't do that when the Kents were around.

The Kents. I still didn't fully understand the extreme secrecy he'd insisted on all this time, but he said his parents were protective. I'd once thought maybe they were spies or something, the entire reason for the need for privacy, but I was long since convinced they were exactly what he said: farmers.

Part of me wanted to press for him to tell me *everything.* But I knew he couldn't. And I was certain enough that it had something to do with the flying man and what Clark knew about him. I knew, though, that Martha would not be happy if he told me anything more at this point, especially after they brought him to Metropolis. I could respect that.

For now.

I locked my door, went straight to my laptop, and pulled up my email. This was too much for a text. I typed up an explanation of the encounter I'd had on my way home (only being a little fuzzy on the bad-guys-being-obsessed-with-me part) and suggested we meet at school the next morning to share any new intel. Immediately, a thread of responses started.

Devin was first: *I have something.*

Me: *Whew.*

And then Maddy: *I'll reserve our room.*

James chimed in: *Maddy, you need a ride tomorrow? I don't like the idea of you walking alone, with all this going on.*

I wanted to say, *No offer to drive me, then?* But I didn't.

Maddy shot back: *Thanks, see you—7:30?*

I think we're running out of time before they start whatever their endgame is, I typed. *See you in the morning.*

I hated that we were still so in the dark. What good was knowing their names if we weren't sure what they were created to do? Why had the armored test subjects seemed to have become ghosts, lost with no one worried about them? What purpose could a group of runaway teens augmented with that silvery metal serve in the larger scheme of things? Why let them be seen in public? Why would their leaders want me *so* specifically?

I didn't like any of it.

Clark and I hadn't been using the secure chat app on my laptop much, so I was surprised when it pinged with a notification. I guessed I'd forgotten to log out the last time we did.

SmallvilleGuy: *I can't seem to stop thinking about the game.*

SmallvilleGuy: *By which I mean you.*

TheInventor could be watching. I couldn't afford to fill Clark in on everything that had occurred on the way home. That could wait until tomorrow.

SkepticGirl1: *I'd already forgotten all about it. Baseball, wha?*

SkepticGirl1: *I kid, sap. Me too.*

SmallvilleGuy: *I just wanted to make sure you got home okay. I tried the phone app, but you weren't on.*

SkepticGirl1: *Yeah, well, I had to warn my mom about a certain phone call she'll be getting tomorrow.*

There was no response for a moment, and I worried I'd offended him.

SmallvilleGuy: *Was she surprised about me?*

Argh, this was delicate. He'd told his parents about me. I'd told mine a cover story about him, at best. He wasn't the only one with secrecy issues.

SkepticGirl1: *Sort of. With Dad leaving, it was better not to tell her you were coming until today.*

SmallvilleGuy: *Right, well. I hope they like me.*

SkepticGirl1: *Lucy is probably going to embarrass me so much I have to put her out of her misery, so don't get attached.*

SmallvilleGuy: *I should probably let you go, rest up for tomorrow.*

SkepticGirl1: *I can't wait to hear about your big day in Metropolis. I'll text you at lunch so we can make a plan for after school.*

SmallvilleGuy: *My day will be boring until then. ;)*

I resisted the urge to squeal and typed a response.

SkepticGirl1: *Mine too. <3*

SmallvilleGuy: *Good night, sap.*

SkepticGirl1: *Guilty as charged. Night.*

I wanted to have sweet dreams of baseball and non-awkward kisses. Instead I dreamed of being pursued around Metropolis. The streets were dark, and shadows stretched around me. I heard Dabney Donovan's footfalls behind me. I saw a flying boy silhouetted by a moon. The dreams chased me through the night, until I woke up, hoping they wouldn't be doing the same thing during the day.

CHAPTER 17

I knocked at the study room door, and Maddy pressed it open.

"Password?" she asked.

"Josephine Baker," I responded. I was learning not to be surprised at who turned out to have secretly been a spy; I'd thought Baker was just a singer. But Maddy had informed me she was a highly effective informant for the Allies during World War II, hiding messages in her sheet music. Who knew?

"Your memory is getting better," Maddy said, and she swung the door open. James and Devin were already at the table, naturally having arrived before me. Maddy took her usual seat on top of the table. Her T-shirt read The Newsgirls, which gave me a sense of her priorities but not her emotional or relationship status.

"I have the memory of an elephant," I said.

"For passwords, I meant," Maddy said dryly.

"I don't actually know whether elephants have good memories or that's a myth," I admitted.

"They do," James said. "At least for some things—faces of other elephants, in particular. There's a whole theory that they remember all sorts of knowledge their family needs. They're matriarchal."

"How do you know so much about elephants?" I asked James, unable to resist.

"We took a family safari when I was twelve." James shrugged, almost as if he was embarrassed by it.

"You did?" Maddy asked, eyes big. "What animals did you see?"

"All of them," he said. "It was kind of nuts seeing a lion just a little way in front of us . . . I don't understand why people would want to go there to shoot them. Or shoot them, period."

"It does make you wonder why humans get to be at the top of the food chain." I pulled out a chair and dumped my bag on the table. I sometimes forgot what kind of wealth James had grown up surrounded by.

James put his elbows on the table. "I'll show you guys pictures sometime if you want."

"I want," Maddy said.

Devin hadn't said a word yet, but now he spoke up. "Fascinating as the animal kingdom is, do we want to get down to work?"

He had a troubled expression, and that made me instantly ready to focus. "Yes, please," I said. I explained to James and Maddy, "We went to the library together yesterday to try to find info on the Contessa, since there's nothing online. A librarian friend of Devin's found us the title, but way back in the 1600s. We figured it must be fake." I turned to Devin. "What'd you find after I left? Is she real? Or was Boss Moxie just messing with me?"

"For the first three hours of going through those old business journals, I thought that's what was up too," Devin said.

"*First* three hours?" I asked guiltily, thinking of how I'd been living it up at the ballgame.

"Of five total," he said.

"Whoa," Maddy said, impressed.

"What'd you turn up?" James asked.

Devin shook his head. "This is where it gets weirder. I eventually found a reference to her in a business journal that isn't indexed online. It was from the late 1980s, and it mentioned the name of her company. Arcana Imperii. In Latin, it means—"

"I know this one." James held up a hand. "The secrets of power? A charge against Roman governments, right?"

"And I thought your dad wanted you to be a journalist, not a lawyer. Nice Latin," I said.

"Once I linked her to that," Devin said, "I found it mentioned way more often. The company has funded all sorts of weird, interesting, lucrative research over the years."

"You put together the info anywhere, Devin?" I asked, hoping.

He fished in his backpack and handed me a few printed-out pages. "I figured you'd ask."

"I'll pass these around to the rest of you today once I'm done," I said, taking them. "We all need to know what we're dealing with. Why and how has some countess who covers her tracks ended up with Donovan, who also covers his? She didn't look that old, either. Not old enough to have been running a company in the 1980s, much less the 1600s. We're missing something here."

"A lot of somethings, probably," James said. "I don't feel like anything we've found out makes sense. Did Reya say anything else helpful to you last night?"

"Just that they weren't going anywhere, and that they're going to do something soon," I said.

James sighed. "Vaguely ominous is the opposite of helpful."

"Right?" I studied the papers Devin had handed me. The Contessa seemed really interested in technology for someone who had such old money. Then again, I didn't understand the rich all that well. James had taught me they weren't all the same.

"As you probably guessed, the new name didn't turn up anything in the missing kids database," Devin said.

"We still have no idea what they want with all this," Maddy said. "I guess we're hitting the *Scoop* after school?"

The first bell sounded. I felt guilty for not telling them that I had a pretty good idea what they wanted.

Me.

Though I didn't know why.

I'd also meant to prepare them for bringing Clark along, but it could wait.

"Yep," I said.

Devin got up from the table and lingered so the two of us could walk out together.

"What's up?" I asked once Maddy and James were out in the library proper. He was obviously after a private word, but I wasn't sure I could handle it. I didn't want any more of a shadow over the awesomeness of having Clark in town. Of knowing dreamy SmallvilleGuy was even dreamier Clark.

"Maybe nothing," Devin said. "Probably something. I haven't had a chance to decrypt the message yet, but your guy made another contact with the government."

"I thought you said he deleted the bug. How'd you find out?"

"He enabled it again. I can only guess so we'd see this. But he encrypted it, to make me work for it."

"So whatever the message is, it won't be good."

Devin nodded, sympathetic. "That's my guess. I just wanted to give you a heads-up. I'll crack it after school while we're at the *Scoop*. Shouldn't take long once we get there."

"Great," I said, meaning the exact opposite.

★ ★ ★

Lucky for me, we had a reading assignment in second

period. Which meant I could do my extracurricular home-work instead.

The dossier Devin had compiled on the mysterious Contessa del Portenza's business concerns made for interesting reading. She'd been an early funder of all sorts of visionary technology, from undetectable shadow weapons to a company that developed some of the components that Advanced Research Labs had later absorbed and turned into real-sim holotech.

Hmmmm. Maybe the presence of my first article—all about Advanced Research Labs experimenting on teen gamers with shady VR tech—wasn't a coincidence. The CEO of ARLabs had gone down once the revelations went public, losing control of his company.

Flipping through the rest of the papers, I saw no evidence she'd ever had any ties with ARLabs directly. None with Cadmus either, so she couldn't have met Donovan there. In fact, she did fit Boss Moxie's description of having pet enthusiasms. Her company dropped ten mil here, another hundred mil there, pocketed any earnings and moved on to the next whim.

That was how it looked from where I was sitting, anyway.

None of it explained why someone who'd taken such pains to keep a low profile would be involved in a project that was destined to be discovered—that, in fact, was baiting a journalist.

More *hmmm*.

My phone buzzed in the pocket of my messenger bag. The teacher was grading, or pretending to, so I chanced slipping it out. I'd stayed logged into the chat app today in case Clark wanted to send me any adorable photos from the Kents' planned day of museums and touristy stuff.

I did have a message from him.

SmallvilleGuy: *Your crew are popping up around town again.*

This was bad news.

SkepticGirl1: *Thanks.*

I swiped over to the browser, where I had the *Daily Planet* homepage bookmarked. Of course there was nothing there. Perry wasn't going to run an unverified report.

Oh no. Perry. He wouldn't be happy if what SmallvilleGuy said was true.

I went to my next bookmarked page: Loose Lips. The goods were there, ready and waiting. A half a dozen threads, all timed within the last hour or so. I clicked the top one, with the headline: "OMG I saw a dude running crazy fast." The post was short and sweet and essentially echoed the subject line.

I had no doubt the poster was telling the truth.

The next one I clicked had blurry phone-cam video of speedy Todd.

"Ms. Lane, phones aren't allowed in class."

"Uh, sorry," I said with an internal groan.

Waiting till lunch to find out more of what was on Loose Lips wouldn't be easy. Neither would facing Perry and telling him we weren't much closer to a story after he'd told me to get cracking.

Maybe I should just march back to the building I suspected was connected to them and demand some answers . . .

Except there'd never been any sign anyone was there.

They wanted me to come to them.

We couldn't let these guys keep showing up around the city much longer, even if they *were* just making noise and not hurting anyone.

Paying attention in my classes proved impossible. James flagged me down in the hallway right after lunch, and I handed over the dirt—such as it was—we had on the Contessa.

He started to say something, but I cut him off. "More appearances are happening. Right now, today, all over."

He gave me a grim nod. "I know all about it. Have you checked your *Scoop* email lately?"

I shook my head.

He took his phone out of his pocket, tapped the screen, and spun it so I could read the message.

From: White, Perry [Daily Planet]

To: Scoop Staff [The Daily Scoop]

Subject: Status update, 3:45p

More wacko reports pouring in. Have a story update for me. See you then.

Perry White

Managing Editor, Daily Planet

That was short for a Perry email and remarkably bullet-point free. I wondered if I needed to add this to the Perry

Mood Scale, along with loose neckties. First, I'd have to figure out what level of panic it should leave us in.

"Brevity is the soul of wit?" I said.

"Or the soul of an editor who is losing patience," James said. He put his phone back in this pocket and held up the papers. "Thanks for these. I'll hand them off to Maddy before last period."

I'd been meaning to talk to him. Now was as good a time as any. "Uh, James, about Maddy . . . you know she's been having, um, issues with Dante? I just wondered . . . do you still like her?"

James stared at me for a long moment. Then he said, "I know you think you're not just being nosy. But . . . it's really none of your business."

My mouth gaped. I was too shocked to formulate a response.

"See you later," James said, easily, like there were no hard feelings.

Watching him disappear up the red and blue hallway, I couldn't even be mad. He was right.

But I was still new at this, at navigating friendships. So I'd apparently offended one of my few others, James. The fact he'd seemed so unsurprised by it didn't make me feel better either. Today was turning up nothing but bad and confusing news so far.

Meanwhile, I sent SmallvilleGuy a message: *Not safe for you at the Scoop; Perry's called a staff meeting. I'll text you when it's over.*

SmallvilleGuy: *Boo. Can't wait to see you.*

Neither could I, but we'd have to.

★ ★ ★

Taxi Jack pulled up at the curb to let us out at the Daily Planet Building after school. "You guys would tell me if there were really flying people around, wouldn't you?" he asked. "I'd like to see that."

"Sure thing," I said, surprised he hadn't already spotted one of our silvery tormentors in his travels around the city. We'd all been watching out the windows on the drive from school, and—if the others were like me—half-expecting the entire armor squad to show up whenever we hit a red light.

James and I split the fare, and then the four of us stayed quiet as we grimly marched across the plaza and inside. Then it was through the lobby and onto the elevator. We had no way to delay meeting our Perry fate.

At least we were a few minutes early. It would give us a little time to regroup and prepare for whatever he had planned. But as we exited onto the basement level, we could hear the chorus of phones ringing from our office. And as we approached the door, it was already open . . .

"The lights are on," Devin said.

"Perry," Maddy and I said at the same time.

Apparently hearing his name, our boss popped his head out of the door and waved at us. "Come on, everybody in," he said.

We obeyed him to the soundtrack of screaming phones.

He stopped in the middle of the floor, in the open area

between our desks. "I can't hear myself think with all these blasted phones ringing. You can start taking calls again as soon as I leave, but let's take them off the hook for now. Just apologize nicely afterward." His tie was snugly at the neck of his shirt. We glanced warily at each other while we did as he ordered. He waited, seemingly calm. Was this a trick?

"So," he said, when the phone receivers were all laid on our desks. "As you know, Lois and I spent Saturday out at Stryker's Island looking for leads from Boss Moxie. We got a little information, but not a lot."

The others' eyes slid to me, and I spoke up. "We found some information about the Contessa this weekend. She's got a track record as a business investor."

Perry squelched me with a look. "I told Lane I wasn't sure this was still a story, but she assured me she thought it was. She insisted there'd be more crackpot reports of people doing impossible things. She was right."

That was awfully neutral, almost positive. I couldn't tell where he was steering our ship. We'd expected to be in the center of a big storm. I didn't think we were wrong. This had to be the eye of the hurricane.

"The main page of Loose Lips is filled with posts from people like the ones calling these offices. They're claiming to have videos of people running faster than cheetahs and flying like birds." Perry flapped his hands.

There was a real wildlife theme developing today. Maybe James could show Perry his safari photos too.

Devin and I exchanged raised eyebrow looks and I could guess he was thinking the same thing.

Perry continued. "I also told Lane over the weekend that if she was right, then you guys had better have a story ready to go. Do you?"

We were quiet. He knew the answer, so why was he asking? But I was hardly going to speak up and say *that*.

"No," James said, at last, when it became clear Perry expected a response from someone. "Not yet."

"But we're working on it," I said. "And we won't stop until we run it down."

"Good," he said. "Some of you can stay here and take phone calls. At least one of you should be out gathering some news. You should've done that instead of all coming here, despite my message."

As if he wouldn't have yelled at whoever hadn't come. Tricky. I bit my lip to keep quiet.

"I want this story," Perry said, starting to walk out. "The real story. So people know we're the ones they can trust to level with them. I've got a staff report running in the meantime. The police are still just considering this a public nuisance. But that could change. So. Go. Get. Me. The. Story. Understand?"

We nodded as if we were one organism. "Yes, sir," I said.

He didn't correct me and tell me to call him Perry. He just stormed out. So he *was* mad.

"How are we going to do this?" James asked as soon as Perry was gone.

"I'll go out looking for leads," I said quickly.

I'd be less worried about the rest of them if I was the only one in harm's way.

"No," Maddy said. "I should come with you. Keep you from doing something rash."

James set his phone back on the receiver and it immediately started to scream. He had a wild-eyed look about him, and I thought of all the different sightings Devin had to plot the last time. That would have equaled a lot of calls.

"I feel like I have a rapport with Reya," I said. "If I do run into her, she might clam up if anyone else is there."

Maddy measured me, like she was trying to decide if this was a legitimate argument. "Fine," she said. "I'll stay here and help James with calls. When we move on Donovan, though, I'm there. I want to be there when you take down the guy who almost ruined my sister's life."

"Fair," I said. I caught Devin's eye. "Can you do the thing for me?"

Maddy and James shook their heads at our secrecy, but they didn't demand an explanation. Devin crossed to his desk and took a seat. I lingered nervously behind him.

He logged in and pulled up a screen that looked like random letters and numbers to me. In just a few key-stroke-filled moments, he'd managed to decode it into readable text.

It was a message from TheInventor to a .gov email address: I'll have more to tell you tomorrow. You seeing this activity in Metropolis?

Crap. This was the very definition of not good. My mind

raced. He said he'd have more information for the .gov guys—
like my dad—tomorrow.

I'd have to take the risk I'd been putting off. I needed to
contact TheInventor and explain how dangerous it would be if
he kept on with these leaks. I couldn't let him continue to act
without at least trying to give him the benefit of the doubt. I
owed him that much, because he had stepped up to the plate
when we asked last time—and because of Clark's faith in him.

"Thanks," I said, and Devin gave me an apologetic look.

But first, I had some reporting to do. Chefs and singers and
Harriet Tubman weren't the only people who could be spies.
So could I.

I took out my phone and sent SmallvilleGuy a message: *I
need to do some field reporting. Don't let anyone see you, but meet me at
the intersection of . . .*

And I gave him the cross streets up the block from the building we'd found. I still had a feeling about it. All those cameras
had to mean something.

I'd decide what we were going to do there on the way.

CHAPTER 18

The street was busyish when I got there, people heading into and out of shops, walking their tiny or giant dogs along the sidewalk. It was as active as I'd ever seen it.

The old payphone booth that had been turned into a piece of street art by a muralist sat near the corner. It was all shiny bright colors. I decided to wait next to it.

"Surprise," a familiar voice said.

I whirled and hit Clark with a smile that probably had the intensity of a thousand suns. "Hi there. Lurking around phone booths?"

"Is that what this is?" he asked, giving the side of it a gentle knock with his fist and smiling back.

That face is a good face. I trust that face.

There we stood, grinning at each other. He was still real.

And so tall I had to look up a little to fully appreciate his *extremely* good face and those nice blue eyes behind his glasses. He had on a plain blue T-shirt and jeans, and somehow managed to look, well, dashing in them. Dashing? Was that a word people even still used? It fit.

"Used to be," I explained, thankfully still capable of speech. "Now it's just decorative. I guess they don't have these in Kansas?"

"I don't think they have them much of anywhere anymore. It's pretty cool though."

"City art project," I said. "The same one that funded Dante's mural."

"I'd like to see that in person while I'm here." He took a step closer. "How was Perry?"

We were somewhat off the radar in the shadow of the phone booth, its boxy shape blocking anyone from seeing us from the building we were here to case. At least, that was the plan I'd come up with on the way.

We'd had no luck with the front door, so I wanted to check out the back of the building. Maybe there was another way in.

"Insistent we get a story," I said. "I'm supposed to be out tracking down the armored gang, but I thought it might be better to come here."

He poked his head around the edge of the booth. "I take it the place you guys visited the other day is up there. The one with all the weird cameras? I count six."

"From here?" I asked, impressed. We'd only spotted five the other day. And we were more than half a block away now.

Clark shrugged a shoulder. "I, uh, walked past it on the way, thought it might be the one."

I wondered where he'd been coming from, but I let it pass. I'd find out about his day later. "We need a better vantage point. I want to take a look around the back of it. See if we can catch the Contessa leaving, or anyone else. Maybe talk to Reya and Todd, if they come back to home base, if this really is it. Devin turned up some articles after I left him at the library—the Contessa has invested in all sorts of tech projects over the years."

"So Boss Moxie wasn't just winding you up," he said.

"I still think he was trying to do *something*, I just can't figure out what." I used Clark's arm to steady myself—my cheeks heating with a blush the second I touched him—and stood on tiptoe to get a better look up the street. It looked like there was an alley a couple of buildings up from our destination. That might work.

"Let's see how quick we can make it to that alley," I said, pointing.

"You lead the way," he said.

Feeling oh-so-brave, I took his hand in mine as I stepped out of the shadow of the phone booth and steered us up the street. I tried to stay aware of everything around us. But it wasn't so easy. I felt like every one of my nerves had moved to the palm of my hand.

"Lois," he said.

"Hmmm?" I didn't want to meet his eyes, not until we were safely in the alleyway. I might get distracted.

"A guy just left that alley. The one we're going to."

More distracted, I meant.

I followed his eyes to the man he was talking about. He was waiting to cross to the other side of the street. He wore a suit that was meant to convey status, but subtly, and looked highly pleased with himself. It wasn't Donovan, but the face was familiar.

"How do I know him?" I asked.

Clark blinked. "You mean you recognize him?"

I nodded. "Yeah," I said. "I can't remember from where, though."

The man loped across as soon as there was a break in traffic. No way I could let him give us the slip without figuring out who he was.

"Let's go," I said, taking Clark's hand and tugging him along.

He resisted. "What are we doing?"

"Tailing him." I released his hand and started walking, suspecting he'd follow. "We'll cross at the next block."

"Should we be doing this?" he asked.

"Doing what?" I said, speeding up so we wouldn't be in danger of losing him. "We're simply taking a walk on a public street. And staying just far enough behind that he won't notice us."

I expected more protest, but when Clark spoke next there was admiration in his voice. "You know how to tail people?" he asked.

"I, um, might have read about it."

"Of course," he said. "That is something you would read about."

My cheeks heated again as he found my hand with his. I glanced over at him. "So we can pretend to just be out for a walk, if he turns around," he said.

"Smart," I said, smiling a little. "You catch on quick."

We kept the suited man in our sights and traveled a couple more blocks with him, before he turned onto another street. I tugged on Clark's hand to steer him to the same sidewalk, where we'd be directly behind the guy—well, about a dozen feet back.

I didn't want to risk this opportunity . . . and if I had to, I could just confront the man and demand to know who he was. None of the silver-armored kids they were exploiting were here to protect him.

He slowed as he approached a newsstand. I turned to face Clark, and he mirrored my movements, taking my other hand too. So we were just two starry-eyed people out for a walk who suddenly needed to gaze into each other's eyes. Except too much gazing would mean we lost our strangely familiar mystery man before I recognized him.

"You're too distracting," I muttered, trying not to pay attention to him even though he was *right in front of me.*

His eyes widened, affronted. "So are you."

"Hmph." But it was impossible to feel *too* disgruntled while he held both my hands in his.

"He's leaving," he murmured, without moving.

"Oh," I swiveled and started moving again, embarrassed

that he'd noticed before me. "He bought a *Daily Planet*. It almost makes me like him."

He'd unfolded it and was skimming the pages, flipping through too quickly to be reading, while he walked. And not caring one bit when other people had to dodge around him and his giant newspaper. Finally, when he'd skimmed through each page, he dumped the paper in a trash can.

"I take it back," I said. "I hate him."

"I bet he was . . ."

"Looking to see if we'd written about the latest sightings," I supplied.

"Yes." Clark's voice had taken on an edge. "Or specifically if *you* had. I just realized that this is one of the people who's been spying on you."

"Probably," I said, though that was low down on my worry list at the moment. Then I stopped.

Because our quarry was slowing in front of a tall apartment building with a doorman. I scurried closer, hearing Clark's steps behind me. "Lois," he whispered, "he'll see us!"

I reached the sidewalk right behind the *Daily Planet* trasher just in time to see the uniformed doorman swing the glass door open for him and say, "Evening, Mr. Jenkins."

Mr. Jenkins, being a jerk, didn't respond, but sailed through like a prince who couldn't be bothered to speak to servants.

I whirled and ran right into Clark. My mind was racing. The face and the name had finally clicked into place.

"The disgraced ex-CEO of Advanced Research Labs. Steve 'Dirtbag' Jenkins. *Of course.*" I swung out around Clark and began to walk back the way we'd come. "I never actually met him, just saw photos."

I couldn't believe it. But then, oh yes, I could. Now it was all starting to make sense.

"The Contessa," I said. "She invested in some of the tech that ended up in holosets. They might know each other from that."

Clark caught my arm and stopped me. He pulled us over toward the wall of a building, so we would be out of the way of the sidewalk foot traffic. "It also explains why they're so fixated on you. You forced Donovan to move and he lost his financier. Jenkins lost his job and business status because of your story."

But not his doorman building. And wait, what had Clark just said? "You're not saying this is my fault?"

He put a hand on my arm. I couldn't breathe for a second.

"I'm not saying that at all," he said. "You did the right thing—your job—and they were in the wrong. But that doesn't mean they don't have it in for you. Clearly they do. I don't like the thought of anyone wanting to hurt you."

It was a sweet thing to say, but . . . "They haven't tried to hurt me. Not really. Reya said they wanted me to 'come to them' on my own."

"You're not going to, obviously," he said.

Was it that obvious? They were laying some sort of trap, but what if the only way to break this story was to get caught in it? I couldn't promise I wouldn't.

Not now that I knew where their HQ was for certain.

"Not yet, anyway," I said.

"Not yet," Clark said. "Don't you mean never?"

"Never say never. That's from Dickens, you know."

Clark's expression didn't lighten. "You're trying to change the subject."

My phone started to buzz. I pulled it from my pocket and saw MOM flash on the screen.

Crap.

Though, if I was being honest, the interruption was a minor relief. I didn't want us to have our first fight so soon. He usually understood me, and so he *should* understand I'd do whatever I had to.

"Did your mom call mine today?" I asked.

Clark said, "She was going to after I left. To torture me."

"They're going to get along great." I slid my finger across the screen to answer. "Mom, hey, what's up?"

"Lois," my mom said in my ear, "are you out with Clark Kent right now?"

Uh-oh. Maybe I shouldn't have been so grateful about the call. "He's just with me while I'm running something down for the *Scoop.*"

Clark was watching me, and I turned around, feeling a little exposed.

"Well, I want you to come home," Mom said. "No dates without a chaperone until I've met him. I talked to his mom—who's lovely—and they three of them are coming for dinner tomorrow night."

"But Mom, I'm working on a story, really," I said.

"Tough," was her response.

I sighed. "Fine."

Hanging up, I faced Clark.

"How bad?" he asked.

"She ordered me to come home, which is pretty bad for her." I slid my phone in my pocket. "But you guys are coming for dinner tomorrow and I'm sure you'll charm her then. I'm just not allowed to hang out with you alone until she's met you."

I craned my head to look back at Jenkins's building, making a mental note of the address.

"No way," he said. "If you're thinking of talking your way into that building, no way."

"I wasn't," I said, laughing. He did understand me.

He didn't laugh. "I don't want to get on your mom's bad side. You're not going anywhere near that place. You have to go home."

"I should tell the others about Jenkins. What if it's him and not Donovan? But Moxie seemed to confirm Donovan was involved. Still, this gives us a new angle to work—no way he's disciplined enough to stay off the grid. Devin might find something."

I'd almost forgotten in the excitement of newsgathering. There was something else I had to deal with—someone. TheInventor.

"Lois," Clark said, "it'll work out. Don't look so worried."

I waved a hand an inch in front of my face and said, "Worry be gone."

Finally, he laughed, so it worked. He must not have been able to see how much worry was still there.

★ ★ ★

Mom was in the kitchen when I came in, and she poked her head out. "Record time," she said.

"You can thank Clark," I said. "He insisted I come straight home. You really *are* going to like him."

I hope. How could anyone not? He was the definition of likeable.

No kiss today, though. I hadn't even thought to regret it until I was already heading home. I didn't blame Mom—nope, I blamed TheInventor. It was time to call his bluff.

I headed upstairs and logged on to my laptop. I would send a message to my fellow *Scoop*ers about Steve Jenkins's involvement in this Typhon business. But first . . .

I navigated over to Strange Skies and pulled up a new private message box.

Private Message from SkepticGirl1 to TheInventor, sent at 5:05 p.m. EST: *Hi there, A – I think you know that I don't trust you, but our mutual friend SmallvilleGuy does. It's time for us to get on the same page or you risk landing all of us in trouble, not to mention the flying man. I know the intelligence that's been going to your military friends; I don't think you understand how dangerous the information you've sent already could be. And I don't know why, if we should trust you, you included us on that list. Before you do something else, let's talk.*

I hesitated, trying to decide how to sign off, then figured he'd used an initial . . . I could give that much away in the hope of convincing him to level with us.

I look forward to hearing from you with an explanation. - L

Well, not exactly, but I did look forward to resolving this. To not having another secret of mine lingering between me and Clark.

I clicked back over to the Strange Skies boards and spotted a lengthy thread titled "More Weirdness in Metropolis" with the flame beside it that indicated it had lots of responses. I clicked and saw the first post was from a regular, KeithB10, asking whether this could be aliens revealing they were among us.

Ha, I thought. *More like evil geniuses among us.*

Discovering Jenkins's involvement was a huge break, so why did I feel so far behind the curve?

Maybe it was because, other than me on his doorstep, I still had no idea what he wanted.

CHAPTER 19

I yawned for the fifth time so far on my way to school, and decided I needed a strategy to combat my lack of sleep. A faded coffee mug sign dangled up ahead, the word Radu's spelled out at the bottom.

Coffee wasn't something I'd gotten into yet, but this morning was a special case. I pressed open the door and joined the line of patrons waiting for their morning fix. I wondered if anyone here had an excuse like mine.

The night before, I'd sat for far too long watching and waiting, seemingly endlessly, for the little "new PM" indicator to appear on my Strange Skies window, telling me TheInventor had responded. It proved pointless. I finally gave up and went to bed. There was zero chance he hadn't seen my message. Maybe his play was to torture me.

When he still hadn't responded by this morning, I could've told him it was definitely working.

I read all the descriptions of the shop's offerings from a big chalkboard overhead while the line progressed. By the time it was my turn, I'd settled on the most desserty-sounding option. "A double mocha frappé," I told the pale coffee guy. Then, on impulse, "Make it two. To go."

The second wasn't for me, but for Ronda. Principal Butler was one of the few people I knew who'd ever met Jenkins. Aside from Dad, who'd gone in for a meet-and-greet when we first arrived in town. But Dad was still off chasing the flying man, and it wasn't like I could ask him anyway. So Principal Butler it was. He'd wanted to be useful; now I'd see whether he actually could make good on it.

The coffee guy glanced over at me as he finished up my coffees. "Whipped cream?" he asked.

Mocha frappés came with whipped cream? I'd chosen wisely. "Extra, please," I said.

The guy laughed and went crazy with the can of whip, creating a tower of the stuff. I paid, and he handed over the cups. I cradled Ronda's in my left hand, and sipped mine from my right.

"How is it?" he asked.

"I don't even care if I have a whipped cream mustache, that's how good," I said.

Utter sugary chocolate goodness. Coffee was growing on me fast.

The hit of sweetness put some speed in my step too. Yes, I'd go see Butler first thing. I needed to figure out what was driving Steve Jenkins, what kind of man he was beyond a colossal jerk who had no problem experimenting on innocent teens. Revenge wouldn't be enough of a motivation for someone like Jenkins—at least, not *just* revenge. I didn't think. He'd be after some sort of other profit.

Talking to Butler about his personality might help me back that up with fact rather than feelings.

A skinny guy with a loaded-down backpack got the door for me at school. I spotted Maddy, James, and Devin waiting as soon as I made it inside the crowded hallway.

Maddy's T-shirt today said Smarty Dance. A hint to Dante to ask her to the spring formal, or not? "For me?" she asked with a look at the cups. "Also, you have a little . . ." she traced a finger across her upper lip.

"Whipped cream," I said, swiping with my forearm. "Worth it. The other one's for Ronda."

Maddy asked, "Who?"

"Butler's assistant. I'm going to talk to him about Jenkins."

"Aha," Devin said, nodding. "That's not a bad idea. He might be able to give us something. Although I still find it weird you would ever talk to Butler on purpose."

James said, "I could come with you, if you want."

"That's not a bad idea," I said. "He does love you. Again. More."

James shrugged and gave an ironic smile. "Who can resist my charms?"

Maddy laughed. I looked at the two of them, but if there

was anything new happening I couldn't tell. Dante appeared then, and she joined him with a wave to the rest of us.

"Save me a seat in English," I told her.

James and I headed up the hall together, Devin peeling off. "I'm not going to ask anything," I said to James. "About Maddy. I'm sorry about the other day."

"Good," he said.

Of course, now that I'd said that, I wanted nothing more than to ask him again. Instead I said, "How'd taking calls go? Anything interesting?"

"Other than the fact they were from people reporting seeing insane things?"

"Yes," I said, finishing off my coffee and popping the cup in the trash can outside Butler's office. "Other than that."

James frowned. "Do you think it's odd that they aren't really *doing* anything? Other than when they approached us, there's no aggression . . . They're just being *seen*."

I'd had the same thought. "The only aggression is toward us. The being seen is for us too. They know we can't ignore a story."

I was going to have to confess about the photo of me, and about the presence of the Project Hydra story. I hadn't even mentioned that Jenkins had bought and trashed a *Daily Planet* to them in my email report the night before.

My phone buzzed in my pocket. "One sec," I said.

The bell rang and the hallway started to clear out. Since I planned for us to depart Butler's office with late slips, I wasn't in a huge hurry.

SmallvilleGuy: *Did you tell the Scoop guys about Jenkins?*

SkepticGirl1: *Of course I did.*

SmallvilleGuy: *But you still haven't told them about the contents of the folder. Shouldn't you?*

Grumble, grumble. Great minds.

SkepticGirl1: *I'm aware. See you later?*

SmallvilleGuy: *6 sharp. What are your mom's favorite flowers?*

I shook my head. The thoughtfulness of this guy. My mom would undoubtedly think I'd put him up to it.

SkepticGirl1: *Same as mine, actually. Tulips.*

SmallvilleGuy: *Thx. See you then. <3*

James was watching me with a *tres* amused smile. "Something funny?" I asked.

"Tough as nails Lois Lane is head over heels," he retorted. "I'd say it's pretty funny."

"Where's your romantic streak?" I said, trying not to protest. I'd never be able to do so truthfully. "He's here, in town."

James blinked at me. "Your mystery guy?"

"Clark," I said. "He got here Sunday. He was with me yesterday, when I spotted Jenkins."

James was gaping at me.

"What?" I asked.

"You haven't told *anyone* else?" His eyebrows lifted in disbelief.

"I, um, think I mentioned he was coming to Devin. Who

would I tell? He's coming to my parents' house, so they know."
I started to open the office door, then realized what he meant.
"Oh no." My heart fell through the floor. "I didn't tell Maddy.
That's why you're surprised?"

"Excellent deducting, Sherlock. She's going to be hurt," he
said. "You'd better be the one to tell her."

"Then you don't," I said. "Argh." I gentled banged my head
on the glass of the door. "I've got to get better at this."

Learning how to be a friend remained a work in progress
for me, but even I knew this was a shocking lapse. I couldn't
explain why I hadn't told her yet either. Yes, there was the
excuse of things not going well between her and Dante, but
that was weak. There'd been a lot going on . . . I'd been so
nervous that meeting him would ruin everything . . .

Annnd I wasn't used to talking about my feelings. Not out
loud, and not with anyone except SmallvilleGuy.

Which meant the reason I hadn't told Maddy was because I
hadn't wanted to. I'd known Devin wouldn't prod that much.
It wasn't like I'd shared the details with him. I hadn't *wanted* to
share with anyone else how dorky Clark made me.

Clark. He was part of my life. He wasn't going anywhere.

"I'll tell her at lunch," I said.

"Excellent," James said. "Are we going in, or what?"

"Oh," I said. I'd paused with my hand on the door. "Yeah."

Squaring my shoulders, I opened the door and hoisted the
extra coffee cup. "Ronda, my friend, are you in the mood for a
mocha frappé? Extra whipped cream."

Ronda sat at her desk, her hair in a perky ponytail. She

paused mid-typing. "I shouldn't," she said. But then, "Give it here."

I put it on her desk, which was in the outer office waiting area, Ronda the guardian of the hallway that led back to Principal Butler's office.

She gave me a quizzical look. "What's up? Here to steal more tardy slips?"

"I would never," I said, hand over my heart.

Ronda and I both knew the drill. I'd never *admit* it.

"You don't have an appointment with him, and he didn't ask me to summon you . . . so what are you doing here? And you too, why'd you come along?" Ronda asked James, then took a long, delighted sip of her drink.

"We need a word with Principal Butler," I said.

"No way," she said.

I clarified. "We think he might be able to help with a story."

"Oh." She set down the cup. "Then go right ahead. I've never seen him in such a good mood as the week after your dad's press conference, James. He didn't yell at me once."

"You are a goddess, as ever," I said.

"Don't push it," Ronda said, without any ire. She was enjoying the mocha frappé too much.

James gestured for me to take the lead. "You know the way better than I do."

"You don't have to rub it in." But I led us past Ronda's checkpoint and up the little hallway to Principal Butler's office, with its fox-hunting paintings and pretentious leather-volume-lined shelves. It was true; I could've gotten us there blindfolded.

I'd spent a lot more time than I'd wanted to in Butler's office when I first arrived. He'd tortured me by forcing me to have weekly meetings with him every Monday, my permanent file tantalizingly stacked on his desk.

"Hey," I said, remembering something, "you said Butler showed you my file, right?"

James's lips curled in a little smile. "Well, not exactly *showed*. He might have left it out one day. By accident."

For once, James had thoroughly surprised me. He'd peeked. I couldn't help approving. "Not bad, Worthington. There's hope for you yet."

Butler's door was open and he was sitting at his desk, frowning into his computer monitor. I knocked on the frame to give him a moment's warning.

"Yes?" he asked, then brightened when he saw it was us.

Oh, how times have changed.

"What can I do for the two of you? Come right on in," he said.

He even got up to shepherd us into his office, closing the door. He returned to his desk as we settled into the leather chairs across from it. The suit he wore was as shiny and expensively flamboyant as always, with a charcoal pinstripe that offset his silver hair.

"To what do I owe the visit?" he asked with a greedy expression.

He really needed to get out more or take up something exciting as a hobby. Was there a natural way to suggest skydiving or spear-fishing to him?

"We're here about a story." I pitched my voice low as if I was worried we'd be overheard, even here, in the privacy of his office. I felt like the least we could do was dress up the part he had to play and make with some intrigue. "We need your help."

"I suspected as much," he said, as if that was a genius thing to surmise.

James cut in. "We were hoping to pick your brain about someone who used to donate funds to the school—Steve Jenkins from Advanced Research Labs."

Well, that slammed the door on Butler's eager cooperation. "The one you wrote the story about that caused the school such humiliation?" he asked, studying his desk.

Riiiiight, it was the *school's* humiliation that troubled him.

I scrambled to make it better. "We know that you had no idea what he was up to—obviously." *You were too eager to look the other way.* "And no reason to doubt his good intentions at the time. Think of this as a chance for payback."

He looked up, which I decided to take as a sign I was getting through.

"Wouldn't that feel good?" I asked. "To see him go down permanently?"

"What do you mean?" Butler asked. "That sounds . . . dangerous."

I'd have to be careful not to overpromise or make things *too* dramatic, apparently. Besides, I wanted the pleasure of taking down Jenkins—again, for good—myself, along with Donovan and the Contessa.

"We think he's involved in another off-book experiment," I said.

His eyebrows rose.

"Not using students from here," I said. "Not this time. But we were just wondering if you could tell us what he's like."

Where Butler had been mellowing, his face clamped back to tightness. "We weren't that close . . . I don't know."

He clearly thought this was a trap of some kind. And, normally, he'd be right. I shot James a panicked look and nodded for him to take a shot. If anyone could save this, it was James.

"We just . . . um . . . you're such a student of human nature," James said. "You never doubted my dad was a good man. We value your judgment. We weren't implying that you would *like* the guy."

"Oh, I see," Butler said. "I'm still not sure . . ."

"You know the other morning," I said, "when we were out front and we told you that Maddy had a run-in with some people who weren't from here? That was them. We don't want to risk them coming back and dragging you and the school into any more shenanigans."

James shook his head slightly, admiringly, at my attempt to manipulate Butler.

And it worked.

Butler relaxed back in his chair. "I'm glad you thought to come to me. You just want to know what he's like?"

"We're trying to understand him a little better. Anything you can remember might help. Did he approach you at first or the other way around?" I asked.

Butler closed his eyes, like he was conjuring the scene in his mind. He nodded, then opened them. "He contacted me—he invited me to come to his office the first time. The offices are well appointed. Luxurious. Modern. Well, you know that, you've been there." He shifted uncomfortably again. "He was polite enough, but cold. Those tech types, you know? He suggested that there were lots of opportunities for bright young students who liked computers to partner with the company."

"Did he work to convince you?" Not that I thought it would have been hard.

"Or did he let you think it was your idea?" James added.

"None of it was my idea," Butler said, and for once, I believed him. He hadn't hesitated at all before saying it. "He went so far as to ask if he might come to the school, meet some of our students who used their gaming software. That's where it all started. I wanted the school to get something out of it, so I proposed the computers he donated. That's all."

"Mmm," I said. "Was he ever . . ." I thought back to James's words in the hallway. "Was he ever aggressive with you?"

"Yes," Principal Butler said. "When you first came here and—when I told him you were asking about the students, the Hydra program, he wasn't happy. He was rude to me. Told me I should be able to handle 'children.' But . . ."

He had a troubled expression on his face, like thinking back made him realize how screwy all this had been. Too bad he hadn't had the foresight when it was happening.

"But what?" I prompted.

James was hanging on his every word too. This might be something we could use.

"The way he talked about them. The Warheads . . . Miss Singh . . . even you, it was as if he barely thought of you as people. More like bothersome problems. Or, no, not problems. Opportunities, and if not opportunities, *then* you'd be problems. He, uh, talked to me the same way. What you said before about my being a judge of character, well, I haven't always been. Sometimes I looked the other way when I shouldn't have. I do regret what happened with him." He paused. "I don't think he was a good man."

So, if we messed up Jenkins's plans, backed him into a corner, then he might lose it. Revenge takes a cool head to plot and carry out. If he saw the world in terms of problems versus opportunities, he must be after me for a reason. I hadn't been a problem for him, not anymore, not before he started baiting me.

The logical conclusion was that he viewed me as an opportunity. But for what?

"*Is*," I said. "He *isn't* a good man. And yeah, we don't think so either."

CHAPTER 20

I waited by my locker for Maddy. As we were leaving English, I'd asked her if we could have lunch alone. She'd given me a curious look, and said "Sure." I'd gotten more and more nervous as the morning wore on. So much so that when she appeared in front of me, I practically cringed at the sight of her.

"Wow," she said, "that's a new one. Do I smell?"

And I was screwing up already. "Like a rose. Or another flower that smells good. I mean, I assume—I haven't smelled you, so I don't really know how to describe your smell. Which means you smell fine, right?"

Stop babbling.

"What is happening?" Maddy asked.

Just say it.

"I screwed up. And I'm afraid you'll be mad at me. And . . . let's get a table and I'll explain."

Maddy gave me a wary look. "You didn't say something to Dante, did you?"

"No, nothing like that. It's something about me. Something I did. Or forgot to do." I sighed, feeling that every word made it worse. "Something I forgot to tell you."

"Okay, now I'm really worried. Come on," she said, and led the way into the cafeteria and to the food line.

I was the worried one. Maddy was my best friend, and I should tell her things. That was part of the friend deal. It should be *easy* for me to tell her things.

We got our Standard Issue Lunchtime Meals—chicken fingers for me, pasta salad for her—and schlepped the trays to our usual table. I'd already warned off the boys. This was a girls-only lunch.

Around us the various friend groups of East Metropolis High gossiped and made in-jokes and did their usual things, whatever those happened to be.

We sat. I hesitated. How should I start? Shouldn't I have rehearsed this before now?

Maddy finally made a frustrated noise. "In the immortal words Lois Lane would use: spill, you're killing me here."

Fair enough.

"So," I said, "here's the thing. I didn't tell *anyone* about this. Not even my parents until I had to."

Maddy frowned. "Lois . . . you're going to force me to start guessing. Did you commit a felony? Make out with

Devin? Secretly fall in love with Boss Moxie over prison correspondence?"

I blinked. "I don't know which one of those is the most unlikely, but—no, it's definitely the Moxie one. Ew."

She gave me a look. It was a look I was an expert at recognizing, because I liked to fancy myself as somewhat of a master of it. It was a *shut up and start talking already* look.

"You know SmallvilleGuy? My online, um . . . uh . . ."

"Boyfriend, yes." A little crinkle appeared between her eyebrows. "Well, no. I don't *know* him, because you don't *really* know him. But I know *of* him. Did you break up?"

"No. No!" Even the thought of that disturbed me more than I wanted to contemplate. I gathered my hands in front of me, clutching them together. "See, I do know him. I know him *really*. I met him. He's here in town. At this very moment, he is somewhere in Metropolis with his parents."

Maddy stared at me. Then, "What's his name? What does he look like? Do you still like him?"

"He's . . . His name is Clark. Maddy, he's . . . He's perfect. He's Clark Kent and he's pretty much perfect and he's coming to dinner at my house tonight and . . ." I raised my hands to indicate I didn't know what else to say. Trying to articulate the magnitude of us meeting and going out on a story together and my giant ball of nervousness that tonight's family dinner would be a disaster left me feeling overwhelmed.

Not to mention, my concern about how Maddy was going to take me having kept this from her.

She picked up her fork and stabbed a piece of pasta. She chewed it, considering, then she placed the fork onto her tray.

I lifted my hands in an over-to-you gesture. "Well?"

"Your *boyfriend,* your secret long-distance *boyfriend* came to town and you didn't mention it until now? Why?" She lowered her voice. "Were you afraid to tell me?"

"No," I said. I sighed. "Maybe. I don't know. I think I'm just a dummy who's too used to not having anyone *to* tell this stuff. Except him. And obviously I can't talk to him about it."

"You can talk to me about anything," Maddy said. "Understand?"

"Still? You're still friends with me?"

"Yes, dummy. *Obviously.* Friends forgive each other, even when they do something like keep giant, delicious news to themselves."

I nodded. Gratefully. "Got it. No more keeping giant delicious news to myself. It's true, I'd be hurt if you kept it from me."

"So, what's he like? Is he what you expected?" she asked. "Perfect is a little nonspecific."

I could feel myself blushing, but I had the perfect way to demonstrate what I meant. I pulled my messenger bag from the back of my chair onto the table and reached inside it.

"I know this is dumb," I said.

"Dumb is our word of the day," Maddy said. She waited, watching curiously to see what my hand emerged with.

"Anyway, we met for the first time at a baseball game—he loves the Monarchs. He caught this for me, kept it from hitting me, in fact. It was coming right for me. And then, he gave it to me." I pulled the baseball/date souvenir out of my bag and held it on my palm for her inspection. I knew it was silly to carry it around with me, but . . . I liked having it with me. Proof that I hadn't dreamed Clark Kent up.

Maddy looked from me to the ball in my hand. "You're carrying what I've heard you refer to as a 'sports ball' around with you!"

"Yes, I'm aware I don't know everything about the game. But I liked it." I sniffed.

"Huh," Maddy said as I put the baseball away. "This is serious. I'm not surprised you were too chicken to tell me."

"I was not. I've never been chicken in my life."

"Please, I'm your friend—inside that tough-girl shell is a *really* tough girl. But you're motivated by how much you *care*. Being part of Team Lois, it's an honor. There's nothing you wouldn't do for any of us." Maddy picked up her fork and gave me a wicked grin. "Except willingly, openly talk about your feelings."

"Point," I grumbled. It was hard to argue with such a flattering—and on the money—assessment. "Clark's the same way, except not as afraid to discuss feelings stuff. You'll like him."

"When do I get to meet him?"

"He wants to come by the office."

"And he's coming to your place for dinner tonight?"

"At six. With his folks. Thank god my dad's out of town," I said. "Is it okay for me to abandon you guys at the *Scoop* tonight? I could try to come afterward . . ."

I hadn't filled Maddy in on everything related to Strange Skies and TheInventor. It didn't feel like a part of *our* world. And, frankly, it felt dangerous. Like the more people I could keep out of it—especially while TheInventor wasn't answering my message—the better. This was different from keeping Clark a secret.

"No," she said, shaking her head. "Stay home. We'll cover with Perry and keep working on IDing the teens to find their families. Enjoy your time with your no-longer-a-mystery man."

"Just FYI," I said, breathing easier, "we are *not* going to become people who only talk about guys. Our friendship will always pass the Bechdel-Wallace test."

Maddy said, "Yes." Then, "What's that?"

"You know, it's that thing where a movie can pass or fail— it's named after two friends who came up with it, based on something Virginia Woolf said. Sometimes people just call it the Bechdel test, which is kind of hilariously telling . . . that they leave out one of the women who came up with it. Anyway, it has three rules," I lifted my fingers and ticked them off. "There have to be at least two women in a movie, who talk to each other, and not about a dude."

"It is sad that's all the criteria and things fail. And, *yes*, our friendship will always pass the Bechdel-Wallace test," Maddy said. "Except that we're not in a movie. And we can still talk about relationships. As needed."

"Yeah, of course," I said, finally taking a bite of my own food. "Anything you need to talk about? You in the same place?"

"Yeah." Maddy shrugged. "I'm still on the fence. Or the wall. It's nice having someone to make plans with, but . . . I feel guilty even thinking of Dante that way. He's too good a guy for that. But I also think maybe I'm wrong and this is just a phase. I don't want to make a decision I'll regret."

"How do you feel when you're with him?" I asked.

Maddy squinted, thinking it over. "These days? I spend most of the time trying to figure out how I'm feeling. That sounds terrible."

"It doesn't." I thought about Clark, and what being around him was like. "But when you're around the right person, you feel it, you know? That you don't really want to be anywhere else. Not right then. Or that wherever you are is better than anyplace else you might be . . . because they're there too. Look, I'm not a poet."

"Clearly," Maddy said. "Do *you* know? Already?"

"Excellent point," I said, but it was an avoidance and I was pretty sure she knew it. It was too quick. We were too young. I wasn't making any declarations about forever, but what I'd said? It was true of me around him, whether online or—now, finally—in real life.

So what I'd said might not be poetry, but how I felt about Clark was.

★ ★ ★

I was lucky Maddy and company were letting me off the hook at work for the night. Despite Perry's orders to get the story, it wasn't like I could do anything *but* go straight home after school. Once again, the mischief-making had tapered off as quickly as it had started up. Not a single new report all day of our armored pals showing off. I kept expecting them to show up on my way home, but they didn't.

I made it to my room and read the threads at Loose Lips. They were of the conspiracy theory variety—just where were these armored individuals disappearing to? Were they aliens?

I expected to see some of the same at Strange Skies. I all but held my breath as I brought up the page.

There it was. The little *1* over the PM box.

TheInventor had responded.

My spine went straight, posture stiff. I couldn't deny that part of me was afraid to click on the message and see what he had to say. It felt a little like detonating a bomb might.

You're no coward, and you're not afraid of him. You're afraid of the consequences of what he might do.

I clicked on the envelope.

Private Message from TheInventor to SkepticGirl1, sent at 2:35 p.m. EST: *Hello, L – I admit that it doesn't surprise me you feel a lack of trust toward me—I sense that's a common emotion on your part—but I can't help but be disappointed. Anything I have done, I did because of* *evidence of that distrust. It was a test, to see if the source of the tracker on me was, as I suspected, connected to one of you. But I am your friend as well as SmallvilleGuy's. I feel if we could put faces to names, all would be clear. We could be on this same page. I happen to know you're in Metropolis, and as it turns out, I just arrived here too. There's more to the story. I will be happy to tell all to you—and no one else, not anyone in the military—if you meet me tonight. Let's make it 12:30 a.m. at the northwest entrance of Centennial Park. Hopefully, A*

I stared at the message. TheInventor was here. And he wanted to meet. Despite him not spelling it out, his wording held an implied threat that managed to come through loud and clear. If I said no, if I denied being in Metropolis, maybe he would tell everything he knew to the task force instead. I couldn't tell whether he knew SmallvilleGuy, aka Clark, was here too.

I didn't like the idea of going alone to meet this guy. In fact, my skin crawled thinking about it. No matter what, I'd have to tell Clark, wouldn't I? TheInventor obviously thought we were both involved in bugging him. The clock on this secret had just run out.

Great.

I hit reply:

Okay. See you then. I might bring another friend. But don't worry, if I do, you won't mind. – L

Assuming Clark still talked to me after I revealed this to him. I couldn't imagine him not insisting on coming along, though. Today was a day when my secrets were being dragged into the light. Maybe I shouldn't have been keeping them.

Which was, frankly, what troubled me the most. I'd almost

screwed up with Maddy, and now I had almost certainly screwed up with Clark. When would I learn?

The only thing I could do now was refuse to play a chicken and face the consequences. At least it wouldn't require talking about my feelings.

I hoped.

A knock sounded from downstairs.

Crap. I checked the time on my phone.

It was 5:55. They were early. I'd forgotten that not everyone considered on-time at least five minutes late, the way my internal clock seemed to.

I jumped up and checked my reflection. I smoothed my hair, pulled down my slightly wrinkled T-shirt. I'd planned to change.

Into what? An elf princess costume?

I heard the sound of Lucy's feet racing down the stairs and of Mom opening the door. I whipped out of my room and then slowed when I hit the living room, taking a breath so I wouldn't appear like some frantic crazypants.

"Flowers, for me?" Mom said. "You know how to get on my good side. Please, all of you come in."

I walked up behind Mom, who was accepting a bouquet of red tulips wrapped in plastic from Clark. The Kents smiled at me and then my eyes locked with those blue ones that had no right to knock me off my feet. Shouldn't the glasses prevent feet-knocking-off? Apparently not.

Because I wobbled, especially when Clark's hand emerged from behind his back with *another* bouquet of tulips.

Purple.

"They remind me of you," he said, fidgeting a little. "Violet."

He meant like my eyes.

I stood there, gaping. My heart fluttered in my chest like it had grown wings and might fly away.

"Lois," Mom said, with an elbow in my side, "can you say thanks and introduce everyone?"

Lucy began to giggle. This jarred my brain back into motion. Clark looked like he might crack up too.

Please don't be too mad at me about TheInventor.

"Shut up, brat," I warned her. Then I smiled at Clark, knowing and also hating how shy I was, and accepted the flowers. "Thank you," I said. "Now I'm two presents in the red. And this is your birthday trip."

"It is?" Mom asked.

"Technically the birthday's not for a couple of months. Seventeen. But we thought we wouldn't make these two stay apart any longer," Martha said.

My mom made a noncommittal noise and I could tell she was curious just *how long* we'd been apart to begin with. Martha and Jonathan were both semi-dressed up, him in slacks and a collared shirt and her in a flowy dress.

"Mom, this is Martha and Jonathan Kent, and, um, Clark," I said, hoping I didn't sound as dopey as I felt. "Kents, this is Ella Lane."

"Hi, so nice to meet you all," Mom said, eyes narrowing on Clark.

I continued, mortified. "And the half-pint is my *legendarily* well-behaved little sister Lucy. I'm sure you'll be shocked at how quiet she is."

Lucy, not taking my cue, howled with delight. "Oh, no! I talked to Dad on the phone last night and I promised to tell all the embarrassing stories you hate," she informed me.

"You did?" Clark asked, not able to hide a grin.

I cast pleading eyes at my mom. She waved everyone inside, toward the kitchen and our dining room table. "Lucy," she said, "why don't you show everyone to the table while we put these flowers in water and bring the food over."

"The kitchen's right there," Lucy said. "You have to go in it to get the water. And the food."

"Would you?" Clark said, crouching in front of Lucy. "I've been looking forward to meeting Lois's cool little sister."

Lucy blinked. She inspected him. And then she beamed.

I shook my head. *Clark, you know not who you charm.*

Lucy grabbed his hand and Jonathan's and pulled them toward the dining room table. "Voila!" she said.

Martha and my mom laughed, and I couldn't help catching Clark's eye and joining in.

I hope he still looks at me that way after I tell him about TheInventor.

I held the flowers close to my chest, and with a charitable glance, my mom snagged them from me.

"Sit down before you fall over," she murmured to me, amused.

Was it possible to die from blushing too hard? I thought we might find out.

"What are we having?" Clark asked.

"The question always on a growing boy's mind," Martha said.

"Lois's too." The two of them shook their heads at each other. At least they seemed to be hitting it off. "I made lasagna."

"You mean, your world-famous lasagna," Clark said.

Mom paused while arranging the tulips into two separate vases. "Is it?" she asked.

Just like that, he'd charmed her too. It figured my family would get along better with Clark than they did me.

He winked at me, and my heart fluttered again as I slid into the chair beside him and nope, I hadn't chosen to sit because I wasn't sure I could keep standing. Nope, not at all. I'd have to look up the origin of the phrase "weak in the knees."

I found his hand under the table and gave it a quick squeeze. I hoped I'd still be able to do that at the end of the night.

"I need to steal you at some point," I whispered. "I have something to tell you."

He inclined his head closer, picking up on my seriousness. "Everything okay?"

"I hope so," I murmured.

Mom brought over the lasagna—proof I was distracted, I hadn't even noticed my literal favorite smell in the world while she was cooking—and waved for me to get up and bring over wine and sodas and waters. I released Clark's hand and did just that, noticing only when I turned around with them that Lucy had stolen my seat beside Clark.

Ha.

He was talking to her and she was laughing. All right, I could live with that.

I eased down between Mom and Martha.

After we were all seated, an awkward silence descended. Mom said, "We're pretty informal, so please serve yourself drinks and we'll pass plates."

"Good, we like things casual," Martha agreed, and passed Jonathan's plate to Mom.

Clark caught my eye and smiled as he asked Lucy, "So you're getting into flying, I've heard? Going to be a pilot?"

Lucy's face went up in blushing flame—we'd both inherited that from Mom—and said, "Yes. I haven't had lessons yet, but I want to."

"I don't blame you," Clark said, and for the first time I could see how nervous *he* was. I'd have bet anything he was talking to Lucy because he knew more about her than anyone else in my family (besides me, obviously). "I bet you'll be great at it."

Lucy beamed again. "I want to be. Lois told me I'd figure out my calling and . . . I think this might be it. She even said I might be able to be an astronaut."

"Lois is pretty smart," he said.

"Gross!" Lucy said, wrinkling her nose. "But yeah."

Clark sputtered a surprised laugh.

My stupid heart is not going to survive this dinner.

"Lois, plate?" Mom prompted me, and I dopily looked away and handed mine to her.

Maybe this would be okay. While I knew I'd live in fear until it was over, maybe dinner would be survivable and maybe Clark would understand why I'd kept my suspicions about TheInventor to myself for a while.

Maybe everything was going to work out fine.

Except right then, we all turned toward the door, at the sound of it opening. Dad strode through in his full dress uniform, carrying his suitcase.

"Sam," Mom said, "I'm so glad you made it." She shot me a look. "I didn't want to get your hopes up, but Dad called and said he was coming home early."

I looked at Clark, whose wide-eyed panic reflected my own.

Or maybe this was going to turn into a complete disaster.

CHAPTER 21

Dad put his suitcase down by the living room wall, and turned to find that Jonathan and Clark had risen to their feet. Jonathan gave Dad a salute that was right on the money.

"Oh, at ease," Dad said, striding over to join us. "We don't stand on ceremony with family. Were you in the service?" he asked Jonathan. He completed his journey to the table and took his seat.

I wished he was in civilian clothes. The General cut a forbidding figure in his full uniformed majesty—especially when he wanted to. Poor Clark.

Jonathan sat back down and, after a moment's hesitation, Clark followed suit. "No," Jonathan said, "but my dad and both grandpas were. Army."

"They taught you well," Dad said.

Mom cut in with introductions. "This is Jonathan and Martha, and that's Clark. Everyone meet Sam."

"Young man," Dad said, fixing a laser stare on Clark, "you can call me General Lane."

Clark was seemingly frozen in place.

"*Dad,*" I gritted the word.

"Yes, sweetheart?" he asked, tone light, and extended his plate for me to pass it.

"Hey," Lucy protested, "I'm *usually* your sweetheart. Lois is usually trouble."

"Sorry, sweetheart," Dad said, the corners of his eyes crinkling with amusement.

Lucy nodded, as if all right had been restored to the world.

"It's an honor to meet you, General Lane, um, sir," Clark said. He pressed his glasses up his nose.

"Sam," Mom said mildly, "stop scaring the boy. Don't worry, Clark, he can reduce an entire barracks to stunned silence with that look."

"Only when they deserve it," Dad said.

Argh. I tried to catch Clark's eye, but he was clearly afraid to look away from Dad.

"What part of Kansas are you all from again?" Dad asked, accepting his plate and lifting his fork.

"A little town called Smallville," Martha said. "Aptly named. You probably haven't even heard of it."

"Really," Dad said. "No, I have. And what a coincidence, I just came from there—well, there and a few other places in the area."

"That is a coincidence," Martha said. "Most Kansans never even make it to Smallville."

She and Jonathan exchanged a glance. Clark finally shot me a panicked look. I wonder if they'd known why my dad was there or if they were only putting together now that he was the reason they were here.

"Why'd you come home early?" I asked.

"Would I miss this?" Dad asked. "We finished up what we were doing there." He redirected his next words to Martha and Jonathan. "Beautiful little town. The kind I always thought we'd end up in. But instead here we are, at least for the fore-seeable future. I worried there'd be too many distractions for Lois, but—for the most part—she's been doing well here. Loves working at the newspaper."

"I love Metropolis," I put in. *And hate being talked about like I'm not even in the room.*

"It's a little overwhelming compared to the farm," Martha said.

"You guys run the whole place yourselves?" Mom asked her. The two moms separated into their own sidebar about the farm.

"The newspaper, hmm?" Jonathan watched me. "Clark, is this why we have a young heifer named Nellie Bly in the barn?"

Clark was reaching for his water glass and splashed some onto the table.

"Um, yes," I said, blushing again. "Nellie Bly's my hero. And also the cutest baby cow ever."

"You can tell Lois hasn't spent much time around animals,"

Dad said. "We moved around a lot. So, young man—Clark, was it?—what do you think you'll do with your life? Are you going to take over the farm? Any interest in the military?"

"Dad, we're sixteen," I said. "He doesn't have to know what he wants to do with his life."

Why had I never asked Clark this question? I had no idea how he'd answer.

"You know what you want to do with yours," Dad said.

"Touché, but as Lucy pointed out, you always tell me I'm trouble. Clark's not." I smiled, feeling I'd scored a point. I even risked a bite of lasagna.

Lucy was watching our back and forth as if this was in fact a game. I crossed my fingers I could win. Or at least keep up.

"Well," Clark said, "I'm not one hundred percent sure . . . but I know I want to make a difference. I want to be a force for good."

Lucy sighed. "Me too."

Dad considered this, and I could tell by his momentary silence he approved of it. He was probably trying to find fault. But how?

"A little vague, but noble," he said. "Sounds like something Lois would say. So, how'd you two meet? Some game?"

"*Worlds War Three*," I supplied. So what if it wasn't the whole truth? It was truth adjacent. We had "met up" for the first time there. Chats were different. "It's a real-sim holoset game."

"Where'd you even get one of those? I know Lucy has one," Dad said, eyes narrowing.

"James gave it to me," I said quickly. "Clark was, uh, friends with some people who had a team from one of our old schools."

"What do you do in this game?" Dad asked. "Do you fight each other?"

"No!" Clark looked to me with a desperate expression. "We hang out . . ."

"And study," I said. "We're kind of long-distance study buddies."

Martha and Mom stopped their side conversation to give me a disbelieving look. "Really?" Mom said. "That's the best you can come up with?"

I decided not to say a word. I picked up my soda-filled glass and took a drink from it.

"I think it's romantic," Lucy said. "You met each other before you met each other."

Clark nodded, but he didn't speak either.

"It could have been dangerous," Dad said.

"But it wasn't." I put my glass on the table with an audible click.

Don't poke back at Dad, don't poke back at Dad . . .

A knock sounded at the door. I didn't care who it was—silver-footed speedy Todd or Jamie with the wings or . . . *any-one* would do—I jumped up to answer it.

But I was surprised to find Maddy on the doorstep. Night had fallen while I'd been inside.

"Why are you here?" I asked, afraid I'd missed a major story development.

"To meet Clark," she said, craning her neck to see past me. Everyone at the table was riveted to us. "How's it going?"

Whew.

"About as well as you'd expect with General Dad here," I said under my breath. "He came home early. I have never been so glad to see you in my life. Get inside."

"You're welcome," she said, grinning.

"Maddy's hungry," I announced, steering her toward the table.

"Pull up a chair," Mom said, though she sounded disbelieving.

"You must be Clark," Maddy said, sizing him up. "Okay. I say a name, you complete it."

I crossed my arms. "What are you doing?"

"Testing Clark," she said.

"This should be fun," Dad put in.

Lucy placed her hands under her chin, riveted.

"I thought you were going to *help* this situation," I muttered to Maddy.

Clark, to his credit, didn't shrink from the challenge. He said, "Shoot."

Maddy nodded and then said, "Dorothy . . ."

"Parker," Clark said, smiling.

She didn't hesitate. "Ida . . ."

"B. Wells."

"Nell—"

"Nellie Bly," he said, before she even got it out. "Popular topic tonight."

"Time for a harder one." She raised her eyebrows. "Katharine . . ."

Clark's gaze gravitated to me, and back to Maddy. "Graham. Tough-as-nails publisher of the *Washington Post* during the Pentagon Papers and Watergate scandals."

"Are you finished?" I asked.

Maddy smiled and said, "Yes, and he passed."

"Of course he passed," I said. "He listens when I talk."

Martha and my mother both made noises like that was the most adorable thing they'd ever heard.

"I listen to you," Jonathan said to Martha.

"Me too, Ella," Dad agreed. Both of them gave Clark a slightly dirty look, as if he'd gotten them in trouble.

He needed to be rescued. Immediately. And I still had my confession to make . . . at which point he might regret running this gauntlet on my behalf.

"Guys," I said, still standing, "I need to, um, talk to Maddy outside for a second. Clark, do you want to come with us?" Lucy was wearing a NASA T-shirt, which I hadn't noticed before. "You can see, uh, what the stars look like from our terrace."

"I don't know," Dad said.

"I thought you said Maddy was hungry," Lucy said, frowning. Clearly, she didn't want Clark to leave her side. I could relate, but . . .

"I am hungry," Maddy said, sliding into my seat. "And you don't really need to talk to me. Seems like we could give these two five minutes to talk, doesn't it? You know, after my test, which I'm sure was the most taxing part of the evening for him so far."

"We'll be right outside," I said. "For five minutes. Then we'll come back—promise."

Dad and Mom exchanged one of their patented looks, communicating silently. After which Mom said, "If it's okay with you guys," to the Kents.

"It's fine," Martha said, putting her hand over Jonathan's.

Clark bolted up out of his seat and was beside me double-time. I looped my arm through his and towed him toward the back door and onto our brownstone's small terrace. Only letting my nerves flood me once again as we stepped outside. Alone.

There were fire escape stairs beside the stone terrace that ran up to our neighbors' and my parents' windows. We had a few straggly plants in pots, but nothing fancy. Not even a table and chairs, so we had to stay on our feet.

"Nice rescue," Clark said. "I like your family, though. They're nice."

"Mom's nice. Lucy's developing a crush on you, and Dad . . ."

"Yes?" he asked, tension returning to his voice.

"Must like you okay or he'd never have agreed to give us even five minutes alone."

Clark made an exaggerated sweep of the back of his hand over his forehead. "Now, how about these stars you claim to be able to see from Metropolis?"

I nodded. "Fewer than Smallville, no doubt. Sounds like

Dad and his friends came up empty, at least. He didn't seem suspicious of you guys being here."

"Yeah, I'm going to hear about that later."

I walked toward the back of the terrace and swept an arm at the sky above. "Behold," I said. "Our stars."

"Beautiful," he said. "The stars. And, well, you."

He took a step nearer to me, and then another. We stood a few inches apart, me staring up into his face. It was dark back here, the few stars and the windows of the brownstone the only illumination. This would be the perfect moment for a kiss.

I could sense we were both thinking it, and Clark's face tilted down. So of course I chose to blurt out: "I have something to tell you. You're not going to like it."

He didn't move away. "Oh?"

I put a hand against his chest, and then dropped it to step away. I needed space. I needed to not see him get farther away as soon as I put distance between us. I turned away, which was a little cowardly—but I didn't know what my face would show once he was upset with me.

"It's about TheInventor," I said.

"What about him?" he asked. His voice came closer again.

I still couldn't bear to face him. I stayed turned away.

"He's in Metropolis," I said. "And he wants me to meet him at twelve-thirty tonight at Centennial Park."

"Why? How?" he asked. "I thought he wasn't on the list."

"He wasn't," I said. "Do you still trust him?"

"Not the way I trust you. But, yes."

"Clark, he wasn't on the list." I sighed. "He was the source of it. I had Devin track him online. Because I didn't trust him. I thought he might be playing double agent. I still think he is. My dad, I overheard him mention that they had a source on the inside at Strange Skies—back when we were dealing with the fake flying man sightings. TheInventor supplied that list to call my bluff. I messaged him and asked for us to come clean with each other, for him to tell us if he's on our side. He told me he knew I was here, in Metropolis, and that he happens to be too."

Silence stretched between us. I stared up the city's practically nonexistent stars, my mind gone blank of even the existential despair that felt appropriate to the moment while I waited.

And waited.

Our five minutes was ticking away. I had no doubt my dad would show up at the door to retrieve us if we pushed it.

Finally, Clark broke the silence. "So you lied to me."

"No," I said. "I kept a secret. It's different."

Sort of.

"Okay. Yes," I said. "I didn't want to say anything until I was sure. I know you consider him a friend."

"And then?" he asked. "When you were? Why didn't you tell me?"

"I'm *still* not one hundred percent sure," I said. "Not of anything except that TheInventor sent that list to my dad. And that *maybe* he was supplying intel to them before too. That's why I'm telling you now."

"No," he said, "you're telling me because of this meeting. Lois . . . you shouldn't go alone."

I faced him. "I'm not going to ask Devin or James . . . or Maddy. Or . . ."

"Me," he said. "Or me."

"I'm not going to put you in that position. I just hope you can forgive me. I hated keeping the secret from you." I met his eyes. The dark made it less painful. "I really, really did. I wish I hadn't."

He was silent again for a long moment, gazing down at me. "Who would I be to give you a hard time for keeping a secret? You were doing what you thought was right." He reached out and pulled me into the circle of his arms, against his chest. "It'll be okay."

I leaned into him. His arms made me feel safe. In a completely dorky way.

"I'm *not* asking you to come tonight," I said. "Because I don't know if your parents would allow it—I'll be sneaking out. But I'm going to the northwest entrance of Centennial Park. Just so you know. In case I disappear or you want to know or something. If you decide to come, I'll see you there."

"Got it," he said. "We'd better get back inside."

"Yes, we'd better."

But neither of us moved for a long moment.

"I'm still sorry," I said against his chest. "For the secret."

"Me too, for mine," he said.

Which, of course, I still didn't know.

He pushed me back and his lips gently touched the top of

my forehead, and I thought—again—that this was it, we were going to kiss. I prepared to make sure my forehead didn't knock off his glasses again. I held absolutely still.

And then his hand drifted down my arm to take mine, his other steering us back to the door and opening it to let us back inside.

"That was six minutes," Dad said. "Just so you know."

Everyone laughed except me and Clark.

CHAPTER 22

My family was sound asleep later that night when I slipped out our front door as quietly as possible and rushed up the street to meet Taxi Jack at the end of our block. The night was cool, and I zipped up my jacket against the chill.

When I reached the car, I climbed in the passenger side.

"Where to?" Jack asked.

I told him the park and which entrance.

"A little late for a picnic, isn't it?" he asked, putting the car in drive.

"Good thing I'm going to, um, interview a source instead." I paused. "You don't mind waiting?"

"If you ever ask me that again, I'm going to be offended, Lois Lane. I'll stay out of sight so I don't spook the source," he said.

We went quiet as he drove us across the city, still lit up. Metropolis never fully turned its lights off, just dimmed them a little. The late-night neon was a comfort.

Getting out of the house hadn't presented any problem. Everyone was sound asleep by the time I'd gotten up and dressed again at midnight. They hadn't stayed up late; Dad was tired from his trip. And my parents completely believed I was ready to retreat to my room as soon as the Kents left, since I was exhausted and somewhat peeved from the constant embarrassment of the evening.

Not that it mattered.

Maddy was still my friend. Clark didn't seem to be angry for my secret-keeping—which was a relief, after that heart-stopping moment when he'd realized I'd lied to him.

Now I had to pray I was wrong about TheInventor, and that I hadn't made a mistake even telling Clark where the meeting was. While my encounters with Donovan had made me a tad more cautious, I didn't mind walking into danger on my own. Not the concept of it, anyway.

But the idea of steering Clark into it—just like my other friends—well, that was another thing entirely. That I didn't want any part of.

Maybe he wouldn't come. Maybe I should text him not to come.

We were already driving alongside the outside of the massive park, though, streetlights illuminating mostly empty sidewalks.

Taxi Jack slowed and said, "You want to get out here? Your

entrance is right up there, on the left."

"Sounds good. I'll text if I need you, otherwise I'll come right back here."

He pulled up to the curb. "No problem," he said. "I'm listening to an audiobook from the library. *The Three Musketeers*. It's pretty good. A classic."

Shaking my head at the fact a taxi driver was undeniably becoming my friend—oh well, he was a handy one—I opened the door to let myself out. "I like Porthos the best."

"Hey, me too!"

I rolled my eyes and set off up the street, imagining Taxi Jack listening to the swashbuckling story Dad had read out loud to me when I was a kid. I'd liked the banter and sword-fights, even though I discovered later on that he'd skipped plenty of the good parts. I'd also longed for a close-knit set of friends like D'Artagnan's, each so different and yet utterly loyal to one another.

How funny it felt to realize I had that now.

I saw a tall figure ahead, near the open gated entrance, and sped up. It was Clark.

He came.

I'd figured he would, but I hadn't admitted to myself how hopeful I was to have him here. At my back.

Despite the reluctance I felt to put him into *any* danger. But I contained multitudes—I could feel both ways at the same time, happy and wary.

He had on a jacket too, but his was open to reveal the same plaid button-down over a T-shirt he'd worn to dinner. His hair was a little messed up from the breeze. Seeing him was good. Really good.

"You probably shouldn't have come," I said as I approached.

"That's some welcome," he said. "My parents must trust you a lot. Because they were semi-okay with it when I told them I had to go with you on a story."

"You told them?" I squeaked.

"Don't worry," he said. "What are the odds they'll talk to your parents again soon?"

"Very, very poor, I hope." I glanced around us and detected some movement off to our right.

Someone was headed in our direction. We both turned to check out who it was.

There was a guy in a trench coat shambling toward us, and I nodded my head. "Do you think that's him?"

Clark squinted. "I think it's a drunk guy," he said.

The guy wobbled toward us, and when he got nearer, I could smell that Clark's diagnosis was correct. He reeked.

He also grabbed Clark for a second and then broke away with his wallet in hand.

"Hey!" I protested, digging in my bag for the whistle Dad insisted I carry. There had to be security around here somewhere. Otherwise, I'd practice some of my self-defense on him. No way he was taking off with Clark's wallet.

But in a flash, Clark raised his hand and caught the guy's shoulder, stopping him from taking off. "Hang on," he said. "Wait."

It was directed to me and to the man.

"Why'd you try to grab my wallet?" he asked the guy. His voice was calm but commanding.

"Clark," I said, "you can't interview a mugger."

"It wasn't that stealthy of a mugging." He gave me a half-smile. My stomach flipped over. He spoke to the man again, "Can you answer?"

"Hungry," the man said, voice as shaky as his legs. He needed a good shave and a better shower. "Drank too much. Didn't keep anything for food."

"Can I have my wallet back?" Clark asked.

The guy sighed. His nose was ruddy and his bloodshot eyes watered up. He extended Clark's wallet back to him.

I watched, gaping. Clark, the criminal whisperer.

"Thank you," Clark said. He reached into the wallet, pulled out a twenty-dollar bill, and handed it to the guy. "For food, okay?"

"For food," the guy said, and took it. "I'm—I'm sorry about that. I just forget sometimes. That I shouldn't just take things."

"It's all right. Just try not to do it again, okay?"

"Okay." The guy nodded and then walked off. After a few steps, he started whistling.

Clark turned back to me, shifting nervously from foot to foot.

I shook my head at him. The security lamp above us shone on his face, gleaming off his black hair and glasses. I couldn't quite find words.

"What?" he asked. "About to give me a speech about how I'm a sucker from Smallville who just got taken advantage of?"

"No," I said, wonderingly. "How did you know the guy wouldn't try to fight you or pull a weapon or something?"

"I didn't," he said. "But sometimes if you have faith in people they'll surprise you. Mom and Dad taught me that. Risk is the price of believing most people want to be good."

"And twenty bucks," I said. "Seems like a small price to pay."

I offered him my hand, knowing I would never meet another person like Clark Kent. "Let's go see if our friend is our friend," I said, promising myself that I'd try to have more faith too.

Centennial Park was a marvel of tall trees, open green spaces, and flower gardens. When I'd been here during the day, it smelled of hot dog carts, the chlorine in the water fountains, an undercurrent of whatever was in bloom. At night, there was a smattering of noise in the distance, but less activity. The air had a fresh, breezy quality. It was quiet enough to hear the leaves rustling above as we walked along the broad paved path.

"How far past the entrance should we go?" Clark asked.

"We're a little early," I said. But then I pointed. "There's someone on that bench up ahead."

The bench sat under another of the security lamps that dotted the park, and the person stood as we approached. The light gave us a good view of him.

"It can't be . . . him." Clark said. "Can it?"

Because the person who stood there to meet us? It wasn't the pasty adult tech genius I'd expected. No, this boy was close to our age, maybe a year or two older at most. He had a lean face and shaved head, and he was wearing clean, preppy, and obviously expensive clothes. Not that I knew enough to gauge the labels, but they clearly were designer of some variety. The cut was too fine for anything else.

When we reached him, he smiled at us. It was a cool smile, hard to read or take at face value.

"Hello," he said, "Alexander Luthor, pleased to make your acquaintances in the flesh. You can call me Alex."

CHAPTER 23

We stood for a moment in the sort of silence only shock can bring.

"Luthor," I repeated his last name, trying to place it. The boy's words had been silky smooth, practiced.

"You've probably heard of my dad," he said.

I glanced at Clark. "We thought you'd be older."

"Who's *we*?" Alex said, tossing a look at Clark.

Not for a second did I trust this guy, same age as us or not. But I held out my hand to shake his. "Lois Lane. And this is . . ." I hesitated. We hadn't discussed whether we'd reveal Clark's online pseudonym to TheInventor or not.

"Clark Kent," Clark said, stepping forward to shake his hand next. Clark was several inches taller than him.

"Firm grip." TheInventor—Alex Luthor—leaned forward.

"I thought the same about you two. That you'd be older. You *are* SmallvilleGuy?" he asked Clark.

Clark nodded, then lowered his hand to take mine. Alex followed the movement, raising his eyebrows but refraining from comment.

"Who's your father?" I asked. "You said we'd have heard of him."

"Billionaire, blusterer, bully . . . goes by Alexander," he said. "He runs a number of companies. His latest is a media start-up—Loose Lips is its primary site."

I grimaced. *Figured.* "I wouldn't call Loose Lips media," I said.

Clark interrupted, chiding me gently. "Let's play nice."

Oh right, I was trying to have more faith in people. "Sorry," I said.

Alex shrugged. "No apology necessary. It's a blight," he said. "Like I said, my dad's a bully. He stole my Skies code for it too. Speaking of which . . ."

So that's why the site's operation had seemed so intuitively familiar. "Our military snoops," I said. "You've been supplying them with information."

"Actually," he said, "it turns out that after I scared the spooks off, I discovered dear old Dad had been giving them a heads-up about things. While he was stealing my code."

I examined his face, wishing I was a human lie detector. "Why would your dad care?"

"He doesn't, not about much," Alex said with a delighted laugh. Clark's fingers tightened on mine. Alex continued, "The military had asked him if he had any knowledge of someone like our mysterious flying man. He happened to have seen the threads on the site and suggested they try the technique they did—announcing the sightings."

"And you didn't tell us this originally, because . . . ?" I asked.

"I like you," Alex said.

Somehow it hit me the wrong way. "I'm not sure if it's mutual. That wasn't an answer."

He really laughed then. Clark said, "Lois . . ." But I could tell he didn't know what to make of this slick, strange guy either.

Alex stopped laughing. "I didn't know until later. I had to dig to find the record, because I wasn't suspicious of myself. Not until I found out Dad had been messing with my code. And I did supply the list of usernames to my dad's contact."

"So I was right!" I said, trying not to enjoy it.

"About?" Alex said.

"That you were trying to put them on our tail. You're a double agent."

"Uh, no," he said. "I trust you both to cover your tracks . . . Except for that bug whichever one of you attached to my computer. That's why the list existed. I was hurt by that."

"Oh," I said, guiltily. "I asked a friend to do that."

"So it *was* you," he said. "Well, or your friend." He squinted at me. "I would never have guessed you. I assumed it was Clark. And I wouldn't have made or supplied the list unless you hit first."

He was slippery. It was hard to tell if anything he said to us was truth or lie or something in between.

No matter how much I wanted to, I couldn't blame him for being upset I'd tried to track his movements. His explanation made sense based on what we knew.

"I have only one question for you," Clark said.

Alex lifted his hands. "Shoot. I'm an open book, to mix metaphors."

Clark didn't take his eyes off Alex. "Are you our friend or not?"

It was a simple question. But even though the question echoed my earlier words, I wasn't sure it could have a simple answer. The "our" from Clark made the rhythm of my heart quicken, the implication that Alex could only be friends with us both or not at all.

"Yes," Alex said. "I don't have many friends. I value you both."

A gust of wind blew past us. I waited to see if Clark believed him. He'd read the mugger correctly, so I would trust his decision here.

"That's good enough for me," Clark said. "So how do we *be* on the same team now? We need to get rid of the people snooping around without causing any more problems. Or crossing any lines."

Alex angled to face me instead of Clark. "Is my word enough for you too?" he asked.

Clark looked at me expectantly. Finally, I said, "It'll do. For now."

"Did I mention I like you?" Alex said, grinning.

"You did," I said.

I still planned to keep my eyes wide open where Alexander Luthor was concerned.

Clark released my hand and took a seat on the bench. The tension between the three of us defused a bit at the motion. He was good at that, I realized. Being the peacemaker.

I sat next to him and asked, "What do we do to get rid of these government guys for good?"

"You don't need to worry about it," Alex said. He perched on the arm of the bench. "I figured out how to lock Dad out again, so he's gone. And I won't have any reason to communicate with them again."

"Yeah, well, I'm still on the list," I said.

"What about you?" he asked Clark.

"We don't think they found anything in my town," he said. "Your IP tip worked."

Alex clapped his hands and considered. "I could send them a cover story, Lois, about you."

He must not have figured out that my dad was among the people looking, which was somewhat of a relief. There was almost a . . . childlike quality to his movements at times, a weird counterpoint to his precise, adult-sounding phrasings.

He pursed his lips. "On the other hand, I didn't supply IP addresses. The odds of them finding you based on a screen-name in Metropolis are extremely low. Although . . . you used the same IP for some of your postings at Loose Lips, and that

268

made it clear where you were. That's how I found you." He snapped his fingers, having a stream-of-consciousness conversation with himself. "I can hack in, fix that. I know exactly where the exposure is. I'll get rid of your account and posts. Poof."

He smiled at me, waiting for me to praise him or something.

"Um, thanks," I said. "That'll work."

"No problem, easily done." He peered down at us and said, "So, what do you think about the flying man anyway? Is he real?" And then he started another stream of consciousness. "Do you think these reports of strange things here in Metropolis are real? I think *you* do," he said to me.

"I know they are. I'm working on a story about them."

"Oooh," he said.

Clark's hand drifted to my arm. *Why had I said that?* Oh well, Alex knew my name. It's not like Google wouldn't reveal where I worked.

"I'm a reporter, remember," I said. I'd told him that much when we met up in the game before, when he'd also been going to great pains to conceal his own identity.

"Right," he said. "So what's the operating theory? Who are they?"

Clark nudged my leg with his own. "He might be able to help you."

I still wasn't sure I trusted Alex—that it could be so *easy* to resolve my doubts. But there was the faith thing. And Clark's seeming certainty he was okay, coupled with the fact Alex clearly *was* better at this tech intrigue stuff than even Devin.

Maybe he could turn up former home addresses for the silver squad for us.

Or the elusive reason for the whole project, and why they wanted me in particular.

"I'll send you some first names," I said, "if you can dig up anything on them, it would help. We think they're all missing teens, but we haven't had any luck finding their families. The other names I'll send are behind the experiment, we're pretty certain. I need proof of what they're up to and to catch them at it. I need a story." I pictured smug Steve Jenkins tossing that copy of the *Daily Planet* in the trash, and Dabney Donovan's cool unconcern with anything resembling human decency. The Contessa standing, waiting to toy with me on the street. "I refuse to let them to get away with this."

"I can't wait to get started!" Alex rubbed his hands together in eagerness, another gesture that barely made sense for someone our age. "Just tell them to me. I have an excellent memory."

It was almost like he'd been pretending at adulthood before, and now that he trusted us, he'd relaxed into this rambling little kid optimism. But, then, if he wasn't used to having friends . . . I felt a sudden pang of sympathy for him.

"Ready?" I asked, and then ran through the teens first, then the others. I added, "We think the Contessa donated to a homeless shelter here, but it was anonymous. Just in case it helps."

"It might. I hate to dash," he said, "but I'd better head home and get cracking on this." He stopped for a second, though.

"Why are you here too? In town, I mean?" he asked Clark, like it hadn't occurred to him before.

"Why are you?" Clark asked.

"Dad came to meet with people at Loose Lips. He dragged me along. I have a tutor, no school to miss. Not like you guys," he said.

"I'm here with my parents, birthday present," Clark said, and nothing more.

Good.

"Ah, well, I'll be in touch ASAP, Lois," Alex said with a wave. "I hope I get to see you both again while we're all under the same sky."

He strode off, but I waited until he was out of sight, disappeared through the entrance to the park before I spoke. "He's . . . odd," I said.

"No kidding," Clark said. "But he seems harmless enough."

"Only because he likes us," I said. "If he can find anything, though, I'll owe him."

"Nah," Clark said, "I declare you even."

"Come on. Since you forked over your twenty, I'll give you a ride home."

Clark jostled my shoulder with his. He asked, "You have a car?"

"I have Taxi Jack," I said.

But I lingered on the bench and so did he. Maybe this was *finally* the time. The kissing time. *Finally.*

Clark stood up and held out a hand for me.

I looked up at him and sent *kiss me, you fool* thoughts in

his direction. Then again. *Kiss me.* He did not magically pick them up. Apparently I didn't have even marginal telepathic abilities.

Disappointing, especially because I wanted a kiss to happen to an embarrassing degree.

"Lois?" Clark asked, softly, hand still extended.

Not to an embarrassing enough degree to ask *out loud.*

I took his hand. "This way. He'll be ecstatic to meet you."

★ ★ ★

We dropped Clark at his parents' hotel in the cheesy tourist paradise of Glenmorgan Square after he and Taxi Jack chattered nonstop all the way. I stayed quiet. We'd averted crisis, but somehow I still felt in a vulnerable position.

Taxi Jack arrived at the end of my block, and stopped there. He knew enough not to take me to the front door unless it was daylight out.

"I like your young man," he said.

I started to protest that he wasn't my young man, but why? "I'm glad," I said.

"He's shy, though. You may have to make the first move," he said.

"Boundaries, Jack," I said. "Boundaries." Why did older people always want to make an embarrassing fuss over the relationships of teenagers anyway?

"*Taxi* Jack," he said, then drove away as soon as I got out.

I shrugged and started for home. My phone vibrated in my

pocket, and I had a moment's hope it was TheInventor with answers already. More likely it'd be SmallvilleGuy making sure I got home okay and wishing me a good night.

Instead it was a group text from Devin to me, James, and Maddy: *This is bad.*

It included a link, but instead of checking it out I shot back a response: *What are you even doing up?*

It *was* two in the morning, after all.

Devin's reply was, *Never mind that, read the link.*

I scrolled back up to his original message. The link went to a local TV news homepage. I clicked through to a story with a headline that made me gasp:

Man Injured in Unusual Dust-Up.

The article related the statement given by the victim, who had suffered from a broken arm. He claimed he'd been pursued by four teenagers matching the same descriptions of those involved in the weird activities all over town in recent days. The kids had then picked him up and dropped in the roadway, where he was hit by a car.

I tapped out a message: *Why would they do this?*

James shot back: *I'm awake now. Maybe it was just a matter of time until they did something like this.*

Maddy: *Time we're now officially running out of. (Although could this have waited until morning? I like sleeping.)*

She answered her own question: *Probably not. Once Perry sees it . . .*

She was right. Now that another news outlet had a story,

Perry would no longer be patient. What were they doing? I could have been wrong about them wanting me after all.

Someone had gotten hurt. I couldn't help feeling guilty that I hadn't moved fast enough to prevent that from happening.

A boy brushed past me, fast, then wheeled on his heel. Speedy Todd. Was he here to hurt me?

My apprehension must've shown in my face—or maybe it was the defensive stance I took. I put one foot in front of the other and put my fists up to shield my body, just like Dad had taught me.

"I see you've heard the news," Todd said. "If you're wondering, that *was* your fault."

Too close to the mark. I wanted to cringe, but then I realized how wrong he was. "Really? Because *I* don't remember hurting someone, just because I can, because my masters told me to. I won't take the blame for what *you* did. You don't have to do these things. Let me help you. All of you."

Todd shook his head. "All they want is you. They said to tell you they want to talk to you, just talk. And only to you. You know where we are."

"Why?" I asked.

"Come find out," he said, "and keep anyone else from getting hurt."

He streaked back past me fast enough to blow my hair back. He was gone by the time I'd blinked.

Not for a second did I believe that all they wanted was to talk. But maybe I didn't have a choice. It hadn't been my fault they broke that guy's arm, but the next time . . . if I *could* prevent someone else getting hurt and didn't? How could I live with that?

I crept the rest of the way home and slipped inside the front door. I waited for Dad to bust me, which seemed almost inevitable. But he must've been more tired than I thought.

No one met me. I made it all the way upstairs to my room.

My phone buzzed again, and this time it was a message in the app. No reason not to use it—or not stay logged in—now that Alex was supposedly on our side.

It wasn't TheInventor, but Clark.

SmallvilleGuy: *Did you see the news?*

SkepticGirl1: *Yes. Perry's going to want a story. More than he already did.*

I considered revealing my encounter with Todd. Clark would only tell me that I had to be careful. So I kept it to myself for the time being.

SkepticGirl1: *Night.*

SmallvilleGuy: *Talk to you tomorrow.*

CHAPTER 24

I walked to my locker to swap out my books after lunch the next day. Distracted was too weak a word for my state of mind. Not that I was scattered, I wasn't. I was the opposite, frustrated and focused on my real problem.

Now that TheInventor didn't take up as much headspace, all I could think about was getting this story, saving Reya, Todd, Sunny, and Jamie, and taking down Donovan, Jenkins, and the Contessa in the process.

Realistically, school wasn't any longer today than ever before. But it felt like the longest school day in the world.

We were waiting, and that was exactly what it felt like. We should have been acting.

Or, rather, I should.

After Todd's latest visit, was it time for me to march up

that alley and hit the back entrance that must be there, alone? Stop waiting for the armored squad to come to us? Would TheInventor turn up anything helpful? This was the first time I had not just rushed in and followed my instincts, and it wasn't working out.

I was beginning to actively regret it.

Clark had texted me that he wanted to visit the *Scoop* in the afternoon and help however he could. I still hadn't told everyone about the photo of me or my articles in the folder. I knew Clark thought I should, and it was possible he would force the issue.

I hadn't mentioned Todd's latest visit to anyone else. It would only cause them to try to keep me from a confrontation that was becoming inevitable.

I closed my locker door and spun the dial—and ran smack into Dante. He gave me a nervous grin and set me back on my feet away from him. "Lois?" he asked. His T-shirt had a few paint splatters, as usual. "I wondered if I could grab you for a second before class?"

Dante being so tentative was unusual.

Crap. I'd promised Maddy I wouldn't interfere, and I meant to keep that promise. She'd been horrified by the very idea that my confession the other day involved talking to him about her.

"Of course," I said. "Unless it's about Maddy. You guys should talk to each other."

"We should?" he asked, watching my expression like it might give him a deeper insight.

Don't screw this up. Don't say anything you're not supposed to.

"Um, you know what I mean. If there's something to talk about." I started to walk.

"I think you know there is," he said. He was the nicest guy, there was nothing accusing in his voice. "I've been trying to talk to her. I asked her to the dance this weekend and she said she wasn't sure if she wanted to go."

Hmmm. She hadn't mentioned that.

He went on. "I just want her to be happy . . . and I feel like she isn't anymore. My question is, what can I do about that?"

"Wait and see? Maybe it's just a phase." *Why did I say that?* I should keep my mouth shut.

"Does she like someone else?" he asked.

"No," I said. "I don't think so."

"Has she said anything to you? About me?" He shook his head when I looked over at him. "I know you can't tell me that. But . . . could you tell me what to do?"

He was serious.

I stopped moving. "You are both extremely excellent people who deserve to be happy," I said. "That's all I can tell you. You don't want relationship advice from me, whether things are going good or bad. Trust me."

Dante considered that. "I do trust you. This helped."

I resisted asking in what possible way it could have, and went to a class where I knew I'd struggle to pay attention.

* * *

After school, my friends and I ferried over to the *Scoop*

together by subway. The others were vigilant for interruptions from our armored attackers, but I didn't bother to keep my eyes peeled for them. I knew they wouldn't show, not unless I was alone.

Which presented a slight problem, because I wanted to meet Clark out front. The others made for the Daily Planet Building's revolving doors, and I said, "I'll be in as soon as Clark's here. Should be any time."

"I've already met him, you know," Maddy said, with a superior air.

"Yes, we've heard," James said. "Poor Lois, she can't even stand to miss out on a few seconds with the guy."

"I think it's cute," Devin said. He lifted his phone. "Maybe I should take a picture for your future scrapbook."

"If I could kill with thoughts, you'd all be dead right now," I told them.

They laughed and left me to my post.

I waited by the wall where speedy Todd had been the other day. This time I did stay on high alert.

I hadn't mentioned to Maddy—yet—that Dante had talked to me. But that was only because I hadn't been able to grab a moment alone with her.

I wouldn't have been surprised if the armored gang showed up again now that I was solo, but they didn't. Clark, however, was right on time.

"You know anyone who can give me a tour?" he asked, long legs covering the concrete between us quickly.

I smiled at him, and then realized I was *just* standing there smiling at him. Like the world's biggest dork. He came closer, and on complete impulse I rose onto my toes and pressed my lips to his cheek.

"Hi," I said. Then, obviously, I started walking extra-fast across the plaza to the lobby doors. "One tour coming right up."

My cheeks were burning. *His* cheek had felt like fire beneath my lips.

A hand took mine, and he tugged me around to face him in front of the revolving doors. I took a breath and said, "Yeah?"

"Thanks," Clark said.

"Oh, uh, that was, um, nothing," I said, and whirled around. "Right this way. Everyone wants to meet you."

You could just kiss me right now and then I wouldn't feel so awkward about having pecked your cheek.

We headed to the guard desk, where Tommy, the freckle-faced redheaded guard I'd slowly won over, was on duty. "Who's this?" he asked.

"My friend." Heat flooded through me. I was terrible at life. "My boyfriend, Clark."

Clark made a little noise at the word, but then scribbled his name in the visitor book.

"You take good care of our Lois. We're fond of her around here," Tommy said, grinning.

"Clark already met the General," I said. "Isn't that enough?"

The guard fake-shivered. "He came here once. I'm still scared."

"Right?" Clark asked easily.

Tommy laughed and I waved for Clark to follow me past the super-fancy elevators to our grim gray one that went to the basement. "Now, I've told you, our office is not glamorous. Get your expectations in check."

Clark's eyes darted around the lobby, before settling on me. "This is pretty impressive. I don't care what you say."

The elevator doors slowly eased open, and we got on. I pressed the B button. The elevator doors creaked closed and it ground into motion.

"Is this safe?" Clark asked.

"Probably not," I said. "So Dante asked me about Maddy today."

"What'd you tell him?" Clark asked, as if he was bracing.

"That he should talk to her."

"Do you think they'll make it?" Clark asked.

I was forced to shrug. "I don't know. But I like him."

"But there's only one of us you like enough to, um, call . . . your boyfriend?" Clark asked, voice shy. He lifted a hand to my cheek.

Suddenly the elevator was moving too fast. Or maybe time ceased to move at all.

Nope. It only felt that way. The elevator stopped and the doors slid open, but I wasn't ready to get out.

"No," I said, breathier than I wanted, "I mean, yes. I have only one friend boy. Boyfriend, I mean."

Clark smiled, the best smile on earth, and then leaned down and pressed his lips against my cheek, the way I had his outside.

Kiss me, I thought. *Kiss me for real.*

And maybe he would have, if . . . "Lois!" James said. "Hurry up!" He was standing outside the elevator.

"We were on our way," I said. "Until you ruined it. James, Clark. Clark, James."

James reached out and shook Clark's hand, and Clark used his shoulder to prevent the old elevator doors from closing on us. "Nice to meet you," he said. "What's the rush? Has something else happened?"

James spoke in a hush. "Dante broke up with Maddy."

"What?!" I didn't mean it to be so loud. I lowered my voice. "What?"

"I know," he said. "He sent her an email. She says she's fine, but . . ." He flapped his hand, as if I was urgently needed, and then preceded us up the hall.

Clark caught my eye.

"I didn't say anything I shouldn't have," I said. "I swear."

"Hey," Clark said, "I know."

Somehow his easy belief I hadn't screwed up made the situation better. I sped up, wanting to see how Maddy was doing.

Which appeared to be . . . fine. When we reached the door, she was sporting her fancy headphones and humming along to whatever she listened to while she typed.

"See?" James said, before going over to his own desk.

I didn't. She appeared completely normal.

Clark made a slow spin, taking in the entirety of the Morgue.

"Like I said, it's not much to look at." I tried to remember my first experience of coming in here.

"Are you kidding?" he asked. "This is the room where it happens. I can't believe I finally get to see it."

Devin got up to come meet us.

"Clark, Devin," I said. "Devin meet Clark, aka SmallvilleGuy, in real life, finally."

Devin attempted a cool handshake of some sort, but had to settle for a regular one. "I'm glad to finally meet you in person," Clark said.

"Likewise," Devin said. He and Clark finished their handshake. "Even if you're the reason I never bothered asking out Lois."

Clark smiled at him. "Good call."

"Some days I have regrets," Devin said, shaking his head tragically and leaning his hand on the top of my desk.

Clark frowned. "Well . . ."

"Devin," I said, "stop that."

Devin cracked up. "I'm just kidding. Oh my god, you two are adorable. Ignore me. Did James tell you?" Devin asked me. "She just read his message and then informed us and put on her headphones."

"Yes, and sheez." I couldn't believe Dante broke up with her over *email*. He wasn't a jerk, but it was a jerk move.

I stalked over to Maddy and gingerly pulled her headphone away from her ear. "You want to tell me what happened?" I asked.

"Dante dumped me in an email," Maddy said cheerily. She put her earphones around her neck.

I gave her the stink-eye, the look I'd give someone who I intended to break in an interrogation. "Let's go out into the hall and talk."

"We don't need to," she said. Spotting Clark behind me, she said, "Hi, Clark!" Then, "Margaret . . ."

"Bourke-White," he said. "Famous photojournalist, mostly for *LIFE Magazine*."

She squinted. "Molly . . ."

"Ivins, or as Lois calls her, 'the funniest political writer in American history.' Nice try."

"You're good," she said.

I just kept looking at her. "You win," she said, "but we don't need to talk about it. We have other things to do. Important things."

"We'll be right back," I said, pulling her out of her chair.

I tugged her out and up the mostly darkened hallway. "What happened?" I asked.

She gave me a look, and I could see a little of the wounds she was hiding beneath her cool exterior. Her T-shirt read Never Say Lie.

"Like I said," Maddy studied her shoes, "he dumped me."

"Why?" I asked. "It wasn't . . ." *Because of me? Something I said?*

"Wasn't what?" she asked.

I might as well tell her. "He came to talk to me after lunch. I swear I didn't say anything."

"I know," she said, "he said so in the message. I guess it was what you didn't say that decided it."

I placed my hands against the wall and gently banged my head against it for the second time this week. "Why did I screw this up? I'm so sorry. I'll fix it. I'll talk to him."

Maddy's hand landed on my shoulder. "No," she said. "It wasn't just the email. When I saw him at the end of the day, he asked if he could make me happy. Very, very serious about it. I told him I am happy, just not *happier* when we're together. He said he needed to think about that, but apparently it didn't take long. In the email, he said that you told him we should both be happy. And then he said that meant he had to break it off."

"Well, that's stupid," I said. "He'll never find anyone better than you. And he should have done it in person."

"But he'll find someone better than me *for* him. And likewise." Maddy pushed her hair out of her face. "We both tried. Lois . . . there was this moment, when I saw the email and read it, that I felt this kind of sinking feeling. Embarrassed. But then I felt relieved. Because he broke up with me. The wall was gone, immediately. He said he thought I would hate it less if he did it this way, in a message, and he's right. I wouldn't have wanted to face him. I hated all these 'talks' we've been having." She paused. "You know, I think we're still friends, even. I need to get stronger. He did me a favor, but I shouldn't have put him in that position. I should have just told him it wasn't working anymore and I wanted out."

I couldn't quite believe it. "You're taking this awfully well."

"You were right. If we were meant to be together, I'd know. Besides, boys, gross," she said. "More trouble than they're worth. I mean, except Clark, obviously."

"Obviously," I said.

"A boy who knows the name of every famous female journalist I've tossed his way so far."

"Dreamy, right?" I asked.

"Dreamy," she agreed. "Back to work?"

I nodded, which was good . . . because Perry was coming toward us up the opposite hall. He extended a finger at the office door. "In here, now."

It seemed Clark was about to get the full *Scoop* experience.

"We were just heading back in," I said.

"Good, because when I checked for copy, it's funny—there still wasn't any," Perry said. "And all the TV stations have stories about this guy's cockamamie experience from last night. He can't give enough interviews. I don't believe for a second someone flew him into the street, but I don't know, do I? Because we don't *have* what's really been happening—"

Perry was still talking when we entered the office, but the moment he saw Clark, he stopped. "Who are you?" he demanded.

Clark opened his mouth and held out his hand, but then Perry waved dismissively. "I don't care. If you can get this story, you're hired."

Wide-eyed, Clark dropped his hand.

"Lane, was I wrong to trust you with this story? Should I reassign it to someone upstairs?" Perry's gaze swept over all of us, leaving burning shame in its wake. "Or are you going to get the definitive take you promised so that we can save the *Planet*'s reputation?"

"We're going to do the last one," I said. "Wouldn't you rather we be right than fast?"

"I'd like both," he said, steam practically coming out of his ears. "If I don't have a story by tomorrow morning, it's over. I'm pulling the assignment and reconsidering what type of reporting you will be doing in the future."

And, with that, Perry about-faced.

"Well, I promised you a tour," I told Clark, after he was gone and definitively out of earshot. "Welcome to our world."

"Wow," Clark said. "And I thought my parents could make me feel guilty. I don't even work here and I feel like I messed up. What are you going to do?"

"Get the story," I said.

"Yeah, how are we going to do that?" James asked, sounding defeated. "We've been trying."

Devin said, "I got nothing new."

They were all looking at me, expecting a solution. Funny enough, my phone buzzed right then and so I knew who it must be. My parents would have phoned. Everyone else who was likely to message me was in this room.

TheInventor: *Sending addresses to your email. I found all four. Wisconsin, Ohio, Jersey.*

"I've got something," I said. "Original addresses for our missing teens," I continued, heading to my desk and sitting down to log on to my computer. "A friend of Clark's . . . and mine . . . tracked them down. I'm forwarding them to all three of you. They weren't from the Metropolis area. That's why we couldn't find them. We should call the families, let them know where their missing kids are. They'll come get them, won't they?"

"It's hard to believe they wouldn't," Maddy said.

I prayed she was right.

"Lois," Clark said, "did you tell them?"

Gah.

"Tell us what?" Maddy asked him.

"It should come from Lois," Clark said.

I knew he was trying to help, but . . . I gave him a desperate *butt out* look. He didn't look away.

Thankfully, my phone buzzed again. I held up a finger. "One sec."

How was I going to get out of this? I needed to get this story—for all our sakes.

TheInventor: *I also found four properties your Contessa's been paying the rent on. Including this one—I'm checking it out.*

He'd attached a photo. It was the building with all the weird cameras.

SkepticGirl1: *No, don't—*

TheInventor: *I just figured out how to get in the back door.*

I knew Donovan well enough to know that there was no way Alex was getting any messages out once he was inside. When I'd lock-picked my way into the last lab he had set up, everything on my phone got wiped on the way out by a security measure he had in place. I could only imagine his experience with us had made him more paranoid.

This is just great. Alex Luthor stole my plan. Now I have to go save him.

Clark appeared at my shoulder. "What is it?" he asked.

I clicked out so he wouldn't see my phone screen.

Todd had said they wanted me to talk. Well, they were going to get me.

I couldn't afford to sacrifice a friend, even one I didn't fully trust. Nor did I want anyone else in this room getting hurt. I could imagine how the Kents would look at me if I got Clark in trouble. Martha would sternly forbid us from ever seeing each other again.

"Bad timing," I said. I excelled at cover stories. "My mom needs me to come watch Lucy. Dad's out and she got called back to campus for a meeting."

"Can Lucy come here?" Maddy asked. "Perry didn't sound like he was going to wait."

"Good idea. Mom's already left, so I'll go get her and bring her back here," I said.

"I could go," Clark offered.

"No," I blurted.

He raised his eyebrows.

"It's just, she's already half in love with you," I said. "She won't be able to take the heartbreak when you leave if she feels like you were on a date."

Clark's head ducked in embarrassment. "Oh. Right."

I channeled my inner commander to keep my friends distracted. "You guys can make the calls while I'm gone. We'll regroup when I get back. Maybe if we can get positive IDs . . . Some help from the parents . . ."

"On it," James said.

By the time I came back, it wouldn't matter that Lucy wasn't with me. I texted Taxi Jack a mayday to meet me out front; he sent back a confirmation immediately. I slung my bag over my shoulder.

"What about me?" Clark asked. "You're sure you don't want me to go with you?"

"You can help—everyone loves you," I said, and my cheeks were on fire once more. "If anyone can convince these parents to step up, it's you, Clark Kent. And you can fill the others in on . . . everything."

He nodded, as if I'd given him a sacred trust. He wasn't going to be happy when he found out what I was doing.

None of them were.

It won't matter if you get the story.

That's what I told myself. I even believed it.

CHAPTER 25

Taxi Jack was somewhat relieved I was headed to a nice enough neighborhood, and while it was still light out.

If only he knew.

"You can let me out here," I said when we reached the corner with the decorative phone booth.

"You want me to wait?" he asked.

"No need," I said. Who knew how long I'd be inside?

"All right, well summon me if you change your mind, milady," he said, waggling his many-ringed fingers.

Milady? He was seriously getting into *The Three Musketeers*.

I waited until he'd pulled away, his taillights disappearing into the distance, before I started up the sidewalk. I'd come unarmed except for my wits—what else could I possibly bring? I hoped they were all I'd need.

At least I had an ally inside. *Though he shouldn't be here.*

The blame for that, for anyone getting hurt . . . it weighed on me. I should have come back here the moment their desire was clear.

I was a match for Donovan. And for Jenkins. I'd proved that.

Maybe not for the two of them together with a fancy benefactor, though.

Too bad. I had to be equal to the task. I didn't slow until I had almost reached the building that was my destination—well, until I came to the alley that I was certain would lead to a back way in.

"Here goes everything," I muttered.

I left the sidewalk for the alleyway. The damp brick walls on either side left enough space to allow a single car through. There wasn't anything to speak of besides a couple of dumpsters. I didn't let myself think too much about a girl walking alone down a dark alley being the ultimate bad-idea cliché. I had no choice.

When I reached the end, I glanced up and saw a fancy camera mounted here too. I waved.

And then I was on a smaller access street. It was mostly old fencing and the backs of buildings. I walked past the two other structures between me and my destination.

At the back of the brownstone a set of concrete steps ran down, down, down into what must have been the building's basement and sublevels. A slick door with a keypad and another buzzer setup waited at the bottom, just visible from where I stood.

I could count on my phone not working inside, so I took it out and typed a group text: *If I'm not back in two hours, come looking. I'm at their HQ, you know the spot.*

And Clark would be able to guess how to get in, from our adventure the other day. I said a silent "I'm sorry" for making him worry before I hit send and put my phone in my pocket. The others were used to watching me charge ahead in person. It was my way.

I started down the steep steps, placing my boots carefully. My phone in my pocket buzzed, but I didn't check the message. Finally, when I got to the bottom, I stopped where the shiny black camera mounted above this door would have a clear angle on me. Unlike Alex, I didn't plan on figuring out how to get inside. I thought it would be easy.

I moved forward to ring the buzzer, and spoke into the little speaker.

"You wanted me to come, here I am," I said.

Then I stepped back and mouthed *Let me in* to the camera.

As I expected, the door buzzed immediately to admit me. I grabbed the handle, going inside before I could change my mind and back out.

What waited for me behind the door was . . . nice. Ceiling panels glowed, casting a cool, uniform light. This was a major step up from Donovan's last two shady labs in rundown buildings in the most dangerous parts of town, places he'd had access to courtesy of Boss Moxie's extensive real estate holdings. Everything I could see in front of me gleamed, clean and sleek and new, the very latest and greatest. The Contessa must have paid for some major upgrades. The smooth-walled hall ahead of me still might as well have screamed an ominous *Abandon all hope.*

I turned, thinking maybe I *would* go back for reinforcements—and heard a definite *click* from the door. I tried it.

No love. The door didn't budge an inch.

Okay, that made the decision for me.

The outer walls and the inside of the door had a metallic shine. It was possibly the same stuff that made up the armor the teens wore, but seemed thicker. I touched the door, and it felt cool under my palm. I dug out a pen and scratched it against the metal surface as hard as I could. No effect whatsoever. So I needed for this to not come down to brawn against brains.

Turning, I took a ginger step in the direction of the hall.

"I can't believe it took you so long to give in," said a voice overhead, a man's and unfamiliar.

"Is that you, Dirtbag Jenkins?" I asked under my breath.

"You'll have to speak up if you want a response. Or just keep coming. We're waiting for you."

"I'm not here to give in," I said, raising my voice. "Just so you know."

The speaker made a noise, and then another voice came over it. "What is the meaning of all—" This one was more familiar. Donovan, I thought. But it cut out before I could tell for sure.

"Be right there," I said, keeping my voice loud enough so they could hear. At least if Alex was with them, he would know I hadn't abandoned him here. That I was on my way. Maybe he'd come up with a plan too.

I wasn't going to abandon all hope. Not today. Not ever.

I shrugged off my nerves as best as I could—which wasn't much—and started to walk up the slick-walled, immaculate hallway. As I walked, I checked my phone and saw the expected but unwelcome words: No Service.

Figured.

I also saw the message I'd gotten before I came in. It was from Maddy: *Lois, no! Don't give them what they want—which, according to Clark, is you.*

He'd told them all, apparently. And it was far too late to turn back. Soon enough, I'd know *why* these people were after me. That was something.

I worked to control the sound of my footsteps as I made my way up the hall. For all I knew, the stealth might buy me a second or two to assess the situation when I finally found someone. The interior of the building didn't appear to be filled with cameras like the outside, so it was possible I wasn't yet visible.

Which meant no one here feared a threat from within.

I had a theory about that metal along the outer walls, that it helped create a kind of isolating barrier for the building. That we were in a fortress of sorts.

Reya appeared at the end of the hallway. Todd, Sunny, and Jamie joined her.

"We knew you'd come," Todd said, and then laughed.

Reya shot him a disapproving look. "She's going to be one of us. Be nice."

No freaking way was I going to be one of them.

Jenkins couldn't be delusional enough to think I'd obey his commands. Best not to say that to them, though, not yet.

"I am?" I asked, moving closer. There was no turning back, not without Alex. And not until I had enough to nail the guys who'd brought these runaways here. "We could all leave here together instead."

Sunny said, "I'm afraid not," her mask catching one of the lights overhead. "You can't give us what we want."

"It's not as bad here as you think," Jamie added. "We have a purpose, a place."

Working for very bad people. Not a good purpose, not a good place.

But I could relate to the sentiment. No one knew better than me how much that meant, how hard a place and a purpose would make you fight.

"Those are good things," I said. "I know your families probably weren't . . . what families should be."

"You don't know anything," Todd said.

"We found their names and addresses, your real families'. My friends are calling them right now. I bet they'll want to see you, all of you," I said, sweeping my eyes across them.

"Bring her," the man's voice said over the speakers.

Todd was the one who scoffed. "If you believe our 'real' families will save us, you don't know anything. I don't even know why our new parents want you. Reya, they told us what to do."

"Sorry," Reya murmured, then grabbed my arm with one of her cool metallic hands. "Right this way."

She directed us into a waiting elevator around the corner. Her hand was strong as steel on my arm, and I knew it would be useless to fight.

The elevator operated by key, and when Jamie twisted it, we went farther down.

"Where are you taking me?" I asked.

"You'll see," Todd said.

How long would it be before my reinforcements arrived? Would they even be able to get into this fortress when they did?

Don't think that way.

They would make it here and inside eventually. They had to, right? Alex had managed it. I just had to get the information I came for and stall.

It wasn't much, but it was a plan. Men like Steve Jenkins and Dabney Donovan were arrogant, overconfident. That made them vulnerable.

The Contessa was more of an unknown, but maybe I'd be lucky. Maybe she wasn't even here.

The elevator car stopped after going down two levels, and I knew my luck had run out when the doors opened.

The glam queen stood in another short sleek corridor, waiting. She was in a long gown and extremely high heels, like she'd planned an evening out. Diamonds glittered around her neck. She raked her eyes over me from head to toe.

Reya and I got off the elevator last, and the Contessa motioned for her to bring me over. We stopped in front of her.

"Those shoes must be killer on your feet," I said. "Or you have excellent balance."

"Lois Lane," she said, "at last we formally meet. I'm the Contessa del Portenza." She waited expectantly. Was I supposed to be impressed?

"It's hardly an introduction if you use a fake name. Who are you really?" I asked her. "The Contessa name you stole goes back hundreds of years. It's not yours."

She tilted her head, like I'd finally gotten interesting. "Oh, but it is. You know what they say, there's no money like old money."

"You're four hundred years old?" I scoffed.

Reya's hand tightened on my skin. "Ow!" I said.

"Sorry." The apology matched the immediate loosening of her grip.

She hadn't done it on purpose. She was afraid of this woman. There was a reason she'd drawn her with a dragon. I realized something else . . .

"Reya, you drew the logo too, didn't you? On the backpack?" That was why the art style was different from the Ismenios logo. It was familiar from her other piece.

"Before," she said, her free hand flexing. "Yeah. She described it to me."

"We must make use of our talents while we have them," the Contessa said. "For some of us, like me, that may be a long time indeed. Whatever fortune gives us, it is our responsibility to make something of it."

"Fortune? Is that what we're calling abductions and experimenting on other human beings these days?" I asked. I was ignoring her claim of being ancient . . . for now, anyway.

The Contessa smiled. "I see it now, why you are the center of their obsession. You're a fiery one to be so young."

Ugh. I hated being patronized.

She spoke to Reya then. "Were you abducted? Or were you given shelter and a home?"

"We weren't abducted," Reya said. "We had nowhere else to go." When the Contessa's eyebrows raised, she added, "We're happy to be here."

"You see, there are always people who need a home, who will do anything for one," the Contessa said.

"You're a monster," I said.

Reya gasped.

I went on anyway. "You're the Echidna to someone's Typhon. Steve Jenkins, right?"

"Everyone has a monster inside them, Lois," the woman said, unconcerned that I was dropping Jenkins's name. "Don't you know that?"

"Is that a trick question? Because no, not everyone has a monster inside them. I don't."

And neither did my friends.

The Contessa's eyes narrowed. They were hard.

"Stop playing with our recruit," a man's voice said, and the infamous Steve Jenkins himself rounded the corner and joined us. He had an expensive haircut, and a more expensive suit, sedately tailored. He was shiny and soulless, just like the inside of this building. "Bring her in here."

Showtime.

First, I had something else to say to the Contessa. "If I were you, I'd choose my investments more carefully. I have no reason to like you, but I also wouldn't have had any reason to want to ruin you—too bad you chose the wrong partners. I guess you live and learn."

The Contessa laughed. "Good luck." I wasn't sure whether the words were for me or for Jenkins.

"I said bring her in here," Jenkins said, and vanished back around the corner.

Reya towed me in the direction Jenkins had gone. I turned my head to see the rest of the silver squad and the Contessa herself following us.

I thought about what James and I had learned about Jenkins, and tried to figure out what to say that might rattle him.

We emerged into a large open warehouse-style space, with training equipment toward the front—futuristic versions of a treadmill and the kind of obstacle course the military used in basic training—and a well-lit lab toward the back. All this made Donovan's last shady lab space look like a kid's garage.

"Impressed?" the Contessa murmured.

Don't show them fear. "Not the word I'd use."

"Children, you can go," Jenkins said with a dismissive flick of his wrist.

So he *was* playing the father figure to them, not Donovan. That made more sense. They'd probably never heard Donovan's name until I used it. Assuming he *was* here somewhere . . . which I did. That other voice had sounded too familiar not to be him.

Reya released me. Quietly, she said, "Don't fight them. We don't want to hurt you." And then the four of them, with their various silvered elements, left.

So there was no hope of convincing them to help me.

"Come on," Jenkins prompted. "I didn't expect you to be shy. You like infiltrating labs, don't you? I expected you'd come running back with Todd as soon as you saw the contents of the folder and had a chance to ditch your friends. You almost held out too long. But I suppose that's all right, since everything is working out just as we wanted."

The Contessa walked toward him, her heels clicking on the floor, and I knew I didn't have any choice but to approach him too. The stupid folder *had* been a trap. I hadn't fallen for that one.

"So, which do you think I am," I said, "a problem or an opportunity?"

Jenkins smiled, but it was humorless. "It never occurred to me to think about you at all, until Moxie suggested it. He made me see that you're both. A problem *and* an opportunity. Just like Donovan."

Boss Moxie. *Of course.*

No wonder he'd been so eager to give me tidbits when I went to visit him.

I realized with a sinking feeling that the bad guys weren't the only overconfident ones here. I was also guilty. Moxie had suggested whatever this was to Jenkins, and he'd known Donovan would jump at any new funding partner for his research. He'd have known about the Contessa's past connection to Jenkins. He'd united my enemies, deftly engineering all this out of the venomousness of his heart to punish me.

Only someone who'd been around as long as Moxie could wait so patiently for revenge and manage it without getting his own hands any dirtier.

Jenkins shook his head in mock dismay and continued, "Poor Dr. Donovan, a genius left out in the cold by you, with no one to help guide his work."

"I was hoping he'd freeze," I said, drawing a frown from Jenkins. He wanted me to be afraid. I was, but I still refused to give him the satisfaction of showing it.

Like we'd summoned the Donovan devil by speaking of him, he appeared, striding purposefully around a partition that looked transparent from our side but hid what was beyond it. He was in his bubble of contained psychopathy, as usual, gliding toward us as if he was separate from his surroundings.

"You got an upgrade," I said coolly, gesturing to indicate the warehouse space.

After a long moment, he replied. "And apparently you're getting one too, girl." His gruff voice sent a chill through me. "Though I wish I'd been consulted before you were chosen."

Jenkins groaned. "Get over it already. She's exactly who we need."

I am not. But why did Jenkins think I was? "Where is Alex?" I couldn't even think about escaping this subterranean lair until I located him.

"Right this way," Donovan said.

I frowned as he led me, the Contessa and Jenkins trailing, around the partition.

"Lois, why did you come?" Alex asked from his perch on a stool beside a gleaming steel countertop. He gave me a big grin. "These people are up to some intriguing work."

My pulse spiked, my heart drumming.

I came to rescue you.

But did he need rescuing?

CHAPTER 26

I put myself between Alex and Donovan, despite my doubts. What if I'd been wrong to place *any* trust in Alex?

Jenkins wore a predatory smile; the Contessa had what I was beginning to consider her trademark haughty air. And Donovan, well, he was gazing at Alex with something remarkably similar to approval.

Think, Lois. Stall, Lois. Have faith, Lois.

"I'd begun to doubt you'd ever get her here," the Contessa said.

My heart picked up its staccato rhythm.

"Though this has been entertaining," she went on, "you could have given Dr. Donovan some notice. He doesn't deal well with surprises."

"Of course I do," Donovan said. "I'm a man of science. Adaptability is almost as important as vision."

This was a business partnership between three of the worst personalities ever. At least I *prayed* it was only three.

"I knew she'd come eventually," Jenkins said. "I was never worried about that. She's too cocky not to."

So the Contessa's comment about getting me here hadn't been directed to Alex after all. *Whew.* But why were they speaking so freely in front of him? If I acted surprised, that might make things worse for me.

"You should talk, disgraced ex-CEO dirtbag," I said. "What about you, Dabney Donovan? Ready to go visit your creation in prison yet? I thought you promised me I'd never see you again."

Donovan's expression transformed into an irritated frown. "It wasn't my choice," he said, casting a deeper grimace at Jenkins. But then he looked me over and said, "However, you're as good a subject as any. Healthy, of the right age."

Subject. And Jenkins had used the word *recruit* earlier. What were they playing at? Why would they want *me* as part of their experiment? I still didn't understand the point. This was way too elaborate to be *just* about revenge for anyone involved.

"Wait a second, doc," Alex said, and stood up. "What does any of this have to do with Lois?"

"Allow me to explain." Jenkins gave Alex an indulgent smile and held up a hand to keep Donovan quiet. "We've always planned five members of our beta Typhon team. She's so curious and likes using her brain so much—I kept putting Donovan off about a fifth subject until we got her here. He thinks he can not only give her enhanced hearing, fusing his new alloy to one of her ears, but strengthen her neural connections to make her smarter. You'd love being smarter, wouldn't you, Lois?"

"I will *never* work for you," I said in horror. "No matter what you do to my brain."

Alex put a hand on my arm. "You could use me instead—my dad would hate it, and I also have a good brain. The best brain. Probably better than hers. Sorry, Lois."

I glared at him.

"We need Lane," Jenkins said, almost regretfully.

"Your time will come, young man," the Contessa said. "I see a bright future for you."

I couldn't resist asking any longer. I trained my eyes on Alex. "You're not *with* them, are you?"

A sharp intake of breath was his response. "Of course not."

He sounded offended. I'd made the situation worse. But still . . . "Then why are they talking to you? Being friendly?"

"The boy has an excellent mind," Donovan said. "He managed to defeat our locking mechanism on the door, the strongest in the building."

Alex shrugged.

Donovan approached me with a long, thick syringe. "But why do you need *me*?" I asked them, moving away from him—only to find my back against a countertop.

"Not you, so much as your father," Jenkins said. "I'm not ready to get out of the arms race yet. This is our ticket back in."

And with that sentence, everything clicked into place.

Yes, this had been about me, but not because of me. It was about my dad. The military's research funds. I thought of the obstacle course I'd seen on the way back to the lab.

They were going to make me part of their "beta Typhon team" because Jenkins thought it would force Dad to welcome them back into lucrative business with open arms. He thought Dad wouldn't be able to say no, not if his daughter's safety was at stake. They probably thought Dad would see what they did to me as an upgrade too. I'd become a military asset, along with Reya, Jamie, Sunny, and Todd.

"Ah," the Contessa said, "now she gets it."

Problem was, they didn't know Dad like I did. "You really think General Lane, who has commanded men in wars, is going to be extorted by you? Because of me?" I asked.

"Your dad's a general?" Alex said.

I shot him a quelling look.

"You'd be surprised what fathers will do for their daughters—especially when they see it's in all our best interest," Jenkins said. "Once you're part of our team, it's the only way he'll have access to you. And we're quite confident his colleagues will want access to all five of you, and the next generation, and the next. Think how useful you'll be on a battlefield, or in covert operations. We *were* trying to lure you here, but we've also been . . . advertising the possibilities by sending the team out and about. Your delay gave us time for that. So thank you, Lois Lane." The level of smug he directed at me was nauseating. Then he said, "Dr. Donovan, it's time. Let's get this done."

Alex tried to shield me, but Jenkins wrestled him aside with ease while Donovan advanced.

"It'll only hurt for a moment," Donovan said, taking my arm. "Alas."

"Hey," Alex protested. "Don't do that!"

I swept my leg out to take Donovan down, but he got the needle in my arm anyway. And then everything went very, very dark.

* * *

I woke up and immediately started fighting. Or I tried to. My arms and legs were pinned down.

No, strapped down.

I strained my head up and saw that I was in a smaller laboratory. Here were Donovan's missing file cabinets, lining the wall directly ahead. To my left, there were a few dark computer terminals, and the makings of what looked like an impromptu surgical theater. Which, I realized, I was in the middle of.

I looked to my right. A file lay open on a steel surface beside me, and Dr. Donovan sat next to it. He was preparing some shiny . . . instruments. Sharp ones too.

"Oh no," I said, trying to shrink away, only to be prevented by the straps.

He glanced over.

"You're awake," he said. "That's unfortunate." But he shrugged and carried on with polishing one of the pointier tools in his selection. "Would you like to know what I have planned for you?"

"Not really. I got the gist." They wanted to get in my head—literally. They were going to give me extra-strong hearing and also make me the brainiest member of Team Typhon. I considered searching for any humanity Donovan might possess, so I could appeal to it, but going for his self-interest seemed safer. "If you let me go I bet I can convince my dad to help you—maybe he could even get your clone back . . ."

"I can always make another one," he said, whistling that serial killer whistle. He stopped after another moment. "Do you want to know why, after some reflection, I now consider you a good subject?"

"Because you're a crazy mad scientist."

Donovan said, "Seems that's your type—your little friend has promise. I'm going to have to figure out how to get rid of his memories of being here. But from what he tells me, his father probably won't notice he's missing for a few days. I have time to play around."

With Alex's brain, he meant. So that was why they had talked in front of him. It didn't matter. They'd just erase any information they didn't want him to have. "What is *wrong* with you?" I asked.

Donovan scribbled a note in the folder and closed it. "I'm not the one who believes my opinions carry more weight than those of a genius," he said. "I was put here to do great work, and I plan to. There's always been someone in my way. First the do-gooders at Cadmus. Then you. But Jenkins tells me no one is more encouraging of experimental research than the military. And so you have become the perfect test subject in an instant. Finally, I have the prospect of support from people who will not block, but clear, the path for progress."

"I'd hardly call wrecking my brain progress. And he's wrong."

He shook his head. "Wreck, no. Not that you can understand, but I'm doing you a favor. When your neural networks reach their full potential, you'll understand. Your intellect will be too great not to. Jenkins and I believe you'll naturally assume your place as head of the team. We can learn so much from the five of you before we produce the next generation . . ." He stopped and rose. "We may as well get on with it. I'll be back. Jenkins wants to witness the procedure."

He pressed a card against the door, and it clicked open. He left.

The door closed. I immediately strained against the arm and wrist bands.

"Be calm. Methodical," I murmured to myself. *And whatever you do, don't look too closely at those things he was polishing. Definitely don't think about what's going to happen if you can't get free.*

Wait.

The bindings holding me were straps. That meant they fastened—which in turn meant they could also be loosened. I worked at the one above my right hand first, pulling against it as hard as I could.

I had to get out of here.

I wasn't getting improved, not for anything.

I wriggled, straining my wrist against the strap, twisting my hand—

My right fingers slipped through the binding. Quickly, I unbuckled the left, sat up, and leaned over to undo the ones at my ankles.

A groan sounded from somewhere behind me.

"Hello?" I asked. "Who's here?"

I finished freeing my feet and was able to get off the gurney.

Behind mine was another gurney, with another person strapped to it.

Alex.

They must have been planning to keep him here until Donovan's mind wipe could take place. From what I knew of Donovan, if he failed, he'd probably just try to make a clone of Alex.

The world did not need two of him.

"Don't enjoy this *too* much," I told myself, and crossed to the gurney. Where I gave Alex a hard slap on the right side of his face.

His eyes blinked and watered with the sting. "Ouch," he said.

"Wake up," I said. "Hurry."

I knew from Donovan using his card to get out that the door had an electromagnetic lock. Good thing I'd been reading up on different varieties of locks and how to open them. The magnetic kind of doors were fairly easy . . . if you had the right counter technique for them.

And so I had a decent idea about how to get us out of here before the good doctor came back. Alex might even be able to help.

He groaned again.

I undid the straps on his arms and legs. "We don't have much time. Stop moaning and wake up."

"Don't hit me again," Alex said. Then, "This has been such an exciting day. Are you always doing things like this?"

I almost laughed. "You mean almost getting conscripted into some weird experiment army as a business case for my dad? No. We need to get out of this room. There's a couple of options—if we can trigger a fire alarm, the electromagnetic door should open automatically. Safety precaution." I looked around, but I didn't see any sensors or fire alarms handy. Of course. "Can you use any of these computers to hack into the system and do that, or kill the power to the building?"

"You are a sharp one," he said, slightly dazed.

"Focus. Can you?"

"Probably," he said. "But how much time to do we have?"

"Not enough, if you're asking me that question." I cast another panicked look at the door. "We have one more option. So, computer genius, tell me if there's a computer in here that would have a strong magnet in it. Preferably a rare earth metal one. That would also work." *According to my extracurricular reading, anyway . . .*

He scanned the terminals, then pointed to the nearest computer. "That one should."

"And where will it be exactly?" I asked.

"Around the drive and the fan." Yes, I'd known that from my reading too. But I'd never actually experimented and so had only a faint idea what I'd be looking for. I squinted at the machine, then him. "Show me where," I commanded. "We don't have much time."

"Okay, okay," he said, and joined me in hurrying over to the workstation. "Bossy."

"I prefer to think of it not as bossy, but as saving us both from certain doom."

He scooted the computer around so I could see the back of it. "In there," he said, giving the back plate a tap. Tiny screws held it in place.

"Good." Grappling a pen out of my bag, I used the top of the cap to pry out the screws with deliberate twists.

"What are you doing?" Alex asked, interested.

"Haven't you heard? The pen is mightier than the sword." The plate came loose. "Can you, um, find the magnet and get it out for me?"

I moved aside as he bent and fished inside the opening. "I used a different method to get into the building," Alex said, but he came out with the magnet.

"That was a different type of door, too. And you haven't volunteered any bright ideas for an escape plan." I re-stashed my pen and held my hand out for the magnet. Alex pressed the disc into my palm. It wasn't huge, but it wasn't tiny either. Here was praying it would work. "Now we use this to temporarily disable the magnetic lock on the door. It's a thing I read."

"Yes," he said, puzzling it out. "That should work."

While he considered the merits of my plan, I crossed to the door and slid the magnet into place against the lock, adjusting to find the right spot on the door's magnet that powered the lock. I wish I'd memorized the manual on this stuff I'd been reading.

"Come on, come on, come on," I chanted. "Work. Please work."

The door clicked open.

I flashed Alex a triumphant grin and tossed the magnet to the floor. "Time to sneak out of this place."

He grinned back at me. "This is all so exciting."

My sense of triumph evaporated when an alarm began to sound. The timing had to just be coincidence. Didn't it? Donovan was paranoid, but they wouldn't have *every* interior door keyed to an alarm, would they?

Which meant something *else* might have set off the alarm. Some*one* else. Maybe even plural someones.

"I think that might be reinforcements," I said, praying I was right.

"Who?" Alex asked.

"Clark and my friends from the *Scoop*."

I looked at him. It was my fault for not trusting my friends. It's what had gotten us trapped here and almost gotten both our brains scrambled. "Unlike you, I have a lot of them. Is that why you were talking to Donovan, Jenkins, and company and being nice to them? Because they were friendly?"

"You're lucky," Alex said, ignoring the question. "We'd

better get going. Oh, hello!" he said distractedly, to someone up the hall.

I turned to find Reya and Todd advancing on us. "They sent us to secure you two down here. Someone breached the perimeter," Todd said.

"Crap."

I ran through my options. I had self-defense training. If I had to ditch Alex temporarily, I could come back for him.

Reya came closer and said, "I'm sorry we have to do this." She extended her hands to literally strong-arm me.

"No, don't be sorry," I said, and dodged below her fingers. I shoved Alex in Todd's direction and bolted up the hall. "Be too slow to catch me."

Speedy Todd would give chase, obviously, but I collided with someone else first. Someone who pulled me toward him with strong hands, and who I knew immediately, through sheer instinct, not to fight.

"Lois," Clark said. "Thank god. This way."

Relief flooded through me. When I looked back, Todd was frowning at the two of us, like he knew he'd be no match for us both. Not even with Reya at his side. "You won't get out of here," he said.

"We will," I assured him. "You could too."

Todd shook his head like I still didn't understand their position.

"I can't believe you did this," Clark said, leading me toward a hallway that was filled with smoke or some sort of fog— there was no fire smell to go with it. "And alone."

"Not alone. Didn't you see Alex back there?"

"Oh," he said. "I was distracted. And I'm getting you out first. I'll go back for him."

I didn't argue. I wanted out of here, and the faster, the better. Clark opened a door and there was a stairwell, filled with more fake smoke. Before I realized what was happening, Clark scooped me into his arms and started up the steps.

"This is dangerous," I said. "You can't see! Put me down!"

"Oh, *now* you're worried about what's dangerous." He made no move to release me, and I decided not to protest again. Arguing would only make our journey to the outside *more* precarious.

"Alex came here," I said. "I couldn't just leave him on his own . . . although he seems to like these guys."

"You know what's going on, then?" Clark asked, and I detected curiosity.

I nodded and let myself relax against him, soaking in the scent of him. Steve Jenkins had intended for Dabney Donovan to break my brain and armor up my ear, make me so smart I didn't know right from wrong anymore. He wanted to take me away from my friends and make me part of the twisted team he'd created.

All so he and his mysterious benefactor could seduce my father into business with the three of them. I never saw this revelation coming, but now that I had the truth I was more eager to bust the three of them than ever.

"I know enough," I said. "Enough to write a story."

CHAPTER 27

When we reached the back door, it hung open in an off-kilter way that made me think Clark must have removed the hinges or something. Clark sat me down gently on the concrete at the bottom of the steps, kissed my forehead, and said, "I have to go back for our other friend."

No one else had showed up to try to stop us. But I worried. "Are you sure it's safe for you to go back in alone?" I asked. "What if they trap you in there?"

"I'll be fine," he said. "Your friends are waiting around front. Go let them know you're all right."

"Be careful," I said, and pressed a kiss to his cheek. He headed back inside to the hallway. I called after him, "If you're not out in ten minutes, I'm coming back in!"

Then I pounded my way up the steps and to the alley. Three

welcome faces waited at the far end of it, huddled together on the sidewalk: Maddy, Devin, and James.

They saw me and let out a cheer.

A few random passersby gave odd looks, but this was Metropolis. They went on their ways as Maddy rushed forward to meet me. Devin and James were close on her heels.

"How are you, besides insane for coming here by yourself?" Maddy asked. "You okay?"

"I'm fine," I said. "But should we go back for Clark? He has to get someone else out."

"Are you kidding? He wouldn't even let us go around back," James groused. "Said he'd be better off going in alone than us taking the risk of getting captured too. Something about navigating through heavy fog on the farm. Which was Maddy's idea. The fog, I mean."

"What was your idea?" I asked, my words coming a little shaky now that I was no longer inside that lair. That had been closer than would ever be comfortable.

I had the story, but thinking of Reya, Sunny, Jamie, and even jerky Todd still left me with a sympathetic pang of guilt. I didn't know any way to help them, besides getting them free of Donovan, Jenkins, and the Contessa. It didn't feel like enough.

"One that would make you proud," Maddy said. "You know those Halloween vapor balls? Your influence rubbed off, because I bought a bunch on sale last fall."

"Aha," I said. "The smoke that wasn't smoke. Smart."

"We *were* debating whether to go in after Clark," Devin

said. "But you came out before we made a decision. Who'd he go back in for anyway?"

"Alex Luthor—I'll explain later," I said. "Well, no, I'll explain now. He's TheInventor and it turned out he was a friend."

"What's TheInventor?" James asked.

Maddy said, "My thought exactly."

"Someone Lois knows online," Devin said, explaining for me. "Who she wasn't sure about."

I still wasn't one hundred percent on Alex. I hesitated, torn between waiting here and tearing back in there. What if Clark and Alex encountered the entire group, determined to keep them there?

But sprinting back into danger for a rescue proved unnecessary. Clark appeared at the end of the alley, supporting Alex with his arm as they walked quickly toward us. We hurried to meet them.

"Let's get out of here," Clark said.

We were back on the sidewalk in broad daylight in seconds flat, where none of the people passing by us would know anything strange was even happening right under their noses.

Not until they read my story, anyway.

"Where to?" Maddy asked. She pointed at a familiar cab waiting just up the street. "We called Taxi Jack. He confirmed that you'd come here. He's ticked at you, by the way."

"The Daily Planet Building," I said. "We are taking these guys down. They are never going to hurt another soul."

"Should we go back in for those weird kids?" James asked, his moral compass pointing true as always.

"What did their parents say when you called them?" I held my breath. Maybe the families would surprise us all. Maybe the four of them did have a place and purpose without the bad guys.

"We only managed to call three before we had to rush here," Devin said. "But they weren't receptive."

"Poor guys," Maddy said. "I can't even imagine."

"Parents shouldn't be so horrible," Clark said, unmistakable anger in his tone.

"Ha!" Alex put in. "Never meet my father."

I hesitated, thinking of the group's reaction when I told them we had their parents' contact info. They'd obviously been right. "We leave for now," I said. "If we can get rid of their new 'parents' by sending them to jail where they belong, I think then we'll have a shot at reaching them. At helping them. They want a place."

And there was still the fourth set of parents. I'd call them myself.

But . . . that wouldn't take away the kids' new abilities. Still, we could deal with that problem once we'd gotten rid of the first one. My guilt twinged again.

We piled into the taxi, Alex squeezing in up front with Devin. I sat next to Clark in back, my legs tucked over his, with Maddy and James wedged in beside us. Taxi Jack gave me a stony glance in the rearview, but he said nothing. He put the car in drive as soon as we were all in.

"Are you okay?" Clark whispered to me once we were moving. "I was so worried I wouldn't get there in time. I didn't know what to do."

He had taken a risk coming after me. I knew that much. His overprotective parents wouldn't approve. "No," I said. And I raised my voice to talk to all of them. "I barreled right in there, right into their plan. I told myself I was doing it to protect you guys, but I was just trying to protect myself. I thought I could handle this on my own."

"You more or less did," Alex said.

"That doesn't matter." I shook my head. "It could have gone another way."

"Yes," Taxi Jack said, finally deigning to speak to me, "it could have. Not that I know what you're talking about, except you've got to stop worrying us like this, Lois."

I couldn't help smiling. "I'll try."

Maddy raised her brows at me. "Does this mean no more secrets?"

"It means no more secrets to protect *me*," I said.

Clark tightened his arms around me. I could feel his breath against my neck, and it was . . . distracting. "I'm just glad you're okay," he said.

"Yeah, I almost wasn't. They were going to make me part of the experiment so Dad would let them back into the military research game—that was Jenkins's plan all along."

"They were going to increase her neural function," Alex said. "And give her super-hearing. I tried to volunteer instead."

"P.S." I reached up and touched Alex's shoulder. "Donovan planned to do a mind wipe on you."

That—finally—made Alex go quiet.

There was still something about him that didn't seem right to me. On the other hand, if his dad was as bad as he said, maybe that was understandable.

"Everyone, this is Alex, by the way," I said, feeling a little guilty.

My friends introduced themselves and Alex gave them big, goofy grins, whirling around in the seat to face James and Maddy when it was their turn, much to Devin's squirmy discomfort. This kid needed to get out more.

Once everyone had officially met, Devin had another question. "What about the Contessa?" he asked. "What was her story?"

"I still don't know," I said. "She kept claiming she really is the Contessa, the very old real deal from the 1600s. She's a strange one, even compared to those two."

"Do you think they'll run?" Clark asked.

"No," I said, thinking of the fortress-like building, with its workspaces hidden below ground, and about how none of them were scared to blackmail my dad. "I think they'll wait to see what my next move is. Which is why it's going to be on the front page of the paper. Can you go faster, Taxi Jack?"

"Your wish is my command, milady," he said, and sped up.

* * *

A scant ten minutes later, Taxi Jack screeched up to the curb in front of the Daily Planet Building. Devin, Maddy, James, and I piled out. But I poked my head back in to see what Clark was doing.

"You coming?"

Alex stayed in the front seat.

"Unless you need me, I'd better get back to the hotel," Clark said. "Mom already texted."

"We can drop you on my way," Alex said. "Though I'd love to go see the Daily Planet Building from the inside."

"Not today," I blurted. "Another time."

Alex shrugged. "I am exhausted. And exhilarated, but mostly exhausted."

Clark caught my eye and almost laughed. I crouched down to hug him and at the last moment aimed my mouth for the side of his lips.

Gah.

He smiled at me and said, "We'll talk later?"

I nodded. The door shut and they pulled away into traffic. My friends and I started for the front door and *our* place in the world.

"I have so many questions," Maddy said.

"Me too," Devin said. "The first one is . . . Luthor as in *Alexander* Luthor? The zillionaire?"

"His son," I said. "Is zillion really a thing?"

Devin shrugged. "Might as well be when you're that loaded."

"Doesn't sound like he cares much for his dad," James observed.

"True story," I said.

But I was distracted, already putting the lead for this story together in my head. By the time we navigated through security to the elevator and down to the office, I was ready to type.

I sat at my desk immediately and powered up my computer.

When reports of teenagers with unheard-of abilities and metallic armor began to surface, the Daily Planet immediately launched a thorough investigation. The shocking findings include names that will be familiar to the business community of Metropolis, and in one case, to legal authorities . . .

I went ahead, outing Dabney Donovan as Steve Jenkins's new business partner. To keep things factual, I only called the Contessa an investor and used Arcana Imperii—her company's name. I explained that Jenkins had decided to restart his unethical research on four homeless minors estranged from their families—names withheld for protection, but their newfound abilities detailed—and launched a scheme intending to force one of the *Daily Scoop*'s reporters into the experiment in order to get back into the world of military contracts.

The others were gathered around, reading over my shoulder as I typed, with gratifying gasps every so often. The loudest came when I typed in the words "possible connection to jailed mobster Moxie Mannheim. The scheme appears to be motivated in part by reports on his criminal activities run by this newspaper."

"Really?" James asked. "It was Moxie."

"Yes," I tossed over my shoulder. "He was the one who got the ball rolling on this."

"Which is why he was so quick to let you visit him," Devin said. "So we weren't wrong to tease you."

"Not completely anyway," Maddy added, beating me to it.

I grunted and went back to typing. Once I was finished, I asked James, "Spellcheck and send upstairs?" I directed my next query to all of them. "Is it too editorial?"

"No," Devin said. "It's what happened. You were involved."

Maddy was scowling. "You were a lot nicer than I'd be."

James finished his pass and sent the story off to Perry. We waited, quiet and tense, to see if he had any feedback. It was getting later by the second.

I jumped when our desk phones started to ring. All four of them.

Frowning, I picked mine up. "*Daily Scoop*, yes?"

A distracted woman in my ear said, "I just got a video of the flying one. They're out again."

"What? Where?"

I scribbled down an address, recognizing the street, and hung up. My colleagues were taking similar calls.

"What are they doing?" I asked. They were being spotted right outside their headquarters.

"Trying to lure you back would be my guess," Maddy said, hanging up her phone.

Perry burst into the room then, holding a printout. "I read it on the way down," he said, waving what had to be my story around. "You stand by all this? It's factual?"

"I believe so, yes," I said.

"Okay then," Perry said, doing that thing where his eyes glazed a bit as he thought and talked at the same time. "We'll get it on the front page, released first thing tomorrow. We won't put it online until then either. A true exclusive." He focused back in on me. "No one else has this, correct?"

"No," I said. "But as you can probably hear, the experiment's subjects are making some trouble tonight."

"We're going to sell a lot of newspapers tomorrow—I'll

head out to cover the new stuff for a sidebar until I can get someone else to come relieve me," he said. "The cops will help get them home."

I nodded, hoping he was right.

"Good work, Lane," he said, and with that, he turned on his heel.

Why did I not *feel* like what I'd done was praiseworthy? The others were smiling and laughing . . . and then back to taking calls.

"Where's the last number?" I asked. "The last of our silver armor squad's parents?"

"Oh, here," Maddy said, holding her receiver and rolling over to me. She handed me a printout with numbers and names on it. "It's the last one."

The name above it said T. Andrews. It must belong to Todd's family. I dialed, then waited for someone to answer.

A woman did. "Hello?"

"Um, hi," I said. "I'm calling because I think I know where your son Todd is."

"We don't have any Todd," she said. And hung up.

The silence in my ear was painfully loud.

"No luck?" Maddy asked.

I shook my head. My heart ached for him, jerk behavior notwithstanding. "I can't believe it."

But I could. I just didn't want to. I spent a moment wishing the best for all four of them, even Todd, who'd always been so rude to me. I wished them a good place, a good purpose.

I wished I could do more than wish for it.

CHAPTER 28

I'd seen enough of Taxi Jack, so I decided to give him a break. I hailed a cab outside the Daily Planet Building to head home—before my parents sent out a search party. The woman driving it was perfectly happy to stay in her own little world. She made no effort at conversation.

I didn't want any chance encounters with our armor-alloyed friends before my story dragged them into the light of day, so I had her drop me off right in front of our brownstone. It was only 11 p.m., after all, the latest I could stretch curfew when Mom and Dad knew I was at the *Scoop*.

Given the role I played in it, I guessed I'd better prepare them for the story.

As much as I could.

But Dad emerged from our building before I even made

it to the door. In his everyday uniform, he barked, "Save that cab!"

"Wait," I told the woman. Then I asked him as he approached, "Why? Where are you going?"

"There've been news reports of a flying man in the city tonight," he said.

We stared at each other. I was reliving that night two years ago in Kansas, when the flying man had saved us. When the flying man had changed things for both of us. I thought maybe he was too.

But I saw something else, something beyond that memory. If my story ran, it would make everything worse. The world's eyes would be open to possibilities it might not be ready for yet. Dad would never stop looking for *our* flying man, not once he had proof it was possible. That group of armored cast-off kids would end up god knew where, separated from each other, probably as lab rats.

Could I give this a happier ending?

The only thing it would take would be sacrificing myself, my front-page story, my pride. And if that was what it took?

The answer was yes.

I bent to the window and told the taxi driver, "Go on."

She shrugged, and drove off.

"Lois," Dad said, "what are you doing? Now I'll have to wait for the car service."

"Good," I said, "by the time it gets here, you'll know where to go. Where *we* need to go. I need to tell you something. Some things, actually."

Our street was mostly quiet, mostly dark. I could hear noise from a few open windows, but that was it. It was Dad and I alone in the night, standing together, looking for answers. The echo of that night in Kansas wasn't lost on me.

"What do you need to tell me?" he asked, concern in his voice.

This was it. No chickening out. "Dad, on your list of names—I'm SkepticGirl1," I said. "And SmallvilleGuy is Clark. I've been looking for the flying man too, and Clark's been helping."

"What?" he asked. He took an involuntary step back, stunned.

"Listen," I said. And I related to him the story of the Typhon beta experiment, only I put my emphasis on the flying boy *here*. Even though he wasn't the one Dad was looking for.

Dad was determined to find a flying man? Well, he would. I believed that he could and would help this one. It wasn't a lie to protect me. It was to protect someone else, to protect the truth until the right time.

"I need your help, Dad," I said. "We tracked them down. I know this boy with wings must be who we saw that night. They'll lie, claim they weren't doing experiments in Kansas— but I don't believe it. Donovan or Jenkins must have before they came here."

Dad had been remarkably quiet. "It would seem so, if this lab complex checks out. Why are you telling me this? Why not put it in the newspaper?"

"I almost did," I said. "But I see that's not the best. I know you'll do the right thing. You have to promise me that you'll take down Dabney Donovan, Steve Jenkins, and this Contessa del Portenza. They go to jail, not on your payroll."

"After they threatened my daughter? You bet they will," he said.

I smiled.

We never know whether people deserve the credit we give them, but sometimes we have to trust in them anyway. It was a joy that I'd been proved right.

"And you'll take care of the others? They want to keep their family, each other, but if they decide to leave at eighteen, you have to let them," I said.

"We can always use smart young people. If they agree, I'll make sure they are treated well, and that they get to stay together."

I waited.

"And that they can leave when they're eighteen if they choose," he said. "Anything else?"

I shook my head, and then I hugged him tight. He folded his arms around me. "Thanks, Dad. I'll get them to say yes."

The sleek black car from the service he used pulled up. It would have a military driver.

"Lois," he said, opening the car door and holding on to the top before we got in, "you shouldn't have been looking. I told you not to talk about it with anyone."

"You're just mad I found him before you did," I said, crossing my fingers where he couldn't see.

"Hop in," he said, waving me into the car. "Lois, I'm proud of you. I don't say it enough. Where are we headed?"

I gave Dad the address we needed to go to. He made some calls to arrange extra military heavies to join the police who'd apparently already set up a roadblock at the scene. I'd get the story taken care of as soon as we finished this, and I could go to the Daily Planet Building guilt-free. Hopefully Perry would still be there, and I could convince him of a different, better truth.

By the time we arrived at the block where I'd almost become a whole new augmented girl, Dad's orders were already being efficiently carried out. There was a smallish crowd gathered on this side of the roadblock and several jeeps and vans had parked along the street behind it, some blocking cars into street spaces. A line of soldiers, accompanied by city police, waited on the other side of the flashing lights.

Our driver pulled up behind a jeep, and Dad and I climbed out.

The sidewalks along the street had been cleared, the businesses all dark at this time of day. I followed Dad's eyes up . . .

To where Jamie flew above the street, zig-zagging from one side to the other. I scanned the blocked-off pavement and spotted three people gathered on it below him, dead in the center of the road. "They're in front of the HQ," I said. "They must be terrified."

I looked again, but still didn't spot Perry in the crowd.

Just then, the sound of a helicopter's distinctive chopper blades came from above, lights spearing down from it and illuminating Jamie, then Reya, Sunny, and Todd below.

Reya and Todd stepped back from Sunny as she angled her head toward it. I saw red beams begin to glow in the air.

"Get that out of here," I said.

Dad walked over and gave the order, and we heard the helicopter back off moments later. He came back. "What do we do?" he asked.

"Let me go talk to them," I said.

"Lois," Dad said, a warning.

"I'll be safe. You're right here. You're proud of me, and you trust me, remember?"

"I should have known you'd use that against me." But he swept a hand to indicate he was giving me a chance and went over to the line of cops and soldiers to wait.

I started my march up the center of the street. I had no doubt there were people covering me as I walked, and I prayed that the four Typhon teamsters would keep calm until I could convince them this was for their own good. If anything threatening happened, I knew Dad wouldn't hesitate to act to protect me.

Sunny recognized me first, and she grabbed Reya's arm. There was another roadblock on the opposite end of the block. The three of them faced me as I neared them, and Jamie set down beside Sunny.

"Are you stupid?" Reya asked when I was in earshot. "You got away. I thought you didn't want to be one of us. They said you'd come back, but I said that was nuts. What are you doing here?"

"They're still inside, Jenkins and Donovan and the Contessa?" I asked.

"Yes," she said. "We're their defense. We're not supposed to let anyone past."

Just when I'd assumed I couldn't be any angrier at those three. What scum they were, sending teens out to fight their battle. I had to show these guys I was on their side.

"Todd," I said, "I talked to your family. You were right."

His head ticked down, and I cringed at the defeat in the small gesture. He'd known, but it still hurt to hear it. How could it not?

"But *I* was right too," I said.

He took a step toward me that seemed almost involuntary. "What do you mean?"

"You all want a purpose and a place, right? There's no going back home for any of you." I moved two steps closer, and that was as far as I was willing to go. I heard the chopper in the distance, hovering somewhere nearby. I couldn't push Dad on this. "But I think you have to know by now that the people who did this to you are not good. Look around. They're not going to protect you. They're not your family. They tossed you out here like bait. *You* are each other's family now. And I think you want it to stay that way."

The four of them exchanged looks, and Reya broke from the pack to stand directly in front of me. "What are you saying?" she asked.

I had to convince them. I couldn't let this end another way. "Do you trust me?"

"No," Todd said.

But Reya nodded yes. "I think I do." She turned to catch Todd's eye. "And you trust me, don't you?"

"Always," Todd said, without hesitation. Sunny and Jamie nodded to her that they did too.

"I trust my dad," I said. "That's who your guys wanted the attention of, and they got it. He can give you a safe place. He promised me he'll let you stay together."

"He's military?" she asked.

"Yes," I said. "But I truly believe he won't make you do anything you don't want to. You know there's nowhere safe for you now, if the world finds out you really exist, with the things you can do. There are a lot of bad men out there." I thought of the Contessa. "And bad women. At least this gives you a chance to stay with good ones instead."

She considered, looking at me instead of the others. They kept their eyes trained on Reya, waiting for her call.

Finally, at last, she nodded. "We deserve some good people for a change," she said. "It's a deal."

I wanted to fall to my knees with relief. And turn and stick my tongue out at the HQ beside us. I didn't do either.

"Come with me," I told her, and waved them all to join me. I led them to Dad, who strode out to meet us. "You can take the building," I said. "But first, meet Reya, Todd, Sunny, and Jamie." The four of them nodded as I said their names. They looked less frightened than I expected, but then, they'd been through more than I could imagine. "Meet my dad, General Sam Lane."

"You can call me Sam," he said, using his kindest, least intimidating manner. "Lois told me what happened to all of you. It's not right. We can't change that, but we can do our best to help you move forward."

Todd and Reya exchanged a glance, and then Todd met my eyes. He didn't say thanks, but his grateful expression was the next best thing. There was zero mockery in it. For once.

It was time for the next step, which was even scarier than all this had been. It was time to tell Perry we had to pull the story.

"You haven't seen Perry, have you?" I asked Dad, talking low.

"Here? No," he said. "Why?"

I held up a finger and fished out my phone to text Perry: *Are you still on-site? I'm here too. We need to hold the story.*

He texted back right away: *Left a while ago, a stringer's there. Headed back to type up my story for the web. Too late anyway. Front page printing now.*

Crap.

Apparently my noble intentions were going to be harder to carry out than I thought.

When I spoke to Dad, I did my best to keep my newfound panic from showing. "Can your driver give me a lift to the Daily Planet Building? I really need to get back there and pull my story, write something that will keep this from becoming a scandal." I paused. While I was here I might as well ask. "And, um, could I maybe get a quote from General Lane?"

He almost laughed. I saw it, and scowled. "I'll give you a quote, but you can't run it until we have everyone in custody. We'll be moving in on the building any minute."

"Deal. The car?" Pride was earned, and—ironically—I had

to sacrifice mine and save the day before I could afford to feel it for myself again.

"Right." Dad looked around, and then, frustrated, told one of the soldiers nearby. "Can you find my driver?"

The soldier hustled off.

"You have your notebook?" Dad asked.

"Always," I said, and handed it over, along with a pen. Dad quickly jotted something down on a blank page. When he finished, he handed it back to me. I skimmed and saw the words: " . . . plotted an attack on civility in Metropolis, threatening to destroy public safety . . . removed peacefully through an unprecedented partnership between the Metropolis police and the United States Army . . ."

"You're really going after them, huh?" I asked.

"I gave my word. Besides, it's what they did."

"Sir?" Dad's driver interrupted.

"Tim, get her over to the Daily Planet Building," Dad said.

"Yes, sir," the driver said. I waved to Dad, and Tim and I hurried back to where he'd parked the car.

It was going to be okay. Maybe.

Perry might fire me. But I had fixed this part and now I just had to fix the story—there was too much on the line not to. Too many other lives.

I climbed into the backseat of the car. As the soldier got us headed in the right direction, I pulled out my phone.

My next text went to Devin, James, and Maddy: *I made a huge mistake. We have to stop that story. Devin, can you pull it from the website so it won't go live in the morning? Does anyone know where the printing presses are?*

I'd never seen them before. As far as I was concerned, the papers just magically showed up on newsstands and front stoops every morning.

I drummed my fingers waiting for a response. In the meantime, I logged on to the chat app to fill in Clark.

SkepticGirl1: *I'm pulling the story. Dad's taking care of the bad guys.*

SmallvilleGuy: *Why?*

SkepticGirl1: *He'll stop looking for the flying man. It'll be over.*

SmallvilleGuy: *You don't have to do this.*

SkepticGirl1: *I do—it's better this way. The only way to keep the world safe for now. It'll be better for those teens. Dad will give them a place.*

SmallvilleGuy: *<3*

SkepticGirl1: *I gotta go. Gotta stop the presses.*

James texted back with the info—the presses were two doors down from the main entrance of the Planet Building.

Whew, at least they're not across town.

I texted Maddy, James, and Devin: *Meet me there ASAP.*

And then I asked the soldier behind the wheel, "Tim, was it? Can you drive faster?"

The driver obeyed, as if I was his commander instead of Dad.

CHAPTER 29

When we reached the press building address, I jumped out of Dad's car to find my three *Scoop* colleagues waiting for me on an otherwise deserted sidewalk.

Maddy looked like she'd gotten dressed in a hurry. I was pretty sure the shirt under her jacket was a pajama top—its marching elephants were the first thing I'd ever seen that wasn't a band name on something she was wearing.

The soldier pulled away. Dad had sent a text that everyone was in custody. So at least I'd have a replacement story for Perry. I'd put it together on the way over.

"What's going on?" James asked. "Why the sudden change of plan?"

"Devin, did you get the story pulled from online copy?" I asked.

"Obviously," he said. "Though we do want to know why."

"Because we can't run that version of it. Where's the door?" I asked.

Maddy strode over and opened the one farthest right in a bank of glass doors. A cacophonous roar met us.

"This guy called ahead to verify our credentials," she said, speaking up and pointing to a security desk. A man with a beard in a blue uniform sat there.

"Lois Lane?" he asked.

I nodded.

"You guys can go on in," he said. "No one answered, so they must've been on the floor."

Once we were past the desk and out of earshot of the guard, I looked at the others. "Why are they letting us in here?"

"We told them we needed to *look* at the press room," James said, stopping. "So now tell us why?"

I would have to explain. And I had to shout, given the roar ahead. "We're going to say it was a hoax, and the military is handling the arrest of the three people who orchestrated a fake attack on Metropolis. I have a quote from Dad."

"But why?" James asked, frowning.

"To protect someone," I said. "To make sure those teenagers end up with a home base, their lives not ruined." Asking them was almost as scary as asking Reya and company had been, but I needed to know . . . "Do you guys trust me?"

All three of them nodded immediately. "Yes," they said, at the same time.

"Good, then let's go," I said, a sentimental lump in my

throat, and we started moving again, crossing into the area that housed the source of the cacophony.

"Stop the presses!" I shouted as we raced past the printing behemoths in the cavernous warehouse.

Copies of the fresh hot *Daily Planet* front page I was desperate to stop kept rolling off the enormous, roaring machines.

I struggled to be louder, the smell of hot ink and paper assaulting my nose. "Stop! The! Presses!"

The ruinous racket continued without pause. It completely swallowed the clatter of our feet as we sprinted across the concrete flooring.

"Where are the people?" I shouted to them.

"This way!" James turned and mouthed to me, pointing toward a back corner with an elevated office.

It did in fact look like there were people up there—at least two standing at the windows watching us approach. I grabbed one of the finished, folded newspapers off the end of the next row of presses as we blew by and then put on a fresh burst of speed.

I had to make them understand.

The presses had to be stopped. I'd take whatever punishment Perry meted out to me. Nothing was worth this story running. Not my pride, not my job. Nothing.

James stopped and waved for me to take the lead at the stairs. I pounded up them and bolted straight through the office door without knocking. The people we'd seen from below were a man and a younger woman, standing above a bank of computers and control panels that looked like they dated to approximately the middle of the last century.

"Stop . . . the . . . presses!" I panted after I got the words out. I held up the newspaper at their frowns. "This story can't go out. I said stop the presses."

"Who are you?" the man asked. He was maybe the same age as my dad, silver-haired with a kind but currently bewildered face.

"Lois Lane from the *Daily Scoop*. I wrote this story," I said. "And it can't run."

The headline shouted out at me from the front page I held. It was the *worst* possible headline, making my point for me. I stabbed at it:

Flying Man Spotted Over Metropolis Explained

"Ooh, sounds like a good one," the woman said. She was younger than the man by a decade, and pixie small. She reached as if to take the page and skim it.

"Can you stop them or not?" I said. "I'll take the heat. This story can't go out on the stands. We've already pulled it off the website."

The man gave me another frown, and then shrugged. "That call has to come from upstairs. And you're not upstairs."

"We can't just call up there?" I asked hopefully.

"They put the policy in place because a reporter *did* what you're trying to do. Ten years back. You could have someone stationed up there. The order has to come from editorial directly to us. There's a code word. Sorry."

There was no way I'd convince Perry over the phone.

Crap. Thanks, ten-years-ago stranger. Who was probably fired.

I looked at the headline again. And I sucked in a lungful of ink-scented air, then whirled, motioning for the others to let me pass. I ran as if my life depended on it, though it wasn't *my* life I was most worried about.

I dashed back out the way we'd come. I had to find Perry and make the presses stop, one way or another.

★ ★ ★

We made it back to the main entrance and up to the newsroom floor in record time. I barreled out of the elevator, shouting, "Perry! Perry White, get out here!"

I heard my friends make tortured sounds, and we drew confused glances from the handful of reporters still at their cubicles this late. I knew they were envisioning my immediate dismissal. I might as well make this good, since that's exactly what I was risking.

Perry stalked out of his office and then pointed a finger at its door. "Get in here. What is wrong with you? I just got back, and now you're caterwauling in the newsroom."

"We have to stop the presses," I said, panting, out of breath. I was *not* caterwauling.

Perry handed me a glass of water off his desk as soon as I followed him inside. "Drink this."

Devin, Maddy, and James appeared in the doorway.

Perry waved them into his office as well. I didn't even have a chance to enjoy his view of the city at night. I sucked down some water and then said, "Let me explain."

"Go right ahead," Perry said, sinking into his chair. "This should be good."

"You have to pull my story off the front page," I said. "Pull it, period."

"Why?"

I took a breath, marshalling my strength. "It was a trick. We've been duped. All the things people saw—that we saw—were elaborate pranks using tech and optical illusions."

"Keep talking," he said.

"The same guys are behind it—they wanted to make us look stupid."

He shook his head. "I saw some things tonight. Before I came back . . . I fell for it too. But what do we run if not this?"

"The military are taking the teenagers who were used into temporary custody. Those are the people you saw. They're also seeing to the arrests of Jenkins, Donovan, and Portenza—they wanted to make us look bad. It was all Moxie's suggestion, just like the story said." That much was true. "I have a statement from my dad, but you can also call him to confirm."

I scribbled his number down on a post-it and handed it to Perry.

"I will," he said. "You're more certain of this than last night's story?"

"Yes. Can you, um, please stop the presses? We can do the part where you fire me afterward."

Perry picked up his phone and punched in a number. "Eagle eyes," he said to whoever answered. He paused, then, "Yes. Stop it. Trash the old ones. A new front page is coming."

He set down the receiver.

"The password will be changed," he said, sweeping his eyes across all four of us. "So don't get any ideas about using it."

"But they're stopped?" I asked. "Destroyed?"

He nodded. "Now, let me ask you a question, Ms. Lane or any of the rest of you. Do you have any idea how much of an expense doing that was? What it costs the paper to halt a print run in progress? Not just in terms of the confidence of our subscribers who will get their papers late, but monetarily?"

"I know it's a lot," I said, before James could chime in with an exact figure or something. "And it's my fault. I'll devote my next fifty years of paychecks to cover it . . . as long as I'm not fired."

Perry gave me a long, hard, considering look.

"No," he said, finally. "The *Daily Planet*'s reputation is worth more than a single day of printing expenses. You did the right thing. Do you know why we have a policy that requires an editor's call with a password to shut down the presses?" he asked.

I shook my head. *I'm not fired. I'm not fired.*

"I did something similar. But in my case it worked. They stopped them because I asked."

"You! Ten years ago!" I couldn't believe it.

Maddy and Devin laughed. James said, "You've changed, Mr. White."

"No, he hasn't," I said.

"You're both right," Perry said. "Now go, get me the story we can run. We can't have an empty front page."

And so I did just that.

★ ★ ★

I was finally headed home, exhausted, having typed up the new story and sent it upstairs. The four of us shared a taxi, too quiet to even talk on the way home.

The cab pulled up to drop me at my front door. I was the last passenger. Except my car door opened as soon as we stopped and Clark peered in. "We have a problem."

"We do?" I asked.

"Alex," he said. "He gave me his dad's address in Metropolis. We'll have to go there. You won't believe him otherwise."

"Get in," I said. "Tell this nice man where we're going. And tell me why."

Uptown. The fanciest part. Of course.

"What'd he do?" I asked.

Clark reached out and took my hand. "He posted his own account of the evening on Loose Lips."

My jaw dropped open. I banged my head gently against Clark's shoulder. "He did not."

"He did."

"And here I was shouting 'Stop the presses!'"

"Really?" he asked.

"It was very exciting. I thought I'd be fired. Turns out Perry did the same thing once."

His hand tightened on mine, but he didn't say anything. I still wasn't used to having him close enough to really touch. Compared to this, I didn't understand how I'd ever thought that inside the game felt real. Real was far more intense.

"You're probably going to have to keep me from killing

Alex," I said to hide the ridiculous detour my thoughts had made.

"You're secretly a sap and you feel sorry for him, admit it." He nudged me with his shoulder.

"Fine. I feel sorry for him." I sighed. "I still don't trust him, though, not completely. He was way too interested in what those guys were up to."

The car pulled up at the nicest building I'd visited in Metropolis so far, which was saying something. ARLabs headquarters and James's parents' place had been no slouches. This one stretched seemingly all the way up to the sky, and I could hardly imagine the views from the top.

A doorman in a pristine uniform didn't bat an eyelash at the two of us straggling in at the late hour.

"We're here for Alex Luthor," I said.

"One moment." He picked up the handset of a red telephone to make a call, presumably upstairs to the Luthors.

A red telephone was a bit much, even for this neighborhood. It wasn't like the president lived here.

The doorman set down the receiver and then crossed the opulent lobby and hit the button to summon a golden elevator. The doors slid open immediately. "The elevator will take you up to the penthouse," he said.

"The penthouse?" I echoed.

"Where the Luthors are in residence," the man said.

We got on the elevator, a gold tube.

"I guess Alex really is a zillionaire," I said.

Clark looked as disconcerted by all the trappings of extreme wealth as I was.

The doors slid open after a zooming trip to the top of the building and we were suddenly in a ludicrously luxurious apartment, with Alex grinning at us both. He had on pajamas that looked as designer as his clothes had, striped with matching tops and bottoms.

"I need you to delete your post from Loose Lips. While I watch," I said. "And never speak of it again."

"You could've texted," he said.

"Somehow I knew she'd want to see proof," Clark said, smiling easily, defusing any tension.

We walked farther into the apartment. An enormous white couch divided into sections with settees on either side dominated the middle of the room. The giant window had a view of Metropolis that rivaled the one from Perry's office.

I still preferred his to this one, I decided.

"So," Alex said, "what you are informing me is that officially the most exciting thing that's ever happened to me did not happen." He flopped onto the couch, where a laptop sat open. "Figures," he said, typing into it. "That seems to be my lot in life. So unfair."

I gave a wry glance at our surroundings, but he didn't notice, absorbed in his screen.

"You'll find the strength to carry on somehow," I said. "You have time."

Then I sat down beside him and watched as he pulled up

the thread—which had only a few responses so far, *thank you, universe*—and deleted it with one push of a button.

"Anyone hungry?" he asked. "I can call out for pizza."

Clark and I looked at each other. I probably had time. At this point, curfew was so far gone that it didn't matter.

"I am starving," I said.

The penthouse elevator doors opened once more and admitted a man in a suit carrying a briefcase. Though he had a full head of brown hair, his resemblance to Alex made clear who he was.

"Alexander, why are all the lights on?" he asked, then frowned when he saw us.

Alex said, "I'm having friends over."

"As long as you keep it down," his dad said. He didn't even ask who we were. Or why we were over so late.

Alex got up and went into the giant, spacious, granite-counter-filled kitchen, presumably to get a menu for our order.

Clark eased down beside me. He turned to face me and took my hand. "Lois? Can I ask you something?"

Like that, my stupid heart went into overdrive. "Um, sure. What is it?"

"Do you want to go on a date?" he asked. "Something boring?"

Alex appeared over us. "Pepperoni okay?" he asked.

"Yes, although it won't be boring," I said, keeping my eyes on Clark. "In fact, leave it to me. You just show up at my house at seven sharp tomorrow night and wear a suit. And you know my preferred toppings."

"You're on. And I do." Clark smiled at me, the best smile I'd seen in a while, maybe ever, and got up to look at the menu.

Alexander Luthor, Alex's dad, was depositing the briefcase by a sliding door that presumably went to his bedroom. I scurried over before he could escape.

"Hi there, sir," I said, offering him my hand.

He looked at it. *You'd think I'm bleeding out my eyeballs or something.*

"Nice to meet you," I said, lowering it. "I'm Lois. Alex is an interesting guy. I guess he inherited your tech savvy."

He frowned at me, eyebrows drawing together. They really did look alike, father and son, the same jawline. "I hire people for that," he said.

That made me wonder whether Alex had been straight with us about his father having been the one in touch with the military. I couldn't follow up with more questions, though, because Alexander Luthor disappeared.

Clark called over, "We're getting pepperoni, green olive, and spinach."

"Spinach, blech!" I said, putting my concern aside for now.

"You need vegetables to live, Lo," Clark said.

"He is right about that," Alex said. "Humans require balanced nutrition or terrible . . ."

I tuned him out and caught Clark's eye. Tomorrow. Finally, a date. In real life.

And I knew just the place for us to go.

CHAPTER 30

The next night I finally understood what people meant when they said they had butterflies in their stomachs. Only I was pretty sure I had dragons and pterodactyls and other flying beasties straight out of *Worlds War Three* in mine.

I was in a dress. It wasn't anything too fancy or frilly, just a short black silk one with the smallest ruffle at the top of each shoulder. I tugged down the hem and squinted in the mirror.

My bedroom door opened. It was Maddy, my mom, and Lucy. Mom put her hand over her mouth. "Honey, you're gorgeous."

Lucy added to the compliment by making kissy noises.

I'd had to get Mom to take me shopping right after school, where I had tried on approximately a jillion dresses in half an hour and went with the simplest. Meanwhile Maddy had on a pink tulle skirt with a cool stretchy black top emblazoned with the words *Spoiler Queens*. She'd doubtless made the shirt herself.

"You're smoking hot," I said to Maddy. "Truly the queen of coolness."

"Why, thank you," Maddy said with a little curtsey.

I had texted my friends the night before and proposed we go to the spring formal en masse. I'd never really contemplated going to a school dance before, but somehow it felt like just the special occasion to mark our victory.

And I suspected Clark wouldn't mind being my date.

A knock sounded downstairs, and my stomach dragons gave another whirl. "That might be Clark," I said.

Lucy darted out of the room. She came right back and, with true disappointment in her voice, said, "Nope. It's James and Devin and a girl."

"Good," Maddy said, "because you're not quite ready." She pulled out some lipstick and advanced on me. I started to cringe away from her. "No you don't," she said.

"Lois, hold still," Mom put in. She and Maddy exchanged a long-suffering glance.

"Fine. I know when I'm beat." I did as they commanded, presenting my face for Maddy's efforts. "You're not sad to not be going with Dante tonight?"

"Stop talking," she said, dragging the wand over my lips. "And no, I never even wanted to go until I got your text. Now it sounds like fun. Anyway, we had a talk today at school and it wasn't even that weird. So I think it's all for the best."

"Good," I said, and turned to the mirror to check out her handiwork. My lips were a soft, sparkly plum color.

Lucy's face appeared right below mine and she puckered her lips. She asked, "Can I have some?"

Mom laughed. "Maybe in a few years, my astronaut-to-be."

Another knock at the door sounded downstairs. This one *had* to be Clark. Lucy zipped out of the room and didn't return.

"I'm ready," I said. "I'm not going to keel over from nerves because I'm totally ready."

Maddy grinned at me. "You do know you just said that out loud, right?"

"Of course." Well, mostly. I gave myself one last inspection in the mirror. Hey, it was me, and I knew Clark liked *me*.

"You're sure about the shoes?" Mom asked.

"Yes." I stomped one of my trusty black boots for good measure. I wasn't willing to sacrifice comfort to the dance gods.

"Then you'd better get downstairs," Mom said. "You know your dad answered the door."

Ack. "Say no more," I said, grabbing Maddy's hand and pulling her along with me.

When we got down the stairs to the living room, Clark stood hesitantly inside the front door while Dad did an impressive job of looming in front of him.

Clark was wearing a charcoal suit with a light blue tie and he looked . . . even better than usual, which was saying something.

Lucy had taken a spot next to Dad, where she could gaze up at Clark. James, Devin, and his date were sitting on the couch, all spiffed up too. Maddy went over to sit on the arm of the couch beside James. Mom moved past me; my guess was to intercede with Dad and make him be nice.

"Um, hi," I said, lingering on the bottom step.

Clark looked past my dad and saw me. His eyes lit up, and he stepped right past my dad, who turned with his mouth open. People didn't walk away from Dad without being dismissed very often.

"Lois," Clark said, coming over to me. He had another tulip bouquet with him. Yellow this time.

I fidgeted. "I know the shoes are dumb."

"No," he said. "They're perfect. You're beautiful." He leaned in a fraction, and a lock of black hair fell over his forehead. Somehow it only made him cuter. "You always are."

My cheeks went up in flame and my heart pounded and I wanted to make everyone else in the room vanish. Why had I proposed a group date again?

We were kissing or bust tonight. It was going to happen. Mom had heated up leftover lasagna for an early dinner and I'd even decided to forgo the garlic bread.

Now would have been a great time . . . if we were alone.

"Thanks," I murmured. Then, louder, I added, "Stop." I hoped my tone made clear I didn't mean it, that it was for the benefit of our audience.

I looked over to find Maddy, James, Devin, and his date, Katrina, watching us.

Maddy said, "The cuteness level of you two together should be illegal."

I rolled my eyes at her. "Are those for me?" I asked Clark, about the flowers.

He gave me a wink, and then turned away from me, back toward Dad. "No, I realized I forgot to bring flowers for *all* the women in the house last time. Lucy, will you forgive me?"

Aha, he wasn't turning to Dad. He was turning to Lucy.

Lucy blinked and blushed and beamed and finally managed to get her hands out to accept the bouquet. She hugged them tight to her. "Thank you, Clark," she said. "You can come visit anytime you want."

Dad shook his head. "Well played, son."

A honk sounded outside, and Mom went to check at the door. "It's your cab. Quick, everyone line up out front for a photo!"

We left the house in a clump and stood and smiled, then piled into a taxi van that barely fit us all. Clark and I got in first, then Devin and his date. I noticed James giving Maddy a hand up into the car, and they sat together in the front row. He smiled at her and said something that made her laugh.

Hmmm . . .

"No interfering," Clark said, low, and offered me his hand. I put mine into his.

"You're no fun." I realized with horror what I'd said. "I didn't mean that, it was a joke."

"I'm familiar with your sense of humor," he said, squeezing my hand.

"Oh, right, good," I said. "There's something you should know . . ."

"What is it?" he said.

"I can't dance."

He took that in, then burst into laughter. "Me neither. This should be interesting."

"Or humiliating." I smiled at him. And he smiled back. We were a couple of grinning fools. "It doesn't matter though."

"No," he said, "not even a little."

The ride to the hotel where the school had rented a ballroom for the dance was full of talking and in-jokes and laughter. But I mostly concentrated on the feeling of my hand in Clark's, on how our shoulders touched. I was determined that we would finally have our kiss and I wouldn't screw it up and knock off his glasses this time.

When the taxi stopped, everyone piled back out. James insisted on paying, and offered Maddy his arm on the way in. She accepted it.

"You guys go ahead," I said to them. "We're right behind you. I just want to talk to Clark for a sec."

Maddy grinned at me, and gave me a queenly wave with her free hand. "See you in there," Devin said, holding Katrina's hand.

"Am I in trouble?" Clark asked.

"No, I just want you to myself for a minute."

The neighborhood we'd gotten out in was a busy one, lots of cute little shops and eateries. "Let's take a stroll," I said.

"Sounds good to me." Clark took my hand in his, swinging

it between us. People in Metropolis usually got growly at this kind of behavior, taking up sidewalk space in a way that screamed tourist. But we must have been too cute for obnoxiousness. Everyone we passed seemed to have a smile for us.

"Hey," Clark said, "I want to take you out one more time before we go home. I have a surprise thing tomorrow. Just for the two of us."

"What is it?" I asked, trying to press away my disappointment that he was leaving so soon.

"You know," he said, "we really need to work on your understanding of the word surprise."

"Just spill it, Smallville."

"I found a movie theater that's showing *His Girl Friday* and *The Front Page* tomorrow night."

"You're kidding!" I said. "My favorite movie! Or maybe tied for favorite with *Madwoman* now. How did you find out about it? What's *The Front Page*?"

"They're both adapted from the same story. It's a special classics follow-up to *Madwoman*. I think I like journalism. Maybe I'll pick up some pointers."

"I can give you pointers," I said, and turned a grin on him.

He swung our hands again. "So . . . why'd you want to wait to go in, besides knowing I can't dance?"

"Like I said, I wanted you to myself for a moment. I'm greedy that way."

"Lois . . ." Clark's expression turned serious as I watched his profile. "You should know, if I ever have to go away . . . I promise I'll come back. Always. This trip. It's made me see how much good there is to do in the world."

"Speaking of cryptic things," I said, pulling him to face me. I looked into those blue eyes that were becoming familiar, and which still made my heart beat faster and my knees weak in moments like this. In most moments, to be perfectly honest.

Stupid eyes. Stupid knees. Stupid heart.

I'd been wondering when we'd talk about this. Now was apparently the time. I'd been thinking about the back door at the lab, about Strange Skies, putting them together with other things.

"Whatever your big secret is, I'll figure it out," I said.

"I know," Clark said, still serious.

"In fact, I probably already have figured out some of it."

The same response, accepting of it. Accepting of me. "I know." He put his hands on either side of my face, cradling my cheeks.

And then I went on tiptoe and he leaned down, and we finally kissed—for real. Our lips fit together perfectly, again and again. Soft, sweet. Real.

Our first *real* kiss was better than fireworks and flying and front-page news all rolled into one.

ACKNOWLEDGMENTS

I wanted to take a moment to say a few quick thank yous here, because Team Lois deserves nothing less. My eternal gratitude goes to Warner Bros., DC Comics, and Switch Press for trusting me to give the first lady of DC Comics a new chapter, and all their support along the way. A special thanks to my editor at Capstone, Beth Brezenoff; marketing doyenne Shannon Hoffmann and her entire team; cover designer Bob Lentz; publicity goddess April Roberts; publicity goddess across the sea Georgia Lawe; and everyone at Capstone/Switch Press. Most of all a thanks to the real Team Lois, the fans of this amazing character both before these books and now, who have been such a joy to get to know and whose support for this series is so very much appreciated. And last but never least, to my agent Jenn Laughran and my partner-in-life-and-crime-fighting Christopher Rowe, who are my super heroes.

GWENDA BOND is the author of the Cirque American series and the Lois Lane series as well as the young adult novel *The Woken Gods*. She has also written for *Publishers Weekly* and the *Los Angeles Times*, among other publications, and just might have been inspired to get a journalism degree by her childhood love of Lois Lane. She has an MFA in Writing from the Vermont College of Fine Arts, and lives in a hundred-year-old house in Lexington, Kentucky, with her husband, author Christopher Rowe, and their menagerie.

Visit her online at **gwendabond.com** or **@gwenda** on Twitter.